Sophie patted his arm. "Honestly, Charlie, I am not offended that anyone would think our courtship was real."

His heart beat faster. Really? Was that so?

"I am a career soldier, but I confess I have no idea how to handle this particular battle. I don't know how to extricate you without damaging your reputation."

"Remember who I am? What I am? Fickle and flighty Sophie." She gave a bitter laugh that wrenched his stomach. "If it comes to that, no one will think anything of it if I break our engagement."

"I don't think of you that way," he muttered. It was the truth. He hated for her to think poorly of herself, when he had seen so much good in her.

She turned toward him, her bright blue eyes glowing. "Don't you?"

"Not at all. I admire you greatly." It was difficult to say the words, but something told him she needed to hear it.

She reached up a̶̶̶̶̶̶̶̶̶̶̶̶̶̶̶̶̶̶
Ch̶̶̶̶̶̶̶̶̶̶̶̶̶̶̶̶̶̶ ̶̶̶̶̶̶̶̶̶̶̶̶̶̶̶ne
tha̶̶̶̶̶

Books by Lily George

Love Inspired Historical

Captain of Her Heart
The Temporary Betrothal

LILY GEORGE

Growing up in a small town in Texas, Lily George spent her summers devouring the books in her mother's Christian bookstore. She still counts Grace Livingston Hill, Janette Oake and L. M. Montgomery among her favorite authors. Lily has a BA in history from Southwestern University and uses her training as a historian to research her historical inspirational romance novels. She has published one nonfiction book and produced one documentary, and is in production on a second film; all of these projects reflect her love for old movies and jazz and blues music. Lily lives in the Dallas area with her husband, daughter and menagerie of animals.

The
TEMPORARY
Betrothal

LILY GEORGE

Love Inspired

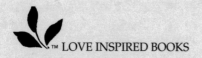

™ LOVE INSPIRED BOOKS

ISBN-13: 978-0-373-82933-0

THE TEMPORARY BETROTHAL

www.LoveInspiredBooks.com

Printed in U.S.A.

Bear with each other and forgive one another
if any of you has a grievance against someone.
Forgive as the Lord forgave you. And over all these
virtues put on love, which binds them all together
in perfect unity. Let the peace of Christ rule in
your hearts, since as members of one body you
were called to peace. And be thankful.

—*Colossians* 3:13–15

For Hoot

Chapter One

❧

March, 1818

Oh, botheration. All the buildings in Bath looked precisely the same. Sophie Handley clutched her bonnet with one hand, clamping it tightly to her curls as she tilted her chin upward. Her intuition fled—she was completely and utterly lost. There was no sign of a haberdashery anywhere on this street. Sophie scoured the directions, written in Mrs. Wigg's undulating hand, once more. Very well. She had come up Charlotte Street, just as the housekeeper instructed. But then, had she taken a right or a left at George Street? Neither. She'd walked straight ahead—yes, that was the Circus, directly in front of her. So should she retrace her steps? Or keep going toward the Circus?

Something splashed onto her piece of foolscap, smearing the ink. She scanned the swollen clouds in the slate gray sky. Botheration—an afternoon shower. Rain fell in fat drops, dampening the foolscap so that it folded itself limply across her glove. And she had no umbrella. Of course. She'd left it behind, as this was supposed to be a mere dash to secure a few buttons for Lord Bradbury's daughter's frock. And yet here she was, lost in the very middle of Bath, with no parasol.

Sophie bit her lip in frustration. She had come to Bath full of purpose and promise, determined to strike out on her own as a seamstress to a wealthy family. And she was coming perilously close to failure, as she could not even go to the shops without getting lost and drenched.

If only there were a way to catch her bearings, but Bath was nothing like home. To find her way in Tansley Village, she had only to note the position of the sun or the moon and then navigate her way across the fields, the sweet moor grass swaying in the gentle breeze. The scrubby hills and valleys were as familiar to her as the face of a dearly beloved friend—but she wasn't home any longer. She gave her head a defiant toss. She had chosen to leave home and come to Bath. And she had chosen a life as a servant. So she had better find her way to the haberdasher and quickly, and then return home to continue work on Amelia Bradbury's riding habit.

She turned back down Gay Street. At the intersection she would try heading in the opposite direction. She shouldered past the milling throngs on the sidewalks, wealthy lords and their well-dressed ladies, scruffy children darting to and fro, and servants soberly dressed in black and white. All of them, every man jack of them, seemed to have an umbrella.

Sophie tossed her now-sodden scrap of paper into the gutter and folded her arms across her chest, holding them closely for warmth. She tucked her chin down, so that most of the moisture rolled off the brim of her bonnet. She assumed a casual air of nonchalance, as though she had forgotten her umbrella on purpose, and hastened her steps along George Street. But oh, it was hard to seem collected when a cold droplet of rain worked its way down your neck and under the back of your frock.

She turned the corner of George Street, colliding with something warm and strong. "Oof!"

"I beg your pardon." Whatever or whomever she had collided with had a lovely baritone voice. "I hope I haven't injured you, miss."

"Oh, no." Sophie righted her bonnet, which was knocked askew by the force of their collision. She turned her head upward, her cheeks hot with embarrassment. "It's my fault, really. I was hurrying along and paid no heed to where I was going."

The brick wall straightened, tilting his umbrella back. His face—she knew that face—

"Lieutenant Cantrill?" she gasped. Of course—she knew he lived in Bath. Her sister, Harriet, had told her that much. But she hadn't seen a familiar face in her two weeks of living in Lord Bradbury's home, so it was rather disconcerting to see someone she knew after drifting along an unfamiliar landscape for so long.

"Miss Handley?" One eyebrow quirked, and a half smile crossed his face. He was much handsomer than she recalled. In fact, when he was at Harriet and John's wedding, she hardly noted his presence. But here, on the sodden streets of Bath, he wore the air of a rescuer, a strong and solid presence in a sea of the unknown and strange. He tilted his umbrella over her and offered her the crook of his elbow. "Are you quite all right? Do you need assistance?"

She shook out her wet skirts and took his arm. It was his damaged one, the one he'd lost at Waterloo. Her fingertips brushed against the leather straps that held his artificial forearm to his biceps. His jacket fit snugly over his shattered limb, so that unless she had touched him for herself, she might never have known that he had been injured. Without thinking, she gave his elbow a slight squeeze—so lightly that he might never discern it.

He coughed a bit—so suddenly and so shortly that it might have been to cover a gasp. She didn't mean to embarrass or discomfit him. Why had she done that, after all? Better to pretend she stumbled a bit and had grasped him for support. She tangled her foot in the soaking-wet hem of her gown and lurched forward ever so slightly, and squeezed his arm once more. "Oh, thank goodness you came to my rescue." Sophie affected the breezy tone of voice that always caught men's ears— the lilting and musical cadence that had, since she was a tiny slip of a girl, gotten her everything she wanted. "I am lost and forgot my umbrella. I was at my wits' end, I assure you."

"I see." He steered her through the milling crowd on the sidewalk, managing to set them on a clear path without bumping into a soul or spearing anyone with his umbrella. How extraordinary. She sidled a bit closer, reveling in the feel of being with someone who knew exactly where he was going and precisely how to get there.

He spoke once the mob thinned out. "Where are you going?"

"Well, I was trying to find the haberdasher at the

Guildhall Market. The housekeeper wrote out my directions, for I am new to Bath and get lost easily. And it seems I've done it again." She glanced up at his profile. He wore a stern, almost abstracted expression, his firm lips turned downward and his face bent low, as though he were walking against the wind. "Thank goodness for you, sir. I was quite unsure what to do next." She prepared to flutter her eyelashes and purse her mouth so her dimples would show, but he never looked her way.

"Guildhall Market? That's a bit of a hike from here. You really did get lost, didn't you?" Lieutenant Cantrill turned the umbrella so that the pelting rain no longer touched her gown. "I'll help you find it. Here—let's turn down Milsom Street. It's a good cut-through."

They passed another row of shops—a confectioner's called Munn's, a modiste and a shop that sold nothing but cheese. How extraordinary. A cheese shop. At Tansley, if one wanted cheese, one had to go milk the cow. But of course, they couldn't afford to keep a cow, so they relied heavily on the one shop in the village that kept everything from sugar to foolscap.

They walked in silence as Sophie drank in the sights. She wasn't jaded yet after two weeks out of the countryside. Everything still retained the crisp edge of newness. Sheltered from the rain and warmed by the lieutenant as he strolled along by her side, Sophie permitted herself to relax the tiniest bit and enjoy their walk.

"It's very kind of you," she murmured as he steered her onto another street. She had no idea what this one was called, and would likely forget, anyway. So…why not try to wheedle a smile from her rescuer? "If it's not too much trouble, Lieutenant."

"Not at all." His voice was pleasant but distant. "I live near there, anyway. Was just on my way home."

"Oh, really? Where do you live?" She maintained her light and breezy tone. He would pay attention to her soon, wouldn't he? At least dart a glance her way?

"I have a flat on Beau Street. Near Mrs. Katherine Crossley's flat." He still spared her no glance, and his tone remained polite but disinterested.

"Aunt Katherine! I had no idea you two lived so close to one another," Sophie replied with a merry laugh. "She helped me to get this position with Lord Bradbury. I am on my way to pick up a few notions for Amelia Bradbury—I am her seamstress."

"Yes, your sister wrote that you would be coming to Bath to live here. She mentioned that you might be willing to assist me in my work with the veterans' group." Was that a spark of attention in his voice? She must pursue it.

"Yes, of course I will." He spoke of that charity for indigent soldiers that Harriet was so interested in. Hattie had told her something about it, but she couldn't remember much. Seeing it had caught the lieutenant's interest, she pressed on. "Tell me more about it."

He looked down at her, and a light sparked in the depths of his brown eyes. "Well, I was hoping you and I could work together, as it were. You see, I get on very well with the soldiers, being a fellow comrade in arms. But the widows are reluctant to ask me for assistance. I know they need help, but they cannot bring themselves to ask a man. So I thought perhaps they would feel more comfortable if another woman were there, helping out."

Work together? "That sounds fine." While she had

his full notice, she flashed her dimples by giving him a slow, easy smile. He straightened and turned away from her, a flush staining his thin cheek. So he was susceptible to flirtation, then? She chuckled inwardly. It was so delightful to be walking with a young man again, smiling and talking playful nonsense rather than working away in her sewing room. She had almost forgotten how fun being a woman could be.

"We're here. Guildhall Market." The lieutenant's voice was cold and remote once more, as though he had shut a door between them. She didn't like that tone of voice.

"Oh, Lieutenant. Thank you for getting me here safe and sound." She should release his elbow, but this lieutenant was too much of an enigma to let go—not before she had spent a bit more time in his company. "Do you mind very much waiting for me, and then you can point me in the correct direction back to Lord Bradbury's house? I am so afraid I will get lost again."

His jaw muscle set, and his strong, firm lips tightened. Yet when he spoke, his voice was well mannered and courteous. "Of course, Miss Handley." He strolled with her over to the haberdashers, and bowed as she went in.

As she sorted through the bins to find the perfect set of buttons, she flicked a glance out the streaming windowpane to Lieutenant Cantrill as he stood outside, waiting. He exuded an air of casual power, as one trained as a soldier should. His broad shoulders were encased in a wool jacket that was simply cut but well made. His face was a trifle thin. Did he have a housekeeper who cooked for him? Perhaps one of the ladies at the veterans' group? She'd have to be an old woman, not young and sweet…. An unreasonable pang of jealousy tore through Sophie, and she shrugged it off.

What did it matter what he ate or wore, or even whom he kept company with? Lieutenant Charlie Cantrill was merely her brother-in-law's dearest friend. And while she loved flirting with him—she always loved a challenge, after all—'twas no business of hers what the lieutenant did in his spare time.

Dash it all, Sophie Handley was far prettier than he remembered. When he attended John and Harriet's wedding a few months ago, Sophie was among the crowd in the chapel and later at the wedding breakfast, but he hadn't taken careful note of her. Her cheeks were sallow, and her eyes were still glazed with something like shock back then. Probably their mother's death, which was surely difficult. But still, that creature bore no resemblance to the rosy-cheeked, blue-eyed sylph who gazed up at him as if—well, as if he was a man and she a woman.

He spied her through the window of the shop as she made her few purchases. Even in a sodden calico dress, she was more graceful and attractive than most of the women plodding along the streets of Bath. He shook his head and turned away from the window. Pretty women had always been his downfall. He should have learned his lesson by now.

Mother's letter rustled in his greatcoat pocket. Ah, a reminder of his familial duties: to find a young girl, marry, have children and give up that ridiculous charitable fund for soldiers. Well, Mother might want him to marry someone like Sophie. But he preferred his life of simplicity and generosity.

And 'twas better to set some distance between him and Sophie Handley, unless he wanted to be made a fool of once more. Since Sophie was his best friend's sister-in-law, 'twould be disastrous indeed to find himself being led a merry dance by her.

The door of the haberdashery opened, and Sophie stepped out. "Thank you for waiting." Her voice was lovely. Perhaps she could sing—that would explain her musical tones.

Careful, man. You have your marching orders. Do not become yet another fool.

He offered his elbow once more. "Did you find what you need?"

"Yes." She waved the parcel triumphantly, heedless of rain. "Perfect buttons, so cunningly made of horn. They will set off the riding habit just so." She sighed and snuggled against his side as they strolled along. He stiffened and moved a fraction of an inch away from her—not so much as to be discourteous—but they did need boundaries, after all. If Sophie noticed, she said nothing.

He piloted her down Grand Parade Street. Lord Bradbury lived in the Crescent, he was sure, with the rest of the haute monde of Bath. So they had a good quarter of an hour before they reached his door. Charlie sighed inwardly. He didn't mind the walk so much, but dash it all, it was pouring by now.

Sophie glanced up at the sky and then turned to him. "The heavens have opened."

He nodded, tightening his lips into a grim line. "So it appears."

She paused, causing several pedestrians to push round them. "I hate for us both to get soaked, and since you are so close to being home, I can't ask you to walk me all the way back to Lord Bradbury's. Shall I take a hackney?" She darted a glance around his shoulder, scanning the street.

He hated to waste money on hackneys, committed as he was to a simple life, but desperate times meant hiring a carriage. Sophie would be drenched by the time they reached her employer's if they didn't, and he wasn't about to let her travel on her own. "We'll go together. It will be my pleasure."

He hailed a hackney with his wooden hand—funny how quickly the drivers halted when he used his prosthesis, though how anyone could see it through the driving rain was beyond him. He boosted Sophie inside and gave orders to the driver before climbing in and shutting the door.

Sophie relaxed against the seat, her gold ringlets sparkling with raindrops. They gave her a fairy queen appearance, and he resisted the urge to brush the droplets off with his gloved fingertips. He sat up straight, pressing his back against the cushion, and stared down at the dusty floor. Looking up at her was too dangerous by far.

"Ah, this is so much better. Thank you, Lieutenant."

He could not look up, so he merely shrugged. "It was your idea, after all."

"True." She fell silent, and stared out the window. 'Twas a relief indeed not to have those luminous blue

eyes settling on him. Sophie Handley was a most unnerving creature.

He shifted around, and the letter in his pocket crackled once more. When he got back to his flat, he'd throw
the dratted thing in the fire. It made a noise every time
he moved, and each time it did so was yet another reminder that his family thought him a wretched failure.

"Lieutenant, I cannot help but wonder if something
is preying upon your mind. You seem so distracted."
He could no longer resist looking at her—a magnet
was drawing him to her. "You helped me. Can I assist
you in any way?"

He started to shrug off her offer, but paused. Could
Sophie Handley possibly help him out of this mess?

"I—uh." Charlie coughed, clearing his throat. "I had
a letter from home, and it's all I have been able to think
on this morning. Even when I was working with the
veterans as I was earlier in the day, my mother's words
have captured my full attention. I apologize that I am
so distracted."

"Not at all, Lieutenant." Sophie clasped her hands in
her lap and regarded him evenly. "Letters from home
can be welcome, or they can serve to remind you why
you left home in the first place."

He surprised himself by laughing aloud. How very
true that was. And nicely put, too. "Indeed."

"My sister Harriet's letters are always so didactic.
'Do this. Don't do that.' I know she means well, but it
becomes tiresome to be lectured to in such a fashion."
She smiled, her lips turning up mischievously at the corners, highlighting her dimples once more. "Of course,
with a letter, you can always fling it in the fire. This

makes it a much more pleasant way to receive lectures than standing there in person, taking orders."

He chuckled. He had not been able to laugh about his family to anyone except himself in ages. And laughing to oneself was a bitter, hateful thing. Sharing the trials of family life with Sophie warmed his heart—he did not feel so utterly alone anymore. He glanced up at her once more. The droplets of rain had dried on her curls, but she still had that air of starriness about her. Some women just had that gift of grace, and Sophie was one of the lucky few.

She returned his frank regard, tilting her head to one side. "So, Lieutenant, if we are sharing confidences, you might tell me what your mother wrote that has so plagued you. Perhaps, as a fellow sufferer, I can think of a way to help."

He hesitated. He had never spoken to anyone about his mother and brother's demands before. Not even his best friend, John Brookes, knew how much animosity existed between himself and his family members. But why not confide in Sophie? He really had no idea what to do with his mother and brother, and Sophie might be able to advise him, especially as one far removed from the family and its dynamics.

He withdrew the letter from his greatcoat pocket and held it, running his thumb over the broken wax seal. "As you might know, I work a great deal with the veterans in Bath. This has been my life's work since I returned from Waterloo. But my mother and brother both detest the way I live. My mother wants me to marry and have a family. Robert wants me to return to Brightgate and help him with managing all my family's business affairs." He sighed, picking at the wax with his thumbnail. "I have no desire to do either. My work is very important to me. I wish they would understand."

Sophie nodded, her ringlets bouncing. "Yes, I know just how you feel. When I chose to come to Bath and work a seamstress for Lord Bradbury, Harriet and John were very uncertain of the wisdom of my choice. Fortunately, I was able to convince them both that living at home would in no way make me a more independent person. After Mama died, I wanted to be more than another girl on the marriage mart, looking for a husband. It's all I was groomed for, but when my family's fortunes collapsed and Papa and Mama died, I decided I needed to strike out on my own. And so I have."

The carriage slowed as they turned onto the Crescent. He could just glimpse the well-matched and imposing facades of the most expensive townhomes in Bath—very different from his own two-room flat on Beau Street. Sophie sensed the carriage's impending halt, and began to gather her things.

"I shall think of a solution to your problem, Lieutenant," she informed him in a confident tone. "Just allow me to think on it overnight. I am sure there is a way you can respond to her letter without relinquishing your work with the veterans, or leaving Bath."

The carriage door opened, and the driver helped Sophie alight. Charlie flung the letter onto the seat and followed, opening his umbrella over her head just as the rain pelted them once again. "I shall return in a moment," he called to the driver as he followed Sophie up the path toward the house.

Sophie turned and headed for the front door. Was

she given special privileges as a seamstress? Most servants and maids entered through the back door. As they neared the front portico, he grabbed her elbow. "Miss Handley? Shouldn't we go around to the back?"

She stopped short, and the package she held toppled to the ground. He bent and retrieved it before the rain and mud could do much damage. "Here," he murmured, extending it to her with his wooden hand.

She shook her head as though clearing cobwebs from her mind. "I haven't left the house much, so I forget. Thank you for reminding me." She held her head high and accepted the package, tucking it under one arm. Then she took his elbow once more, saying nothing as he led her back down the path and around the large stone mansion.

Even from the exterior, everything about Lord Bradbury's home spoke of wealth and privilege. Priceless lace curtains graced every window, and he could just pick out a glorious chandelier sparkling in one of the rooms as they passed by. It was no wonder that his lordship could afford to hire a seamstress to work as a personal modiste for his two young daughters. Why, Charlie was no member of the haute monde, but even he knew that Bradbury spoiled his daughters shamelessly, doting on each one after their mother's passing just a few years before.

They rounded the corner and went through the back gate. The garden was budding out in lilies and irises, flowers that nodded heavily in the pouring rain. He helped Sophie up the back steps and took down his umbrella momentarily, as the porch roof offered ample shelter.

He prepared to touch his hat and take his leave, but Sophie halted his progress. "You rescued me twice today," she teased in that same lilting voice that enchanted him before. "You saved me from the wind and the rain, and then you saved me from blundering my way in the front door. There must be some way I can repay the favor. I will give your situation careful thought, and come up with a solution." She withdrew from his side and smiled up at him. "Do you meet with the veterans again soon?"

He blinked rapidly, clearing his mind from the webs of coquetry she spun around his senses. "Yes. I planned to go Thursday morning, after I have attended to a few matters at home."

"Perfect. Then I shall come with you. I can get started on my work with the widows, and tell you of my solution to your problem. How does that sound?"

He bowed. "It sounds fine to me, but won't your employer take exception to your absence?"

Sophie smiled and patted his shoulder. A tingle shot through him at her touch, and he moved a fraction of an inch closer, wanting more of her magic, more of her charm. "Thursday is my day off, Lieutenant. I am at my leisure all day. I shall look forward to spending it with you, if you don't mind me tagging along as you work with the veterans."

"Not at all. Shall I call for you around ten o'clock? We can walk together, and that way you won't get lost." He didn't mean for the last bit of what he said to sound quite so teasing, but Sophie grinned and chuckled.

"I shan't get lost so easily once I learn the buildings

and my routes," she replied in a saucy tone. "I shall expect you Thursday at ten, Lieutenant."

He bowed and held the door open for Sophie as she disappeared into Lord Bradbury's rambling townhome. Then he put up his umbrella and strolled out to the hackney carriage, waiting patiently on the curb.

Funny how one chance meeting with Sophie Handley had changed his whole afternoon. What had felt tragic and utterly insurmountable this morning now seemed a mere trifle. A joke. Something the two of them could chuckle over. His steps, so leaden earlier in the day, now had a definite spring to them. He leaped back into the carriage bound for Beau Street. As they rolled toward home, he tucked his mother's letter in his greatcoat pocket and gave it a satisfied pat.

It was good—very good—to have an ally in the war against his family.

Chapter Two

Mrs. Wiggs was in the kitchen as Sophie entered. Judging from the delicious smells emanating from the oven, she was baking bread. Sophie set her parcel down on the long oak table that the other servants dined at every night, and stretched her hands to the hearth's blaze. She was soaking wet through and chilled to the bone, but a glow warmed her heart. She could not stop smiling, even as miserable as the cold and damp should make her feel.

"Bless my soul, don't you look a sight? Nancy, run upstairs and fetch something warm and dry for Miss Sophie—there's a good gel." The housekeeper dried her hands on her apron and shooed one of the kitchen maids upstairs. "Whatever happened to you?"

"I got lost on the way to the haberdashers, and it began pouring," Sophie replied with a chuckle. "Of course, in my haste to get the buttons and return home, I neglected to bring a parasol."

The housekeeper made a tsking sound under her breath, and stirred up the fire. "I best make you some tea, or you're likely to catch your death."

A commotion sounded in the hallway, and two young ladies burst through the door, giggling and talking breathlessly over one another. "Sophie, you're back. Did you find some buttons for me?" Amelia, the elder of the two Bradbury daughters, danced over to the table, seizing the parcel and clasping it to her bosom.

"Amelia, can't you see she's soaking wet? Poor Sophie, are you quite all right?" Louisa, the younger and gentler of the two girls, laid her head on Sophie's damp shoulder.

"I am quite all right, thank you, my dear. It was a bit of an adventure, actually." Sophie gladly accepted a steaming cup of tea from Mrs. Wiggs, and spooned sugar in it while she waited for the brew to cool down a bit.

"Girls? Where are you?" Lucy Williams, governess to the Bradbury family, called from down the hall.

"In here!" the two imps chorused, and Sophie couldn't stifle a smile as she stirred her tea. The girls delighted in provoking dear Lucy, who proved to be quite a good sport about it all. Lucy strode through the kitchen door, planting her fists on both hips.

"Really, I turn my back for one moment and find you in the kitchen," she scolded. "Is that proper behavior for two young ladies?"

"I don't know if it's proper or not, but the kitchen is the most interesting room in the house," Amelia replied smartly. "Aside from your rooms, and Sophie's, of course."

"I agree," Louisa chirped, flipping a long brown curl over one shoulder. "Here, we can steal biscuits and tea.

In your rooms, we can loll around on the beds and talk nonsense."

"Well, be that as it may, you two must fall into line. Your father returns later this week, and I must have at least a semblance of order and discipline. For his sake, if for no other reason."

Sophie choked, the hot tea burning a path down her throat. Lord Bradbury planned to come home from London this week? She'd had no idea it would be so soon. For the two weeks she had been in Bath, no one had given any indication that his lordship would be in residence at all.

"Are you all right?" Amelia patted her back with a few solid whacks.

"Y-yes," Sophie spluttered, trying to take a deep breath. "I—was surprised—that's all."

"Surprised about Papa? Don't be, Sophie. He's such a dear. You'll love him," Louisa assured her as she took the biscuit tin down from the larder.

"Yes, he is," Amelia added, helping herself to a few biscuits. "He's been so good to us all. We quite adore him. No need to be alarmed, Sophie. He'll take one look at you and be satisfied."

"I don't want him to be satisfied with me—I want him to be satisfied with my work. It's a very different thing," Sophie admonished, draining the last sugary drops from her teacup. Thus fortified, she turned to Lucy. "I haven't had very much time to begin my work. I've only just cut the pieces for Amelia's riding habit."

"I would not worry," Lucy assured her, an encouraging smile lighting her brown eyes. "His lordship is very just and fair, and he knows you've only been in residence for a fortnight. I am certain all will be well."

"Even so." Sophie rose, shaking out her still-damp skirts. "I would feel better if I accomplished a bit more before his lordship returns. Come, Amelia, let us retire to the sewing room. I need to see if these buttons meet with your approval. They were hard-won notions, after all I've been through today." And though they were hard won, they were well worth the effort. Lieutenant Cantrill, with his lean angular face and velvety eyes, drifted across her mind. 'Twould be difficult indeed to keep her mind on her sewing today. But if she wanted to impress his lordship, and keep her position as a seamstress, she had better try to banish the lieutenant from her thoughts—at least until after supper, when she could turn her mind toward his most fascinating problems, and how she might be able to solve them.

Chapter Three

A knock sounded on the sewing-room door. "Enter," Sophie called. Perhaps it was one of the servants to bring her breakfast on a tray.

Instead, her dear friend Lucy poked her head around the doorjamb. "Oh, good. You're alone. I thought perhaps the girls would be with you."

"No, I think they are still having their breakfasts. Why do you ask?" Sophie tossed aside Amelia's riding jacket and rubbed her hands together. Working the buttonholes in that stiff wool played havoc with her manicure. Besides, a good gossip with Lucy always broke up the monotony of the day.

"Something's happened. You've been distracted and vague since you returned from shopping yesterday. And you barely said two words throughout supper last night. What is the matter?" Lucy sank down on the settee beside her, a grin crooking one corner of her mouth.

"I met someone." Had she really seemed distracted? To the point that her absentmindedness was obvious to others? Well, she had been thinking about the lieutenant, after all.

"Really?" A broad smile crept across Lucy's face. "Is it someone I know? You must tell me everything."

"No. His name is Lieutenant Charlie Cantrill." Saying his name aloud was difficult. It sounded so dignified and so…real, when spoken aloud. "He is a good friend of my family's, and he rescued me when I got lost on the way to Guildhall Market. I literally bumped into him as I was trying to find my way."

"Lieutenant Cantrill?" The governess's brows drew together, and she looked off into space. "Why is his name so familiar to me? For I don't know him, but I have heard of him."

"He does a lot of work with the veterans of Waterloo," Sophie added. "I am to help him work with the widows of some of the men who fell during the battle."

"No, that's not it. There was some scandal when he returned from the war—"

"Scandal?" Sophie's heart leaped in her breast, and she leaned forward, grasping Lucy's hands. "Do tell!"

"I'm trying to remember. Something happened. I think he was engaged to one girl and then the engagement was broken when he returned. As I recall, she was rather well-placed in Society, so it was a bit of a to-do." Lucy smiled ruefully. "But since I don't frequent those social circles, I cannot recall much more than that."

Sophie sat back. Well, this was interesting. Perhaps Cantrill was a bit of a black sheep. That made him infinitely more intriguing. "Did he cry off? Or did the lady?"

Lucinda shrugged her shoulders. "I cannot recall."

Why, this added an entirely new dimension to his character. Perhaps his moodiness and serious disposition was a mask for his true character. Maybe he was even a bit of a rake, despite his charitable work. Sophie stifled a laugh at the thought.

"I would watch myself around him, you know," the governess admonished. "Until we know the truth of what happened, you should be on your guard."

"I am to meet with him tomorrow," Sophie replied, her eyes widening at the thought. "I can't miss it. I promised my sister I would help with his work with the widows. The lieutenant is my brother-in-law's closest friend."

Lucinda nodded. "If he is a friend of your family, then perhaps there is no need for caution."

Sophie nodded. "Do you know, I promised the lieutenant I would come up with a solution to a problem he has, since he was so kind as to rescue me yesterday. But I must confess that, even though I have been pondering it, I have no idea what to do to help."

Lucy shrugged. "Tell me. Perhaps we can come up with a plan together."

"Well, his family is very concerned with status and his place in Society. His mother wrote that he must give up his work with the veterans and look for a wife. His brother has ordered him to return to Brightgate and assume some of the responsibilities of the family estate." She sighed. "I understand how the lieutenant must feel. I struck out on my own, and though Harriet supported me, she was reluctant to let me come to Bath at first."

Lucy traced a pattern on the rug with the toe of her slippered foot. "Well, perhaps he could give the semblance of returning to Society and status while still remaining devoted to his cause," she replied, a thoughtful crease marking her straight, fine brows. "After all, as long as he just gives the appearance of being a part of Society—that may be enough to appease his family."

"True. But how could he compromise?"

"I don't know. If his mother is concerned about the lieutenant finding a wife, perhaps he could pretend to be looking for one." Lucy rose and walked over to the door. "I had better go find my charges. I would wager my last pound they aren't in the schoolroom doing their Latin lessons." She paused in the doorway. "Oh, and Lord Bradbury has arrived, and would like to meet with you this morning. If you would go down to his study in fifteen minutes or so, he will be expecting you. He likes to meet all the servants in person and will probably plan out Amelia's Season with you. So be prepared."

"Of course." All thoughts of helping the lieutenant fled. Now she must prove her worth to her employer. Sophie rose, gathering a stack of fashion plates to show his lordship. "I shall go down at once, Lucy. Thank you for your help."

Lucy winked. "Think nothing of it."

Though Sophie had been downstairs a few times since her arrival, the labyrinthine corridors were confusing. And why were all the doors painted the same color? Goodness, it was difficult to know where one was going. The clock in the hallway tolled the hour. She was going to be late to her first meeting with Lord Bradbury. That did not bode well for her continued employment, did it?

In exasperation, she grasped the last latch on the right and rushed headlong into the room. An older man with a handsome and serious face rose in surprise from a massively carved desk. "Miss Handley, I presume?"

Sophie bobbed a quick curtsy, spilling her stack of fashion plates and foolscap on the floor. "Yes. Oh, bother."

He came around the side of the desk and helped her scoop the papers into a pile. "There you are, Miss Handley. Pray be seated." He motioned her to a coffee-colored leather chair poised in front of the desk.

His manners were so smooth, so urbane. Droplets of perspiration began to bead Sophie's brow. She furtively wiped them away as he took his place behind the desk. Then he smiled at her and clasped his hands over his ink blotter.

"You are younger than I expected, Miss Handley." His hazel eyes raked over her figure as if trying to determine the exact day and hour of her birth. "My daughters already seem to adore you."

"Um, yes." Sophie cast about for something intelligent to say. Anything that wouldn't get her sacked. "Well, you see, I am young but I have been sewing for most of my life. I feel I am very talented despite my youth, Lord Bradbury. And I do think I can make some wondrous creations for your daughters."

"Please don't feel you need to defend yourself, Miss Handley." He gave her an easy smile that sent butterflies fluttering in her stomach. Why was she reacting so? He was much older than most of the men she knew— too old for her by half. "I was merely commenting on the obvious."

She nodded uncertainly. He would have to take the lead from now on. She was in uncharted waters.

"My daughters lost their mother a few years ago, and I am being very frank when I say that I am making up for their loss with material pleasures." He ran a hand through his thick black hair, ruffling it a bit. "No girls should have to grow up without a mother. It preys upon my mind."

Sophie tilted her head to one side. Had she come to Bath merely to solve every man's marital woes? "Perhaps you should remarry, your lordship."

He leveled a piercing gaze at her that made her catch her breath. "I may do so someday. However, my first wife was nothing short of remarkable. I don't think I could find the likes of her again…." His voice trailed off.

Sophie nodded and fell silent. Nothing she said seemed to be the right thing to say, so 'twas better to be quiet.

He turned toward the window, looking out on the sleet as it ran in rivulets down the pane. "You are Sir Hugh Handley's daughter, are you not?"

"Yes, your lordship." Any mention of her family connections made Sophie uneasy.

"What makes you take a position in service?" He flicked a glance her way.

She hated having to defend her choices. If her family approved, why should Lord Bradbury care? "I desire to make my own way in the world, doing what I love best," she replied, raising her chin with defiance.

He turned to face her again, an inscrutable look crossing his face. "I see," he replied. "Well, Miss Handley, I give you free rein with my daughters. All of my funds are at your command. Doll them up in any way you see fit."

She leaned forward, grabbing the pile of papers from his desk. "Do you wish to see my ideas, my lord?"

He waved his hand in a listless fashion. "No, I trust your judgment. Nothing too immodest, I assume?"

Heat flooded Sophie's cheeks. "Certainly not."

He stood, signaling the end of the interview. "Very well, then. I hope you enjoy your work. Do not hesitate to come to me if you need bigger lines of credit at the shops."

She grasped her papers in one hand and rose, bobbing a shaky curtsy. "Thank you, Lord Bradbury. I shall endeavor not to disappoint."

Charlie Cantrill opened the door to his club with a sigh. As the son of a wealthy merchant, there were certain things you could give up, though the other fellows might sneer about it. Liquor and light skirts, for example. He had been living as simply as could be following Waterloo and Beth's rejection. And yet, one thing remained eternal and unchanged. Devotion to one's club remained constant, no matter how one might cut corners in other aspects of life.

He nodded as a valet scurried forward to take his coat and hat. Then, scanning the open hallway, he spied one group of gentlemen playing a game of whist in the next room. He made his way to the lounge, where Lord Bradbury lay before the fire, deep into a glass of Scotch.

"Cantrill! What ho, man. It's good to see you." Rising, Bradbury extended his hand toward Cantrill.

"Bradbury, good to see you back in town." Cantrill

shook hands and then sank into the opposite chair. "Tea, if you please." He smiled briefly at the hovering butler.

Bradbury took up his Scotch with a laugh. "Never could understand how you make do without spirits, Cantrill. They've kept me sane these years since Emma died."

"I find myself saner without them." Time for a change of subject. He never enjoyed talking about his abstinence with anyone who wasn't a close friend. Just as he kept his faith close to the vest, he kept other parts of his life from public scrutiny. It was a private matter, after all. "I understand that a friend of mine is recently in your employ."

"Really?" Bradbury leaned forward, cradling the glass in both hands. "Whom are you speaking of?"

"Miss Handley." He found it difficult to speak the words. Why was it so hard to say her name?

"Ah, yes." Bradbury sat back, a satisfied smile crossing his face. "I had the pleasure of meeting Miss Handley today. What a lovely creature. I was quite surprised to find she was seeking employment—because she is a Handley, and because she's so beautiful."

"I believe she wants to establish some measure of independence," Cantrill remarked. He didn't like the light that was kindled in Bradbury's eyes. The man looked too satisfied and pleased with himself.

"Oh, I am sure she would be happy to give up that much-vaunted independence when the right offer comes along," Bradbury said with a laugh. "Pretty young ladies like that needn't stay employed for very long."

The tea arrived, giving Cantrill the distraction he needed to calm down from Bradbury's comment. After all, wouldn't marriage be an excellent thing for Sophie Handley? She was a lovely girl, and would likely get an offer of marriage from someone soon. He flicked a glance over Bradbury. The man was older than him by a decade, and yet retained a distinguished and sportive air. His name had been linked to at least one high-born widow in the past year. Might he be in the market for a match? And if so, why did Charlie's stomach revolt at the thought? It was none of his affair, surely.

Bradbury glanced over at Cantrill. "How is she connected to your family?"

Cantrill busied himself with pouring tea into his cup. "Her elder sister married a good friend of mine— Captain John Brookes. Really, he's almost a brother to me."

Bradbury sipped his Scotch with a meditative air. "I see. And she is Sir Hugh Handley's daughter, is she not? Why on earth would she be working to earn her daily bread?"

"Well, as I am sure you heard, Bradbury, her father died bankrupt. The family estate was sold at auction and the two girls and their mother went to live in a small cottage in Tansley. After her sister's marriage, Miss Sophie came to Bath. And that's really all I know of their story." He hadn't meant to sound rude, but the look on Bradbury's face was raising his hackles. 'Twas none of his affair, and yet…well, he had an obligation to Brookes and to Harriet to make sure that Sophie was protected during her stay in Bath.

"Well, my daughters adore her, but I must make sure she is the proper kind of young lady for the job, you know. I have acquaintances in Liverpool—I will ask around to find out more about the Handleys and what happened when her father died." He polished off his Scotch and rose. "Funny. I expected a spinster. Imagine my surprise when Aphrodite burst into my office this morning."

Cantrill peered up at the older man, trying to read his thoughts. On the one hand, he seemed to regard Sophie in more than just the usual master-servant manner. And yet, he also seemed unwilling to believe that she was a genuinely good girl, one who was seeking her way in the world in a manner that was admirable. He rose, setting the teacup to one side, as Bradbury began to stroll out of the room.

"Miss Handley is a fine young woman, and you have nothing to fear from your daughters associating with her," he responded, willing the flush that was rising up his neck to stay hidden under his cravat.

Bradbury turned back, a gleam in his eye. "Oh, I am not worried about my daughters associating with her. I am more worried about myself." With that, Bradbury quit the room.

Chapter Four

Thursday morning dawned crisp and cool, but at least the rain had stopped. There was even a bit of watery sunshine peeping through the clouds. And since today was her day off Sophie could do exactly as she pleased in Bath. Not that she minded her work, of course. But there were some days when a girl just wanted to lounge in bed, even if she had the most wonderful job imaginable. Of course, her eagerness to enjoy the day had nothing whatsoever to do with meeting Charlie Cantrill. No. It was just a remarkably fine day. That was all.

Sophie turned on her side and stared out the window. One of the kitchen servants would be in soon with her morning cocoa. She stretched lazily toward the ceiling. And soon after, she would dress and ready herself for her morning meeting with the lieutenant. She could wear anything she wanted on this day—no more dark grays and plain bodices. And yet, perhaps one shouldn't dress up too fine for visiting wounded veterans. Her lavender gown with the long sleeves would do the trick nicely.

A knock on the door snapped her out of her reverie. "Enter."

Lucy poked her head around the door frame. "Shall I accompany you this morning?"

Sophie motioned her in, and Lucy shut the door softly. She was becomingly attired in an ink-blue frock that darkened the color of her eyes. Sophie patted the mattress, and Lucy sat. "Pretty dress, Lucy."

The governess smiled. "Thank you. I don't have your skill with a needle, but I do all right by myself."

Sophie rolled her head back on the pillow. "I think I am being too missish if I bring you along as a chaperone," she replied. "Surely Charlie can be trusted. He is a friend of my family, after all."

Lucy grinned, her eyes sparkling. "And it wouldn't be because you want the young man all to yourself?"

Sophie chucked her pillow at Lucy, who laughed and ducked in the nick of time. "I am merely doing my duty by my sister," Sophie said, pursing her lips in a spinsterly manner. "And I want to help the lieutenant as he has helped me. Besides, as a young lady who works, I have little time for romance."

"That's rich." Lucy leaned against the footboard, tucking her legs up underneath her. "From what I understand, his lordship finds you a most admirable young lady."

Sophie pulled her coverlet up so high, the quilt nearly touched her chin. "Whatever is that supposed to mean?"

Lucy shrugged. "Just that. Servants' gossip, you know. But apparently Lord Bradbury thinks terribly highly of you."

Sophie frowned. "How did this rumor start?"

"How does any rumor start? Perhaps he mentioned something to his valet, and from there the story spread like ink running out of an overturned well." Lucy plucked at the quilt. "Why are you so upset by this rumor? If Lord Bradbury is fond of you, it could bode well for your future."

Sophie gave her curls a negative shake. "That doesn't sound very nice at all. I feel much safer working for Lord Bradbury and helping the lieutenant. And that's all."

"Ah, well, then." Lucy rose from the bed with a smile. "Then by all means keep your appointment with Lieutenant Cantrill. I shall spend my morning reading Byron. When you return, shall we meet for tea? Perhaps at one of the shops?"

"Yes. I shall meet you at Molland's in Milsom Street around three, if you please." Sophie threw back the covers, preparing to get out of bed.

Lucy departed with a cheerful wave. "I cannot wait to hear about your morning adventure. Adieu, dear Sophie."

By the time Lieutenant Cantrill knocked on the kitchen door, Sophie was ready and waiting. She had dressed in her lavender gown and tucked up her curls, then added a deeper purple spencer to keep out the spring chill. She had even taken her breakfast at the birch wood table with several other servants, so as not to miss his arrival.

She stepped out onto the back porch and smiled. "What a lovely morning to walk together, Lieutenant. I cannot wait."

He cordially offered his good arm, and she accepted

it happily. As they strolled together, she cudgeled her brain for a way to bring up the topic of his rescue. She stole little sideways glances up at his handsome features, taking in his fine, straight nose and his firm chin. She breathed deeply to compose herself, but was only aware of Charlie's scent—a scent of tweed and oiled leather. A distinctly masculine smell that could, if one were susceptible, make one giddy. Not that she was, of course. She had to stop thinking about him, so she spoke to break the spell.

"What made you decide to involve yourself with veterans?"

"Well, Miss Handley, I am one, you know." He looked down at her with a quizzical air.

"Yes, of course." How stupid of her. "But many young men are veterans. Not all choose to help others."

"Well." He paused a moment, as if pondering what to say, or even how much to tell her. "I lost my arm at Waterloo and it changed my life. I felt a sense of purpose. Some might even say a mission."

"A mission?" She glanced back up at him, thoroughly confused. "Please explain, Lieutenant."

"I felt that, because I did not die on the battlefield, God must have another purpose for me in life. That there must be some reason I was spared. And so, from that terrible day on, I became a changed man. I decided to devote my life to helping others."

She nodded slowly. "I never thought about life in that manner. That God may have a purpose for each and every one of us."

He looked down at her intently. "I believe it to be so."

Sophie turned away from his gaze, her brows knitted

together. A purpose in life? She had never considered such a prospect before. In fact, to be perfectly honest, she hadn't considered anything the Lord might have to say before. She had lived life the way a leaf tossed in a stream might live, buffeted along by the current, catching on pebbles, tossed along without any hope or thought of changing direction.

First there was Lucy's comment about Lord Bradbury. And now Charlie's talk about faith. She opened her eyes wider. She was certainly learning much about life this morning. And she wasn't sure she really understood any of it.

As they neared St. Swithins, Charlie felt his hand perspiring. How would Sophie react? Would the other veterans and their wives take to her? Or would it just be an awkward, interminable morning? Hopefully not. Visiting the veterans was the highlight of his week, and 'twould be a pity indeed if Sophie spoiled everything for him.

"It's…in a church?" Sophie asked, her steps slowing.

"Yes." He gave a curt nod. "Reverend Stephens has been a tremendous help to my cause. He opened the sanctuary to the veterans of Waterloo, and it is there that I meet with them and ascertain what their needs might be."

Sophie tilted her head back, holding on to her bonnet with one hand. "It's beautiful. I haven't been in a church since Harriet's wedding, and very seldom before that. How magnificent the steeple looks!"

The church did look rather magnificent under the streaks of icy sunlight that cut through the clouds. Like most of the buildings in Bath, it was made of stone and tan in color. Its majestic steeple pierced the sky, a beacon that called everyone, saint and sinner alike, home for worship.

He glanced at Sophie's pure profile, tilted back as she drank in the splendors of the view. "You did not go to church often?"

"Hardly at all," she admitted with the frankness he was coming to admire. "Crich is a four-mile journey there and four miles back. 'Twas too far to travel with Mama. And before that, well, church in Matlock Bath was more of a social affair for our family."

He nodded and opened the massive oaken door. Her experience with faith was not much different from his. After all, his conversion happened on the battlefield, not because of any experience he had growing up in his family's parish. "I come here for worship every Sunday. If you like, you may join me. Reverend Stephens is a gifted speaker. I daresay there are few who can phrase the Bible in such clear and understandable terms."

She smiled politely. "Thank you."

That brief response, and the brief, circumspect smile that came with it, gave one the feeling of being rebuffed. Or at least brushed off. He set his jaw. They were here on a mere business arrangement, nothing more.

As they entered the narthex, the cacophony of male and female voices, both young and old, bounced off the walls and the high-pitched ceiling. He spied Reverend Stephens with the veterans, gathered near the altar, while the women and children sat farther back in the pews. "Come, I'll introduce you," he said, hurrying her up the aisle toward the altar.

"Reverend," he called as they drew near. "Gentlemen, I have a new representative here with me."

Reverend Stephens motioned for silence and gave a friendly smile to Sophie. "So I see," he responded gently. "Welcome, my child."

Sophie curtsied. "Thank you, Reverend."

Charlie grasped her shoulders and turned her slightly so she was facing the group of veterans. A larger group than usual today—nearly fifteen men. The good weather must have made it possible for more to come.

"Gentlemen, ladies, Reverend Stephens," he called, making sure his voice carried to the back of the church. "With me today is Miss Sophie Handley, newly arrived in Bath. Miss Handley is the younger sister of Mrs. Harriet Brookes, whose book about Waterloo is making a sensation across England."

The crowd applauded politely, and several women leaned forward as if to hear him better.

"As you may know, Mrs. Brookes has donated the proceeds of the sale of her book to our group."

Many people gasped, turning awe-stricken faces to his. Well, this was the first time he'd made the announcement publicly. And it was a very generous thing Harriet had done. The looks on their faces made him break into a grin. How they would put that money to good use.

"Miss Handley is working for Lord Bradbury in town, but has agreed to be her sister's representative here in Bath. Anything that we want to do as a group, Miss Handley will work to make sure it can happen. Please think of her as you do me—as a friend, a confidante and a colleague." He turned his grin to Sophie,

who was looking up at him with wide blue eyes. "I trust
her. And I know that, together, our veterans' group can
make a real difference in everyone's lives."

The group erupted in applause, several of the men
whistling and stamping their feet. Sophie blushed pret-
tily and bobbed a little curtsy before the crowd. He nodded at her, as if to say, "Go on, say something," but her
rosy color deepened and she shook her curls quickly.

He shrugged. "You don't have to say anything if you
don't want to," he replied in an undertone. "But I must
get started working with the men. Do you want to talk
to the women and children?"

"Yes, of course." She moved to the back of the sanctuary, and disappeared as the veterans began to swarm
around Charlie, talking about Harriet's generous dona-
tion and how they should use the funds.

He spoke with the men for a good hour without taking a break. There was a private who had a wife and
a small baby, but he had been blinded and couldn't
earn an income. How were they to survive? And then
a smaller group of veterans with missing limbs, who
complained that the colder-than-average spring was
making it difficult to move about. For the blind veteran,
Charlie withdrew a stipend of fifty pounds, all he could
afford until Harriet's money began trickling in. And
for the others, they came up with a schedule of therapy
involving taking the waters on a twice-weekly basis.

He spent most of his time with a young ensign, the
former scion of a wealthy family, who had braved the
battlefield at a very early age, and become mute from
the experience. The lad could write down a few words,
and Charlie could scratch out words on foolscap, though

it was hard to hold down the page with his prosthesis so he could write fluently with his right hand. From their exchange, he was able to ascertain that the lad needed help—regular conversation, even if he just listened as someone else spoke. But whom, and when? Ah, that was the problem. He would find some way to help Rowland, but it might take time.

When he finally had a moment's pause, he looked anxiously down the pews to see how Sophie was faring. He hadn't meant to leave her alone for so long. Was she beside herself with nervousness and anxiety? No, quite the contrary. She was sitting in the back of the sanctuary on the floor, with two children in her lap. A group of widows were gathered around her, talking quietly. Sophie was listening intently, replying with a soft word here or a nod there. Her spencer was long gone, as was her bonnet, both strewn across a pew with abandon. As he watched the tableau, a child reached up and touched one of her bobbing curls, which made her laugh.

His heart pounded gratefully. She seemed to be coming along very well. In fact, she seemed to have already won the trust of those widows—women who'd barely spoken two words to him before, who kept their eyes cast down and their lips compressed in thin lines when he asked how he could help them. She was going to be an extraordinary asset.

As the church bell tolled the lunch hour, the group began to drift apart. After shaking hands with a few of the departing veterans, and after expressing his thanks to the reverend, Charlie started up the aisle to retrieve Sophie.

She smiled as he helped her back into her spencer,

and bent to kiss one of the little girls on the cheek as
she left. Then she tied on her bonnet and took his arm
decisively. He sucked in his breath a little at the feeling
of Sophie next to him. She had such vibrancy, such life
about her. His existence, so gray and dull until he met
her, now pulsed with color. She would assuredly make
a man very happy someday.

She exhaled sharply, blowing out a puff of air as they
left the church, turning her head up to the sky.

"Are you tired? I'm sorry. I didn't mean to leave you
alone for so long," he apologized.

"Not at all. I think I got on very well with many of
the women. And the children were darlings," she replied, grasping the crook of his elbow more firmly as
he led her down the steps. "I think the women need
money," she added in an undertone. "Many have no
means of income, and several have children to care
for. Without a steady flow of money, some of them
have been reduced—or nearly so—to rather desperate
circumstances."

Just as he suspected. He stopped, turning to face her.
"You will help me, then? These women, they respond
to you. Together, we can help keep them from turning
to occupations that are beneath them."

She gazed deeply into his eyes. "Of course I will
help you, Lieutenant. Did I not already promise to?"

"Yes, you did. I just wondered if, once you saw how
things were—"

"That I would gather up my skirts and flee in hor-
ror?" She gave a modest chuckle. "Surely I am better
than that."

He couldn't bear the challenge in those blue eyes any

longer. He directed their steps back toward the street. "I do need your help with one other matter. There's a young ensign, named Rowland, who is mute. I think conversation—even just listening to someone read aloud from a book—could help him. Do you think you can help me find someone willing to take that on?"

Sophie smiled, her dimples deepening. "I know just the perfect person, Lieutenant."

Chapter Five

Thank goodness she had gotten an advance on her salary. Sophie sat, cradling her teacup in her hands, observing the hustle and bustle as shoppers filed in and out of Molland's. She needed a fortifying meal and a few moments' peace after her chaotic morning. Even though she feigned courage for the lieutenant, her emotions were deeply shaken. She picked up her watercress sandwich with shaking hands and savored one delicious bite.

Her entire family had been cast into poverty when Papa died. But Sophie never realized how very dreadful poverty could be. Of course, it meant making over Mama's old court dresses rather than enjoying new frocks. And it meant eating potatoes every day rather than having chicken for dinner. And yet, even though they left their ancestral home in disgrace and eked out a meager existence in a cottage, the idea of desperation had never crossed her mind. Why, she had even rejected Captain John Brookes because she no longer loved him after the war.

Love! What nonsense.

Sophie dropped her sandwich and crossed her arms tightly over her chest. What a selfish ninny she had been. The only thing that separated her from the widows she met this morning—women who were facing such straitened circumstances that prostitution suddenly seemed a viable option—was the fact that her industrious sister had kept her from feeling desperate. True, they had discussed taking on jobs in the village. But really, it was Harriet's own demeanor—her insistence on writing a book, her persistence in having it published— that had kept the wolf from the Handley cottage door. And because of her sister's cheerful toiling, she never felt as desperate or as poor as the women she met today.

She tried another bite of her sandwich, but really, it tasted like ashes in her mouth.

The only thing to do is resolve never to be a burden on one's family again. After all, she had gainful employment for the foreseeable future. She would simply have to work hard, save up money and open a dress shop of her own one day. She would never have to worry about Harriet or poverty again.

"Penny for your thoughts?" a cheerful voice interrupted. "Sophie? Are you all right?"

Sophie gave a shake of her head, ridding herself of her reverie. "Lucy." She patted the table and beckoned her friend to sit down. "Thank goodness you are here."

"Did you have a bad morning? How did your visit to the veterans go?" Lucy sat across from her and placed her reticule on the table. "Tea and sandwiches, if you please," she told the waitress with a smile.

"Oh, the meeting went well." Sophie took a sip of her tea. "But really, Lucy. I had no idea how very badly off some of the women are." She leaned forward and lowered her voice to a whisper. "Some of them even consider...selling themselves."

Lucy nodded. "Yes, I know. I can't say I blame them. After all, a woman must do what she can to survive."

Her response was like a slap in the face. Sophie sat back in her chair, her eyes wide. "Surely you don't condone it."

"No, I wouldn't say I condone it." Lucy accepted her tea from the waitress and nodded her thanks. "I would just say that I can understand it. You see, Sophie, I am an orphan. I grew up in an orphanage. Fortunately for me, I have brains and was able to develop them even in that environment. I was able to become a governess. Some of my friends were not so fortunate."

Really, this was astonishing. It was like turning over a pretty, smooth rock in a field and seeing the worms squirming underneath. "But really, Lucy. My family lost everything and I never felt that kind of desperation. Maybe my sister hid it from me. I even turned down two marriage proposals."

Lucy spluttered and choked on her tea. "Beg pardon?" she coughed, dabbing at her eyes with her handkerchief. The waitress returned with a small china plate of sandwiches.

Sophie waited until the waitress left before picking up the thread of conversation.

"Yes, it's true. I turned down Captain John Brookes and another redcoat—James Marable." It was embarrassing to admit it now. Especially as Lucy sat staring at her, looking at her as though she had just sprouted horns on the top of her head.

"Why?" Lucy took a careful sip of her tea, continuing to eye Sophie over the rim of her cup.

"Because I did not love them." Why did it feel like an admission of guilt? After all, Harriet had promised her long ago that she did not have to marry anyone she did not love. Even after Mama died and Sophie was riddled with guilt and sorrow, Harriet promised her she had made the right choice.

Lucy set down her cup with a clink. "Well, then, I must say yes. It sounds to me that your sister did protect you. I envy you your freedom, Sophie. Most young women in dire poverty would marry anyone without delay. No picking and choosing allowed."

"And that's why I am seeking my own fortune." Sophie lifted her chin in the air. It wasn't as if she was lolling about in bed all day, eating bonbons. She worked very hard for Lord Bradbury and his daughters. And she was building a future for herself until she could strike out on her own and become a modiste with a proper shop.

"And so you are." Lucy reached out and clasped Sophie's hand warmly. "But listen, Sophie. Not everyone's experience is akin to yours. We do not all have the same background, breeding or talent to make something of ourselves. And to be perfectly honest, not all of us are as pretty as you." She released Sophie's hand. "You mustn't judge other women for what they may choose to do to survive."

"I don't," Sophie protested. "I am just stunned, that's all. In our days of poverty, I never had to consider such a thing. And it both addles me and humbles me to know that others do. I never knew how hard my sister worked as a writer to save my family until this moment."

A sympathetic light kindled in Lucy's eyes, easing some of the turmoil in Sophie's heart. Lucy wasn't dismayed by her refusal to marry. And for that she was grateful.

Lucy tapped the table with her forefinger for emphasis as she spoke again. "So now that you have this position, what do you wish to do with the rest of your life?"

"I wish for peace and freedom." Why, she could even feel it—the sensation of being lifted up on wings. Not relying on anyone. Making her own way in the world. "I should like to have my own dress shop someday. When Amelia and Louisa no longer need my services."

"And what of marriage? If another proposal came your way, what would you say?" Lucy cocked her head to one side.

"I do not know." An image of brown eyes in a stern face flashed before her mind's eye. Charlie Cantrill. If Charlie asked her, what would she say? And why was she thinking of him, anyway? Theirs was a mere business relationship. "It would depend upon the gentleman, and my own feelings in the matter."

"Ah, *c'est bon.*" Lucy stirred her teacup meditatively. She fell silent, brooding over the steaming brew.

Sophie regarded her carefully. Lucy seemed so lively, so independent, and yet she had no family. Other than her charges and the other servants, she had no one to speak to, to care for. Her existence must be so lonely. She needed to find others to share her life with. Perhaps reading to Ensign Rowland would allow her to branch out, and forge connections with others.

"Lucy, you're so clever." Best to start with flattery. Everyone loved a nice compliment. "There's someone who needs your help. Lieutenant Cantrill mentioned an ensign who is mute. Would you come to the veterans' group with me and read to him? The lieutenant thinks it would be a great help to the young man, and I would love to have your company there."

Lucy looked up, her blue eyes wide with astonishment. "Really? You think it would be a help?"

Sophie offered her most appealing smile. Her plan was already starting to work. Maybe Lucy could find her happily ever after, even if Sophie's seemed remote. "Dear Lucy, I think it would be a tremendous help. For everyone."

Charlie accepted the teacup from Aunt Katherine's extended hand. "Thank you, Auntie." He couldn't help but call her Aunt. Everyone did. In reality, she was John Brookes's aunt—but in practice, she was aunt to them all.

"And so, Charlie," she asked, amusement evident in her tone, "how did Sophie fare on her first day?"

He settled back in his chair, breathing deeply of the scents of oolong and leather. Aunt Katherine's home always made him feel at peace. She managed to live a life of simple luxury, one that made him comfortable without causing guilt. After all, so many people had so little.

"She did quite well, Aunt Katherine. I believe that she will be a tremendous help to my cause. Some of the women took to her immediately—she got their confidence in mere moments, whereas I had been working for weeks."

Aunt Katherine nodded, her wrinkled features softening into a smile. "Good, I am glad to hear it. You know, I was none too fond of Miss Sophie after she broke her understanding with John. He is my nephew and I feel he is a rare gem. On the other hand, matters worked out right. John and Harriet are together, and a better match you'll never find."

He nodded. Everything had worked out for the best, for everyone. "So you are not bitter, Aunt Katherine?"

She laughed, tilting her head back. "Not at all, I assure you. In fact, I am inclined to like Sophie more and more. She is, perhaps, the more spoiled of the two lasses, but she is showing a willingness to work on her own and gain independence that is most pleasing."

Charlie smiled. It was easy to misjudge Sophie. She was so pretty and so vibrant that it was not at all difficult to think of her as a flibbertigibbet, passing over her strength of character. "I think so, too."

"Do you?" The faded old eyes regarded him sharply, as though Aunt Katherine were studying him through a lorgnette. The close regard caused a wriggle of unease to work up his spine.

"Yes." Would Auntie stop regarding him in that fashion? He felt like an insect under a spying glass.

"And what of Elizabeth Gaskell? Do you ever hear of your former fiancée at all?"

The sudden shift in conversation threw Charlie off guard. Like a good soldier, he eyed the terrain warily. What did this abrupt change signify? Why was she bringing up Beth, right on the heels of their discussion about Sophie?

"What I know of Beth I read in *The Tatler*." His

words were clipped and precise. Beth's downward spiral into licentious behavior was a constant source of amusement for Bath—and embarrassment for her former fiancé. He did not like to talk about it with anyone. Not even Auntie.

"So, then. If she is mentioned in the gossip rags, then she is still living a hedonistic existence." Aunt Katherine clasped her hands, laden with rings, together over her stomach, peering at him with eyes that had only sharpened with age. "And where does this leave you, Charlie?"

"Forgive me, Auntie, but I don't understand your meaning." Honestly, the old woman was as mysterious as the Sphinx. John had warned him so, many times in the past. And yet, since she was meddling in others' affairs, Charlie found it amusing. Now, faced with it himself, it didn't seem as funny.

"Tut, tut. There's no need to get testy with an old woman. I only mean to say it isn't right for a young man to live alone without thinking about a wife and family. While your work with the veterans is nothing short of admirable, what are you doing to better your own life, my son?"

"You sound like my mother. Always lecturing me to give up my work and settle down with a wife." And yet, what was so winning about his life? Dinner alone. Walks to the Pump Room. Reading before his cozy fire. It was usually pleasant, but took on a lonely tinge now that he thought about it. "Sometimes I prefer solitude. When Brookes is in town, I have a very active social life."

Aunt Katherine clapped her hands, her rings tinkling merrily. "Ah, but John is now married, and I am sure he and Harriet will have a family soon. He won't have as much time for trips to Bath and army reunions. You must create a life for yourself that is rich and full, young Charlie. While austerity has its benefits, I worry that you are missing out on the very vibrancy of life."

Vibrancy. Warmth. Beauty. An image of blue eyes and hair the color of sunlight passed through his mind. A lively young lady, someone to share his life with. He blinked rapidly, clearing the alluring vision away. "I don't know, Aunt Katherine. Sometimes I think I was meant to be alone. Perhaps that is why God spared me. To live a life of quiet austerity helping others. It's not a bad existence, you know."

Aunt Katherine pursed her lips and shook her head. An unusual quiet descended on the library, broken only by the crackling of the fire in the grate. At length, Aunt Katherine spoke softly. "Not all women are like Elizabeth Gaskell. Not even pretty ones."

"I am afraid all young ladies are more like her than we care to admit." The thread of bitterness running through his tone was surprising, even to his own ears. "Especially…" His face began to burn, a flush he could not attribute to the heat from the fire. "*Especially* pretty and vivacious women."

"Charlie." Aunt Katherine's voice was quiet, the kind of tone she might reserve for a child who had fallen and skinned his knee. "Surely you don't harbor bitterness and prejudice in your heart." She straightened up and offered him a kind smile. She was like a mother in some ways, and it made him blink back sudden tears. He was a soldier, after all. No good to cry. "'Another man dies in bitterness of soul, never having enjoyed anything good,'" she quoted. "Don't allow what Beth did to rob you of happiness."

It took a few moments for Charlie to gain composure. He simply stared out the library window, avoiding Aunt Katherine's gaze while he settled his thoughts. What she said was true. He must get rid of all bitterness in his heart. And yet, it was hard to let go of that anger. It had driven him and fueled his existence for so long, he didn't know how to relinquish it. It had been hidden under a mask of good cheer, at least where the Brookes family was concerned. But Aunt Katherine, with her uncanny powers of perception, had discovered the truth.

When he was of a more reasonable frame of mind, he rose. It was embarrassing to be so emotional. "Aunt Katherine, I must be going. But I do want to thank you, from the bottom of my heart, for your help. I appreciate all you are trying to do for me."

She extended her hand, jewels winking in the firelight. "Tut, tut, my dear boy. I shall meddle with you tirelessly now that John is happily wed." She gave him a wheedling smile. "Your mother may be right, after all. And remember that the Handley girls are made of stronger stuff than I think we often give them credit for."

Her words echoed in Charlie's mind as he walked back to his flat. Why had she added that last bit? Could it be that Sophie Handley was made of stronger stuff than he imagined? Behind that pretty face, was she something more? He let himself into the chilly flat. His housekeeper had the day off, and he hated coming home when she hadn't been working all day. His home seemed dour and cheerless without at least a fire burning in the grate and the bustle of work in the kitchen.

He kindled the fire himself and extended his hand to the blaze. The warmth ran from the tips of his fingers to the pit of his heart. Perhaps he had allowed bitterness to settle and become part of him for too long. Perhaps it was time for spring—in more ways than one.

Chapter Six

"Oh, Sophie!" Amelia cried, flinging herself through the door of Sophie's sewing room. Sophie glanced up in surprise. Shouldn't Amelia be studying with Lucy in the schoolroom?

"Amelia? Whatever is the matter?" Sophie removed a pin from her mouth and stabbed it through the dress form she was working with.

"Papa has agreed to have a dinner party a fortnight from now, and I am to be the hostess. Imagine! My first entrée into Society. So I must have a very pretty gown, you know." Amelia danced around the room, her long curls bobbing as she clapped her hands.

"That is excellent news, Amelia. What do you think of this blue dress I am finishing? Surely it would fit the bill nicely." Sophie stepped back and surveyed her handiwork with a critical eye. A bit more pin tucking around the bodice, and it would just suit her young muse. And perhaps a bit of lace, as well?

"Yes, yes, it's very pretty. But, Sophie, that was the gown I am to wear later in the Season. I want something special for this occasion, something entirely new. Perhaps—" she spun around the workroom, running her hands over the bolts of fabric "—perhaps something in this yellow?" She held out a yard of gauzy fabric, wrapping it around her middle.

A brief wriggle of unease made its way up Sophie's spine as she watched Amelia prance around the room. Here they were, surrounded by luxurious fabrics of every conceivable color and finish. And here was her young charge, dancing around in delighted anticipation of yet another new dress, made expressly to her whims.

Sophie's mind flashed back to the widows, old and young, whom she had met at St. Swithins. Their clothes were so worn and patched, they were almost threadbare. Why should one young girl have so much, while others had so little? Sophie gave her head a defiant shake. It seemed rather unfair. To distract these unpleasant thoughts, Sophie gave her full attention back to pin tucking the bodice, stabbing the pins in place with shaking hands.

"Sophie, is anything the matter? Don't you think the yellow will suit me well?" Amelia dropped the fabric, a worried frown puzzling her brow.

"Oh, no. So sorry, Amelia darling. Bit of a headache coming on, that's all." Sophie managed a small smile for her charge. After all, it wasn't Amelia's fault that she was born into great wealth while others were wanting.

"I am sorry to hear that." Lord Bradbury lounged against the doorway, his arms crossed over his chest. Sophie jumped a little, startled at the sound of his rich, sophisticated baritone. "I was depending upon you to help prepare Amelia for her debut as hostess."

Were none of the Bradburys where they were supposed to be at the moment? Amelia was supposed to be studying. Lord Bradbury was supposed to be wherever a wealthy lord spent most of his day. Honestly, having the peace of her workroom completely interrupted by the family was disconcerting. Especially by his lordship, who always managed to ruffle her emotions.

"How can I help, your lordship?" Sophie stuck the last pin into the bodice and turned to face her employer.

"Well, Miss Handley, Amelia will need some assistance with the finer points of being a gracious hostess. Since you were born into the Handley family, I am sure you know how to manage such an affair."

Another mention of the Handleys. Why was he so fixated on her family connections? Surely he knew that the Handley family never acknowledged or spoke to Mama, Harriet or herself. Everyone, it seemed, knew of her family's downfall, the auctioned estate, the years of penury and debt. She slanted her glance toward Amelia, who was bouncing up and down, waiting for her response with heightened anticipation. How much of her sordid past did she dare reveal in front of her young charge? And yet…Amelia looked so hopeful, her eyes wide and pleading.

"Well, your lordship, I shall try. But I must admit that was a long time ago, and I had little practice myself. My elder sister was the only one out at that time. I was still in the schoolroom." She managed a demure smile for Amelia's benefit.

"Nonsense. I can tell you were born to do it." His lordship flicked an appraising glance over her figure, making her cheeks burn. "Some women have natural grace. Others cannot buy it with all the money in the world."

She acknowledged the compliment with a slight incline of her head. "Thank you, Lord Bradbury. I am sure Miss Williams can also assist, if you like."

He shrugged. "Perhaps. But Miss Williams was not born into quality, as you were."

Sophie's mouth dropped open in surprise. What an astonishing thing to say. And rude. After all, Miss Williams was certainly good enough to be entrusted with his daughters' education. She shifted her gaze to Amelia, to gauge her reaction. But if Amelia felt obliged to defend her teacher, she said nothing. She just eyed Sophie expectantly, an excited smile quivering on her dimpled cheeks.

She turned to face his lordship. He was gazing at her with an inscrutable expression in his dark eyes, a look that made her breath catch in her throat. Whatever did he want from her? It seemed like he always wanted something, gauging her reaction or waiting for an opportunity to, well, pounce. Like a barn cat. Or a tiger. She choked back a sudden nervous giggle. He smiled as though she had finally satisfied his question.

"So? We are in agreement? You will coach Amelia on the finer points of being a gracious hostess." He stepped closer to Sophie, and the simple movement sucked all the oxygen out of the workroom. She took an abrupt step back, knocking against the dress form.

Lord Bradbury lifted one puzzled eyebrow. "Miss Handley?"

"My apologies, sir. As I said, I have a bit of headache coming on." She rubbed her elbow ruefully. "But of course I will be happy to help Miss Amelia."

"Oh, Sophie!" Amelia rushed headlong into Sophie, catching her in an embrace that squeezed the breath out of her. "Thank you ever so much. I shan't feel half so awkward if you are there."

Sophie returned the embrace, smoothing Amelia's curls. "Well, my dear Amelia, I shan't really be present at the party. But I shall be guiding you every step of the way until it begins."

Amelia tilted her face up toward Sophie, trouble brewing in her eyes. "But Sophie, I shall need you there to guide me. Papa, isn't that so? Shouldn't Sophie be at the dinner party?"

Sophie shook her head. "Amelia, it wouldn't be right. I am a servant, after all." She had learned her place well after her first few days of missteps and blunders. And it was a good thing—something that made her proud, in fact—that she was earning her place in the world. Even if it meant the social niceties would often be closed to her for the rest of her days.

"On the contrary, Miss Handley. I think your presence would be most welcome at our dinner party. Not only can you continue to assist my daughter with her entrée into Society, you are rather—" he paused as though searching for the right word "—decorative yourself."

"I haven't any gowns that are suitable." She needed any excuse to back out of this arrangement. Something wasn't quite right. She couldn't put her finger on it, but it was rather akin to being tested. And really, one should know all the rules of engagement before being put to the test.

His lordship waved his hand at the bolts of fabric littering the room, his signet ring glinting in the pale sunlight that poured in through the parted curtains. "Make anything you like, Miss Handley. Surely your talents can extend to creations for yourself."

Sophie froze. A new gown? A creation from new fabric, made expressly for her? Such luxury. She had been cutting down Mama's old court dresses and making them over for an eternity. How would a new dress look and feel? Her imagination surged, conjuring images of a pale lavender frock with a modest neckline, some ruching at the bodice...

"Well, Miss Handley?" His lordship was staring at her, the same inscrutable expression on his face that made her heart flutter. Surely there could be no harm in helping her young charge make her debut in Society, could there? And surely, after her years of sacrifice, she deserved one fine gown.

"Very well, my lord, I shall be happy to assist Amelia with her debut, and I will be present at the dinner party, as well." She tossed him a warm smile of gratitude, which he returned with ease. He was handsomer when he smiled. Much less...forbidding. He turned on his heel and vanished without another word.

Sophie hastened her young charge back to her studies, her mind full of plans. For the first time in ages, she would have a taste of real Society. And, though she hated to admit it, it was a flavor she had sorely missed.

Charlie sat before his hearth, Mother's latest missive in his hands. She was coming to Bath. No longer content with issuing orders from afar, Moriah Cantrill would descend on him in a matter of a fortnight. No letter would dissuade her. She was intent on bending her son to her will. And if he capitulated to Mother, then in no time at all, he would be forced to return to Brightgate. He couldn't give in to one family member without giving in to them all.

The clock on the rough wooden mantelpiece chimed the hour. Blast, he would be late for St. Swithins unless he made haste. He rose, tugging on his greatcoat. Perhaps working with his fellow men, helping others with their problems, would help him, too. It gave him great satisfaction to answer the needs of his fellow men. Their wants were so few and so simple—food, clothing and shelter. Not a man jack of them cared about their position in Society. None would be cowed by Moriah Cantrill, that much was certain. A morning spent in service would clear his mind and help him come up with a solution to his problem—which was nothing at all compared to what these men faced.

Once at St. Swithins, he dove into his work, rolling up his sleeves and toiling away on securing the most basic foundations for the men who served with him in battle. There were fewer men here on Saturday, as most elected to come on Thursdays. But the few who gathered had such gaunt, haunted looks on their faces that he was determined to help them, no matter the cost. A few women huddled in the back, but dared not step forward. If only Sophie Handley were there to talk with them, but of course, one day a week would be the most she could manage with her duties to Lord Bradbury and his family. He would have to set some time and energy aside for the widows when he was done with the men.

"Lieutenant Cantrill! I was hoping to find you here this morning," a musical voice trilled in his ear. He spun around, trying to will away the flush creeping over his face. Sophie Handley. It could be no one but her. Several of the men stepped back in deference, their admiration of Sophie's beauty written plainly across their faces. Funny how a pretty creature could make these men instantly lose sight of their troubles.

"Miss Handley," he replied with a bow. "Are you here to assist? I was not aware that you knew I helped some of the veterans on Saturdays."

"One of the widows informed me of it at our last meeting," she admitted, a sweet smile curving her lips. "I cannot stay long, but I wanted to stop by this morning and assist as much as I can. And you will be proud of me, Lieutenant. I found my own way here."

He chuckled. Her chin was tilted at a proud angle, and her eyes danced with merriment. "Even though you are well acquainted with the twists and turns of Bath, I would be delighted to walk you back home."

One of the veterans guffawed, but then tried to disguise it as a sudden cough. Charlie looked with daggers at the man, willing him to stay quiet. So he wasn't well schooled in the art of flirtation. What did that matter? He was just…answering her in like tone. That was all.

Sophie's eyelids fluttered down over her brilliant blue eyes, and a slight flush stained her cheeks. "That would be lovely." She dipped a slight curtsy. "I'll go see what the widows might require."

He worked the rest of the morning with a curious lightness in his heart. As before, when he made Sophie's acquaintance, all his problems seemed insignificant. He practiced how he would tell her about his latest missive from Mother, how he would reenact her stern warnings, her dire predictions. And she would laugh that silvery laugh—it reminded one of bells tinkling. And he wouldn't feel so blasted alone any longer. So while he helped each man who turned to him, finding sources for clothing, or offering food, or locating shelter, his mind remained firmly fixed on Sophie Handley as she toiled away in the back of the church.

It may have been a kind of sin, but he couldn't shake his mind free.

As they left, she took his arm. "What a pleasant morning, Lieutenant. You know, I think what the women need most is clothing. Not just for themselves, but for their children. I wonder if we could have some sort of sewing bee, where we all join together and sew as a group. Wouldn't that be a practical solution?"

His mind was drifting again, fixating on her pretty profile rather than her sensible words. He forced himself to pay attention. "Yes, of course."

"You seem distracted again," she chided in a cheerful tone. "Pray, what has claimed your interest this morning?"

Ah, now was his chance. "Another letter from home. My mother intends to come to Bath in a fortnight and bring me to heel," he began, aping an aggrieved tone of voice, but was cut short by Sophie's stifled gasp.

"Your family! Oh, Lieutenant, I beg your forgiveness. I promised to come up with a solution to your problem, but I got so engrossed in Amelia's debut that I forgot." She darted her glance up to his, and he forced himself to allow his breathing to remain steady. Having her so close and so engaged in conversation was a heady experience. But then, of course, he would feel that way around any pretty gel. It was just that he had set himself apart from women for so long after his broken engagement to Beth Gaskell.

"Don't trouble yourself." He cleared his throat, forcing the words through his lips. Why was it so hard to even speak when she looked at him that way?

"Nay, I shall trouble myself. If your mother is coming, then the problem is reaching a crisis stage, I daresay." She steered him back down the sidewalk, and they ambled past the shops, which buzzed with activity. "I've given it some thought. I believe that if you at least give the appearance of going along with their wishes, your mother will leave you in peace. In other words, we must strike a compromise. Do you agree?"

That sounded sensible enough. He nodded. "Yes, but what would the compromise be?"

She patted him with her gloved fingertips, and he steeled himself so he wouldn't feel a tingle racing up his biceps, as he always did when she touched him. "Leave that to me, Lieutenant. Tomorrow I promise to have a solution to your problem. Once and for all."

They strolled the rest of the way to Lord Bradbury's in a state of friendly companionship. He meant it all as a joke, of course. Sophie Handley didn't have to come to his rescue. He didn't really need her help handling Mother. But there was tremendous gratification in knowing that, for the next several hours, he would be topmost in her mind.

Why that was so gratifying, he dared not examine. But it most assuredly was.

Chapter Seven

Sunday—a day of rest.

Sophie stretched her hands up to the ceiling. Time to find that solution she'd promised Lieutenant Cantrill. She was mortified that she had neglected his problem since her promise to assist Amelia two days before. Her life had been all a-swither, planning gowns and helping to select the menu and the guest list. He hadn't been far from her thoughts, though. When combing through the guest list, one name had particularly caught her eye: Lieutenant Charles Cantrill. When she mentioned his name to Lord Bradbury, certain there must be a mistake, his lordship laughed. "Don't let his austere existence fool you, Miss Handley. He's the second son of one of the wealthiest merchants in England. He's a member of my club, and a most welcome guest."

That added a whole new patina to Charlie Cantrill's allure. So he came from wealth but adopted a poor lifestyle to help others. He was wounded in service yet refused to rest on his laurels. And he had been most mysteriously jilted by his former fiancée. The lieutenant grew more interesting by the moment. So in helping him find a solution to his familial drama, she would be able to inch that much closer to him. Not that she really liked him all that much. But goodness, it would be lovely to have a gentleman friend of sorts again, one to squire her home and hold the umbrella for her. When he allowed himself to joke, his eyes lit up with a mischievous twinkle, and she caught a glimpse of the Charlie Cantrill John Brookes had talked about before the war.

No use lolling about in bed. She could be at church and by his side in a matter of minutes if she hurried. Sophie bolted out of bed, landing with more of a thud than she meant to. She had only three quarters of an hour to ready herself and hasten to St. Swithins. There would be no time for breakfast, surely. She flung open her wardrobe and rummaged among her plain, serviceable gowns for something fetching enough to catch the lieutenant's eye.

Her lavender gown was still in pieces, ready to be stitched together for the dinner party a week hence. She eyed her wardrobe with mounting frustration. Oh, to have unlimited funds like Amelia Bradbury. In a range of frothy confections, she would certainly catch the lieutenant's eye.

Botheration. The dark blue damask with the pleated bodice would have to do—it was the most attractive one she owned, for it darkened her eyes to a sapphire shade.

She scurried about the room, pulling on her stockings, tossing on her gown and pulling on her black kid slippers. Her hair—oh, dear, her hair. She had no time for a complicated style. A simple ribbon would have to do. There. She looked presentable, if not exactly allur-

ing. She wrenched open the door—and tripped headlong over Lucy, who was strolling down the hall.

"Wherever are you off to in such haste?" Lucy
propped Sophie up by the shoulders, saving her from
tumbling onto the floor.

"St. Swithins. I am attending Sunday services." Sophie righted herself and checked to make sure her hair
hadn't come loose.

Lucy's eyebrows shot up to her hairline. "You never
mentioned going to services before."

"Um…" Sophie unsuccessfully fended off a blush.
Her cheeks were scorching hot. "I only just remembered it."

"Hmm." Lucy stepped backward, planting her fists
on her hips. "This wouldn't have anything to do with
Lieutenant Cantrill, would it?"

Botheration. It was best to go ahead and admit defeat.
The blush told all. She nodded, smiling at her friend.
"He's a friend of my family, after all. Would you like
to accompany me?"

Lucy gave her head a decisive nod. "Of course. Let
me just get my wrap."

Bath was now her adopted hometown, its streets and
alleyways becoming more familiar with each passing
day. She struck out for St. Swithins with confidence.
Sophie and Lucy skirted the Circus, glancing at the
enclosed garden that would surely begin budding soon
with warmer weather, and continued up Bennett Street,
past the gracious, aloof Assembly Rooms. A month or
so from now, Amelia would begin attending functions
at these rooms with her father, and perhaps with Lucy
as her chaperone.

It was beginning to smell like spring, the scent of moist earth and leaves filling the air. For some reason, it smelled of home—like working in the miniscule garden with Harriet at Tansley Cottage. Sophie blinked back sudden homesick tears. Yes, Bath was becoming more familiar, but Tansley would always be home.

When they arrived at the church, it was already crowded with a mixture of Bath Society and the lowlier masses, all milling about the narthex, greeting each other with nods and smiles. What a relief Lucy had come, for otherwise, she might feel quite lost in this crush of people. The lieutenant was nowhere in sight. Sophie fought to keep the disappointment from showing on her face as they chose seats in the pews near the rear of the church.

"Chin up, chicken," Lucy whispered. "I feel certain we shall see your lieutenant soon."

Sophie shook her head. It was no concern of hers whether or not he was here. As the crowd settled, the organ and choir struck up the opening notes of the hymn. Sophie absorbed the atmosphere of the church, the soaring music, the voices united in song. Tall white tapers glowed, casting a gentle light over two lush bouquets of roses that framed the altar.

The reverend stepped up to the pulpit and began preaching on the Beatitudes, his strong, dynamic voice commanding her full attention. Usually, when she was forced to listen to a long explanation of any kind, her mind would drift. She'd begin thinking of her dress, or a dress she'd like to make, roaming the fields of her imagination. But the reverend's words were entirely captivating.

"Blessed are the poor in spirit, for theirs is the king-dom of Heaven." Here was an entirely new view of heaven and spirituality. Sophie sat up straighter, her senses attuned to his every word. Why, all those months when she and Harriet felt abandoned and alone, all those times when want and poverty stared them in the face—they were never completely forsaken. Sophie blinked. They were never entirely alone. How comforting, and how profound, to know that He was there, and cared for them all the time.

A glow kindled her heart, and she glanced out over the congregation. Was anyone else feeling the same spiritual uplift that she was experiencing at that moment? Some parishioners nodded in agreement, others looked rather uncomfortable, still others simply stared ahead, glassy-eyed. Lucy was drumming her fingers on the hymnal. Why, no one seemed to be as enthralled as she was. How very strange. Why wasn't anyone else as moved as she was, as captivated by the thought of not being alone as she was?

Something pulled her eyes from the reverend's smil-ing face. She turned slightly to her left, focusing on the pews near the altar. And there he was. Lieutenant Cantrill was looking directly at her, his dark eyes and thin face reflecting an inner spark, as though he, too, were on fire from the healing words of the sermon. But for once in her life, she could not summon a coquettish smile or even a flirtatious dimpling. Something pro-found passed between her and the lieutenant, and she was powerless to turn away.

When at last Lieutenant Cantrill flicked his glance away from her, Sophie cast her eyes down to her lap.

Her hands trembled and a feeling, not unlike butterflies fluttering in a spring garden, settled in the pit of her stomach. She heard not a word of the rest of the service, and merely mouthed the words to the last hymn.

Lucy leaned over. "Well, I think I see your lieutenant," she whispered. "That fellow with the dark hair and eyes has been staring at you for most of the service. Is that him?"

Sophie nodded.

"Are you quite all right? You look terribly pale." Lucy plied her with her fan.

"I—I'm fine," Sophie stammered.

"We shall have to find a way for you to meet up with him as we leave," Lucy said.

Sophie shook her head, embarrassed by Lucy's constant whispered chatter. "Not now. The service is still going."

Lucy's mouth quirked as though she were hiding a grin. "Ah, how pious we are, even while thinking only of…him."

"Hush." That was quite enough out of Lucy.

The hymn ended with a last, drawn-out "Amen" that echoed well up to the rafters. If the parishioners of St. Swithins were bored with a sermon, Sophie reflected, they certainly seemed to enjoy the singing. Then they jostled and pressed out of the pews, filing out of the three aisles in a noisy, chattering mass.

"Now, to get over to see your lieutenant," Lucy murmured, giving the church one all-encompassing sweep with her eyes, "we will need to leave through the side. You see? He is over on the left. We shall have to fight, but we can make it over."

"But even if we are able to get over to his side of the church, how will we attract his attention?" Sophie followed Lucy, who was graciously applying both her smile and her elbows to fight through the crowd.

"Leave that to me," Lucy called over her shoulder.

As the crowd surged toward the main exit, Sophie and Lucy were able to press through to the left aisle, where the sea of parishioners was considerably thinner. Cantrill was a few feet ahead of them, walking slowly toward the side door with a young man—surely that was the ensign, judging by the slope of his shoulders and his slightly hunched gait.

With an expert flip of her wrist, Lucy sent her reticule sailing through the air, and it landed just inches away from the lieutenant. He stooped down and scooped it up with his hand, turning around to find the owner with a puzzled expression on his thin, serious face. Sophie's heart lurched anew. How handsome he was. The ensign paused beside the lieutenant, his boyish face uncertain and clouded.

"Oh, sir!" Lucy sang out. "You found my reticule. How very good of you." She caught Sophie around the waist and dragged her up the aisle. "It was knocked clear of my hand by the bustle of this crowd." She took the reticule back and smiled at Sophie.

She took the hint and assumed control of the social graces, introducing each to the other.

"Lieutenant Cantrill, Ensign Rowland, may I present Miss Williams. She is the governess for the Bradbury girls, and a dear friend of mine."

"So this is Ensign Rowland? How do you do, sir?" Lucy shook hands cordially with the ensign, who said nothing, his clear green eyes wide and unreadable. "Ensign, I was wondering if you could assist me with a problem. You see, I must instruct Lord Bradbury's daughters in the finer points of elocution and pronunciation, and the best way to do so is by reading aloud." She threaded her arm under his elbow and piloted him toward the door. "But I am so rusty at reading aloud myself. Would you be my audience? I should so like to have your assistance..." Her voice trailed off as they disappeared into the crowd.

"It seems Miss Williams is amenable to the idea of reading to Rowland," Lieutenant Cantrill observed, his eyebrow quirked. "Tell me, is she always so... talkative?"

"I am afraid so," Sophie said with a rueful laugh. It was nice to be standing here, talking with him comfortably. She liked his banter during those rare moments when he allowed his guard to slip.

"Well, then, she will be very beneficial to Rowland. No pressure for him to speak, and a great deal of chatter to listen to," Cantrill replied, and offered her his arm.

They trailed out the side door of the church together, but Lucy was nowhere to be seen. Sophie peered around the milling pack of parishioners once more, just to be sure. No, she had vanished, leaving Sophie quite alone with Cantrill. She wasn't sure if she should be embarrassed, furious or grateful—or some combination of all three.

Charlie directed her toward the stone steps that led down to the sidewalk. "Are you enjoying working for Bradbury?" he inquired in a polite tone.

"Yes. Amelia and Louisa are sweet girls. And Lucy

is a dear friend. She almost makes up for the loss of Harriet." She let it slip before she thought about it. Why would Cantrill care about her feelings of homesickness? He was, after all, only showing his good manners by asking such a feeble question.

"You are very close to your family." It was a statement, rather than a question. She glanced up at his profile, but he was locked away in his own thoughts, his jaw clenched tightly as a fist.

"Yes. But that brings me to your problem, Lieutenant. How well I know the conflict you feel with your family. I've battered my brains about it long enough. I think I may have the perfect solution to your mother's edicts."

The pressure of her hand resting in the crook of his elbow sent a wave of fire down his mutilated arm. He sucked in his breath. Sophie was powerful, more so than she was probably aware, even if she enjoyed flirting. But this wasn't the action of a coquette. Her dark blue eyes—so blue they were nearly black, with a fringe of sooty lashes—held a spark of understanding and empathy. He warmed to that spark, longed to kindle the blaze.

"Really, Miss Handley, you don't have to come to my rescue. I was just teasing, you know. As a grown man, I can well handle my own mother."

"Oh, I know you can." She led him down a few stone steps. "But defying one's family can be quite difficult. I believe in you. I believe that the work you do is good. And I should hate for it to cease just because your mother and brother feel you should be living the life of a Society buck. I wish they could understand, as I do, all that you are doing to help others."

He had to turn away. When she looked up like that, tender and beseeching, he was hard-pressed to remember that she was just being nice. As a family friend. And she had the soul of a flirt. It wasn't as if she really cared for him, as mutilated as he was. Hang it all, she had spurned John when he returned from the war, after he lost his leg. Why would she feel any differently toward him?

He cleared his throat to steady himself and buy a little time to craft an articulate response. "I can't judge them, you know. They feel I should be more concerned about Society—that is all. Going to balls, having a proper calling that supplies a reasonable income. Living in a poky flat in Bath, preferring to live simply and to help poor veterans—well, that kind of lifestyle is rather a slap in the face to their mode of living."

"I see." She finally dropped her hand from his elbow, but the imprint of her touch still burned like a furnace. "So they feel you should be doing things more in keeping with what other men in Society do. Drinking, gambling, making piles of money in a position you don't love.…"

"Courting the ladies," he added, then halted. Heat flooded his face—why had he brought that up? It was beyond ridiculous to mention, especially in light of his all too recent humiliation, courtesy of Beth Gaskell.

Sophie frowned, her dimples deepening. "And that is the reason we must strike a compromise. Tell me— are you ready to hear my plan?"

"I suppose so." He sighed. "But I won't drink or play cards. More's the pity, they say."

"Of course not. But you could court the ladies. More specifically, me."

Chapter Eight

At Cantrill's shocked expression, Sophie swallowed and rushed on. She glanced up at him, her face aglow with excitement. "We could pretend to be courting, you and I. Only whilst your mother is here. That should give her enough hope that you are done with your austere ways, and perhaps she will leave you in peace a bit longer."

That had been the plan all along—in the back of her mind. In her most private dreams, perhaps. She longed to say it—but now, speaking the words aloud gave her pause. It sounded like such a daft promise. Sophie could've bitten her tongue out the moment the words slipped from her mouth. 'Twas certain he would think her a runaway from Bedlam. But Charlie looked so downcast, and so hunted by his own family, that she was determined to help him out. They were friends, and friends helped one another through the darkest times.

"But…what happens after my mother leaves?" The lieutenant had turned a bright shade of scarlet, and she detected a slight stammer in his voice that hadn't been there before.

"Well, then we stop pretending. You can tell your mother that I cried off. After all, I already have that reputation, you know. Everyone knows about my engagement to John Brookes." The tone of her voice was more bitter than she intended. She cleared her throat and attempted to lighten the mood. "We don't have to be officially engaged, so there will be no damage to anyone's reputation. You can just pretend to court me, and your mother will see that you are fulfilling your part of the bargain. There will be no need for you to return to Brightgate, and you can continue your life's work with the poor."

"That's most generous of you, Miss Handley. I honestly don't know what to say." The lieutenant was staring down at his boots, as if they were the most fascinating shoes in the world.

"Say yes, and then start calling me Sophie. It would be silly for you to call me Miss Handley if we were courting." She turned him gently back toward the steps of the courtyard, and gathered her skirts in one hand so she could descend without tripping.

"But it feels like you are doing me a favor, without gaining anything for yourself in return. Is there anything I can offer you, Miss Hand—I mean, Sophie?" He guided her around a crumbling step, assisting her so she would not stumble.

She glanced sideways at him, a smile hovering around her lips. "Don't fret about it, Lieutenant," she rejoined. "I am happy to help a friend. We are friends, aren't we?"

"We are." She watched, fascinated, as a dimple appeared in his cheek. How handsome he was when he smiled. If only he would do so more often. Perhaps, during these next few weeks, she could endeavor to bring him out of his shell. In those few moments they spent together, she discerned that his dour behavior was only a facade, a mask to cover the hurt that his former fiancée had caused him. She didn't know the lady in question, of course, but she would gladly claw her eyes out for the pain she had caused Cantrill.

On the other hand, the lady's defection had left the field open—not, of course, that it mattered to her.

"Sophie!" Lucy's voice rang out from the bottom of the steps. The governess was standing beside Ensign Rowland, waving up at them.

"I must return to Lord Bradbury's," Sophie informed Charlie. "When does your mother arrive?"

"In about a week."

"Then we have time to formulate a plan and make sure we have our stories correct," she replied. "Perhaps we could talk about it when we meet at the veterans' club this coming week?"

"Mother may arrive that very day. She should be here by Friday, but it may be as early as Thursday." He stopped at the foot of the stairs and turned toward her. "If this is too difficult a task, we need not go through with it."

"Nonsense. Send round a letter and let me know what to expect. If your mother is arriving Friday, then she will be here in time for Amelia's dinner party. I shall make sure she is added to the guest list. I can meet her then." Sophie patted his elbow with her fingertips and then withdrew from his grasp.

"You will be present at the dinner party?" His voice betrayed his amazement.

"His lordship has asked to me to take part in it, to help smooth Amelia's first experience as a hostess," she replied nervously. It did sound odd, since she was a servant. Yet that was the truth of it, no matter how strange it might appear to others.

"I see." He shifted his weight nervously, daring to look her in the eyes for the first time since they agreed to participate in the charade. "So I just need to send you a letter?"

"Yes, tell me everything I should know about our relationship, in case your mother asks me any questions. Send it around as soon as you can, so I can begin committing everything to memory. And don't worry, Lieutenant. Everything will be well, you'll see. My mama was an actress, after all. As her daughter, I can certainly assume this role with assurance." She tossed him what she hoped was a bright and careless grin, and then turned to go.

"Charlie," he called after her, his voice echoing a little off the stone steps.

"Beg pardon?" She paused and half turned in her flight.

"You asked me to call you Sophie. Don't forget, you must call me Charlie."

Her heart skipped a beat. "Charlie," she said softly. It was nice to call him by his Christian name. With a little wave, she turned back and ran quickly to Lucy, who was nodding her goodbye to Ensign Rowland. The thin young lad tipped his hat briefly at Sophie and then headed over to where Charlie stood waiting.

"So?" Lucy was grinning, a wide smile that made Sophie laugh. "Did you have a pleasant visit with your lieutenant?"

"His name is Charlie." Sophie sighed, relishing the sound once more.

Lucy stopped short. "Are we on first-name terms, then?"

"Only on a fraudulent basis," Sophie replied. She then divulged the plan, noting that Lucy's eyes got rounder and rounder as she explained it.

"Well, that's daft," Lucy responded when Sophie finished.

"Why? He's a family friend, and I want to help him as he's helped me."

"He's a friend, but it sounds like you want to make him more. Surely, Sophie, you are setting yourself up for heartbreak." Lucy's tone held a polite note of warning.

"Not at all, I assure you. I esteem the lieutenant—"

"Charlie," Lucy interrupted.

"Fine. I esteem Charlie greatly, but I don't want to marry anyone. Haven't I told you that I declined two offers of marriage within one year?" Really, sometimes Lucy's high-handedness could get on one's nerves.

"Hmm." Lucy studied Sophie's face like one would study a fine work of art. "I think you haven't married because you haven't found the right man. And yet, the way you blush at the mention of Charlie's name, I would think you are quite susceptible to matrimony, should he but offer."

Sophie swallowed her annoyance and attempted to carry off the moment with style. "Goodness, Lucy," she replied with an airy wave of her hand. "The way you talk. Charlie is nothing more than a good friend, and I am doing him a favor. That's what friends are for, after all."

"We'll see," Lucy said, her voice betraying a smirk. Honestly, she could be most insufferable at times.

Charlie crumpled up the foolscap and flung it into the fire. He had tried to write down the instructions for Sophie three times already, but kept running up against a brick wall. What was he supposed to say? Everything sounded so bizarre when he put pen to paper. He tried jotting down some ideas about how they met, but it sounded like something in a novel—a poorly written, feverishly detailed novel. And then he tried writing down the number of times they had met, but it sounded like a fantasy. He and Beth Gaskell had really only ever met at assemblies and balls. Now that he eschewed most societal functions, and now that Sophie was a servant, those soirees were out of the question.

She was trying to help him, so the very least he could do was follow her instructions. And yet, he had no idea what to say or do. His heart surged with gratitude. Now he didn't dread his mother's visit—only the aftermath, when the sham was over and he and Sophie must put aside their fraudulent courtship. Because of Sophie, he would be able to stay in Bath and take care of the veterans' fund. Just as her sister's money had made their comfort possible, Sophie's selflessness was making continuing his work a reality.

Had he really just called Sophie selfless? As he'd known her before, as the woman who spurned his best friend, he thought of her as heartless and flippant. And yet, she was generous and lovely. Her few weeks in Bath had worked wonders on her character. Both Handley women were astonishing, in fact.

That brought him up short. What if Harriet and Brookes found out? Even if they knew that Sophie was doing him a favor, they might decide that the matter was simply too fantastic to countenance. And of course, knowing Mother's love of gossip, word would spread to Tansley from Brightgate like wildfire. Was it better to go ahead and inform them of the plan in advance, or merely hope against hope that they would never hear about it?

He turned back briskly to the matter at hand. What should he say to Sophie about their charade? Any time he tried to write it as an epistle, he hated what he wrote. Falling back on his soldierly training, he jotted down instructions as he might lay out orders for his underlings.

We know each other because your sister married my best friend.

We became close in Bath through our work with the veterans' fund.

We are not engaged, but have been courting for a few weeks.

We have no fixed plans for the future.

All of it was true, and yet, spelled out bluntly with pen and ink, it seemed awfully threadbare. But there was nothing more to say. He had tried to dress it up several times and the result was merely ridiculous.

Whatever you do, don't tell Mother we're formally engaged. We will never hear the end of it.

He crossed it out as soon as he wrote it. Sophie was nobody's fool, and a broken engagement would cause more harm to her reputation than to his. And since she was seeking to stay in service to Lord Bradbury, it was in her best interest to stay as free from scandal as possible. His reputation was hardier, since he had already endured one broken engagement and didn't really care about Society, anyway. And coming from the wealthy Cantrills, he could always call on his brother in a pinch. Not that he ever would.

That was all he could think of to say. Anything else was too much. He folded up the missive and sealed it. Then he placed it on the small mahogany table in the hall, where his housekeeper, Mrs. Pierce, would be sure to see it. She would either deliver it herself or post it in the morning, as she did with all his outgoing letters.

There was nothing to do now but wait for Mother to arrive. She would be here within days, and he had no idea what to say to her. At least the matter of his personal life was somewhat settled for the time being. She would still likely decry his frugal way of living, and urge him to move to a more fashionable address. She would probably laugh about his work with the fund, and try to entice him back to Brightgate with the promise of a position in his brother's firm. In fact, the only thing she would probably approve of was Sophie.

Her dancing eyes and careless smile flashed across his mind. Her sweetness of temper and her willingness to help him out of an unlivable situation were definitely the marks of a true friend and desirable woman.

Desirable for some other man, he hastened to add. Not, of course, desirable to a crippled old bachelor.

Yes, Sophie would definitely meet with Mother's approval.

* * *

After receiving Charlie's curt missive, Sophie had nothing more to do or say about their charade. She had hoped for an elaborate letter, explaining everything in detail. And yet, he simply stated what was already true.

Sophie threw herself into preparations for Amelia's dinner party, and the rest of the week sped by in a flurry of etiquette lessons, final menu preparations and practice sessions. The town house, already cleaned and polished, was cleaned and polished once more. Masses of flowers graced nearly every available surface in every available room. During the rush of planning, Sophie saw her employer hardly at all—only once did he nod in passing while she and Amelia worked in the dining room.

Exhausted after her last day of preparations, Sophie collapsed in a heap upon her bed. There was nothing more to be done. Everything was ready. Amelia had been drilled endlessly on grace, poise and proper manners. She was turning into quite the little heiress before Sophie's eyes. The house was stunning and gracious. The gowns were pressed and ready. Tomorrow was Friday, when the real test would begin.

A knock sounded on her door. "Enter."

Lucy ducked in and came to sit beside her on the bed. "Are you too worn out to talk?"

Sophie rolled over, cradling her head in her pillow. "You must know I am never too exhausted for gossip."

"This isn't really gossip." Lucy plucked at the coverlet, her eyes downcast. "It's something…more personal."

This was intriguing. Usually Lucy was positively

bubbly. Now she looked pensive and a bit sad. Sophie sat up. "Yes?"

"Well, you know how you weren't able to go to the Widows' Fund this week?"

"Yes, I was too busy with Amelia. Go on."

"Well—" Lucy kept her eyes downcast. "I read aloud to Ensign Rowland. And spent many hours in his company. Oh, Sophie!" Tears began rolling down Lucy's pinkened cheeks. "I want to help him. I want to make him well." She flung herself down on the quilt, sobbing in earnest.

"Why is that so terrible?" Sophie patted Lucy's back with a gentle hand. "I think it's wonderful."

Lucy hiccupped several times before she could speak. "The struggles he has been through are nothing to mine. Even growing up in an orphanage as I did, my life has not been so difficult. How can I possibly assist him, when I myself have so little understanding of what it means to suffer?"

"Lucy, my dear," Sophie murmured in a soothing tone. "Aren't you getting a bit ahead of yourself? After all, you've only just met the ensign. Charlie just wanted you to begin by reading to him. Simple human companionship is all he needs." She handed Lucy her handkerchief. "I am sure, in time, that with your help, he may overcome his suffering."

"Does Charlie's affliction bother you?" Lucy asked, sitting up on the bed.

"His affliction?" Funny, she had never thought of it as such. Yes, his arm had been shot off, but she felt no revulsion about it. When Brookes returned from the war, his leg gone, she found the changes in him too much to bear. But Charlie—well, his war wound was as much a part of him as his thin face, or the way his eyes twinkled when he joked around. "No. I am not bothered by it at all."

Lucy blew her nose with a decisive honk. "What a pretty pair we are, eh, Sophie? Me with my hopeless desire to cure ills, and you with your sham romance. Surely we two maids have more heartache than anyone in Bath."

With that, Lucy rose from the bed and retired to her own chamber. But Sophie was too tired to sleep. Having spent most of the week living in a blur, she could not calm her mind to the point that blessed rest could overtake her.

She rolled over onto her side, scrunching her pillow under her head. Was Lucy right? Was she destined for heartache if she continued with this charade? Charlie's shocked expression flitted across her mind. He seemed sincerely appreciative of her offer, if slightly taken aback by her brazenness in suggesting it. But what did she feel? Wasn't she just the tiniest bit excited by the thought of being engaged to Charlie—even if the engagement was a sham?

Yes. She tucked her pillow under her head and squeezed her eyes shut. She was excited—too excited for comfort. A niggling feeling of doubt crept into her mind. She had better, just to be safe, guard her heart.

After all, the engagement was only a temporary betrothal.

Chapter Nine

A knock sounded on the front door, and Mrs. Pierce bustled to answer it. Charlie eyed her through the crack in his sitting-room doorway. That imperious rapping could belong to only one woman in the world: Mrs. Moriah Cantrill, widow of the late George Cantrill, mother of the esteemed Robert Cantrill and the lesser-known Charles Cantrill. Mother. She was here, and 'twas time to put his plan into action. If only it weren't so difficult to talk to his family members. Oh, they all had good intentions, but he might as well have been dropped on his parents' doorstep as a baby. He resembled them—in temperament at least—not at all.

Mrs. Pierce ushered Mother into the room. No, pretending that gypsies had left him on a doorstep simply was not possible. 'Twas like looking into a mirror. The same dark hair and eyes, the same thin face. He looked too much like his mother to deny the connection.

"Charles, my son." She removed her feathered cap and velvet pelisse, tossing both to Mrs. Pierce, who nearly missed catching them.

"Mother." He leaned forward and brushed a kiss across her finely wrinkled cheek.

"You may go," she replied, half turning toward Mrs. Pierce. "We should like tea in approximately ten minutes."

Mrs. Pierce bobbed a curtsy and stalked out of the room, shaking her head. Charlie couldn't blame her. He never treated her as his mother treated her servants. In fact, Mrs. Cantrill had a reputation throughout Derbyshire for the brevity of most of her servants' lengths of stay.

"You look thin, Charles. Careworn, in fact." Mother sank into a chair, glancing about the room. "It must be this terrible situation you live in. You must take a more fashionable address, my son. I know Katherine Crossley lives on Bilbury Lane—perhaps you could take a flat in her building."

Already Mother was ordering him about. He clenched his teeth and shook his head. "This flat is perfectly adequate for a bachelor's needs, Mother."

Mother's patrician lips curled in a slight grimace. "Your flat is unbearable. I shan't stay here myself. I am staying with our friends, the Pooles, at their townhome in the Crescent."

Twin emotions pulled at Charlie's gut—elation that Mother would not be around all day and all night throughout her stay, and anger that she hadn't deigned to settle with him in his poky flat. In the end, elation won out over hurt feelings. That was Mother for you. High-handed and snobby.

Mrs. Pierce rushed in with the tea tray.

"A trifle early," Mother admonished.

"We'll take it, anyway, and thank you," Charlie added.

Mother glanced at him, something like a flicker of amusement in her gaze. "Still coddling the servants?"

"Merely treating others as I would wish to be treated."

Mother said nothing more, but busied herself with the tea things. After an agonizing silence, during which Charlie's heart beat faster in his chest, she handed him a cup.

"You know why I am here." It was a statement, not a question.

He sighed. "Mother, before we begin, you must know that we are invited to Anthony, Viscount Bradbury's tonight. His daughter, the Honorable Amelia Bradbury, is making her debut as hostess." If he cut off any discussions at once—especially with an invitation to dine with nobility—surely Mother would let the matter drop for the time being.

It worked. She settled back in her chair, a satisfied glow lighting her features. "Of course, I should love to dine with the viscount," she responded in dulcet tones. "How nice of them to include us."

It was now or never. If he didn't say it now, the moment would vanish in a trace. "There's another reason for our invite."

"Yes?" Mother took a careful sip of her tea.

"I should like you to meet the young lady I am… courting." There. It was out. And it even sounded reasonably natural.

"You are courting someone?" Mother eyed him with suspicion over the rim of her cup. "Whom are you courting, pray tell? Surely not one of the veterans' widows you are so fond of helping."

Hot anger bubbled to the surface, but Charlie steeled himself. "Of course not, Mother. The young lady is Sophia Handley, Sir Hugh Handley's daughter. She is working as a private seamstress to Miss Amelia, and will be present at the gathering tonight."

Mother cocked her head to one side. "Sir Hugh Handley? Isn't the family completely destitute?"

"Yes, Mother. But Miss Handley comes of impeccable breeding, I can assure you." Surely that would quell any further questions.

"Well, yes. That goes without saying." Mother waved one hand listlessly. "It's just very odd, Charles, that she has chosen to go into service. Most young women would not choose such a path. She's not a bluestocking, is she? Or one of these free love advocates, like Mrs. Wollenstonecraft?"

Charlie threw back his head and laughed. 'Twas the first really amusing thing Mother had said. Sophie, a bluestocking? "No, not at all. You'll see for yourself when you meet her tonight. She is accomplished and lovely, and has an amazing talent for needlework. That is why she works for the Bradbury family. She loves to sew, and can indulge her artistry in this manner."

"Yes, well, we shall see, Charles." Mother's expression hardened into one of suspicion and doubt. "I shall reserve judgment on the young lady until I meet her tonight. But tell me truthfully—are you considering marrying the gel?"

"We've only begun courting." He pronounced the words with a snap. "I haven't decided for certain."

"If she is of good breeding, and as lovely and charming as you say, then I shall be happy to see you wed. You both could come home to Brightgate and set up housekeeping there. Robert has a position for you, taking over the mills. In no time, you could have a beautiful home and family, Charles."

A beautiful home and family. Sophie would make some man a perfect wife. She would make a home anywhere she went, simply by living in it. But he loved his work. Home and family meant nothing to him. Only helping others. That's why he agreed to this farce—to keep living the life he had chosen.

But telling anyone in his family about any of this was out of the question. No one would ever understand his feelings on the matter. So he merely nodded. "You'll see for yourself, Mother."

Sophie wove another ribbon rose into Amelia's dark, curly hair. They had settled on a graceful, Grecian style of hair dress, not too elaborate but still quite elegant. Amelia had shooed her own maid away for the occasion, trusting only Sophie to make the necessary preparations. Nothing could possibly go wrong on this night. And since this was her first time wearing her hair up, as well as the first time to act as hostess in her father's home, Sophie was determined to make Amelia look her loveliest.

Sophie glanced at her muse in the mirror, selecting another hairpin from the box on the dressing table. "I think a few more roses at the crown of your head, and then we should be done."

Amelia blinked. "I dare not nod for fear of undoing all your handiwork. But yes, I agree."

Sophie smiled. "You may relax, my dear. You're likely to give yourself a headache by holding so rigidly still. I assure you, I am using so many hairpins, a windstorm could blow through here and not muss a single strand."

Lucy and Louisa were watching, curled up together on Amelia's bed. "Oh, Miss Williams, can't we watch from the top of the stairs? It would be such fun."

"No, I'm afraid not." Lucy smoothed her charge's hair with a gentle hand. "But I have asked Cook to send some of the dinner up to us, and you may stay up an extra hour reading in bed if you like."

"Well, that's something," Louisa grumbled, burying her face on Lucy's shoulder. "But I still think it's awfully mean that I won't even be able to see Amelia's debut."

"You'll hear all about it when I come up to bed tonight," Amelia murmured through clenched teeth. She was still as a statue, hardly batting an eyelash. "And you shall have your own debut in a couple of years."

"Ah, the wisdom of the elder sister," Sophie replied with a laugh. "How often did I hear such advice from Harriet. 'It will be your turn soon enough.' Cheer up, sweet Louisa. You and Lucy will both have a lovely time tonight. I'll sneak up an extra bit of cake for your bedtime snack."

Louisa rolled back on the pillow, a mollified expression crossing her face. "Thank you, Miss Handley."

Sophie stuck the last two roses in place, pinning them down securely with a maze of hairpins that she hid under Amelia's mass of curls. The effect was enchanting, as though some fairy had sprinkled rosebuds over Amelia's hair and they had stayed put. She stepped back, allowing Amelia the chance to see herself in the mirror. "You look beautiful, dear Amelia."

"You do, too!" Amelia turned gingerly from the mirror, gazing at Sophie with shining eyes. "That dress suits you perfectly."

"Thank you." The dress did look rather wonderful. And that was part of her plan. If Mrs. Cantrill really did arrive tonight, then it would help Charlie immensely if she looked her best.

"I agree. You are both as pretty as a picture." A suave baritone voice sounded from the doorway. Lucy scrambled off the bed, shaking out her skirts hastily. Louisa continued to lounge on the bed. "Papa," she called out in a mock-angry tone, "this room is off-limits to you. Only females are allowed."

Lord Bradbury drew back, a hurt expression crossing his face as he placed his hand over his heart. "What? Even if I come bearing gifts?"

"Do you have anything for me? Or only for Amelia?" Louisa demanded, getting into the spirit of their game.

"I would be a horrible papa indeed if I only brought gifts for one daughter," he responded in a wounded tone. "Of course, if I am not allowed—" He took an exaggerated step toward the door.

"No! Let me see!" Louisa scrambled off the bed and flung herself at her father, grasping his elegant evening coat in both hands. "What did you bring us?"

Lord Bradbury withdrew two leather boxes from his

pocket. "For you," he replied, handing one to Louisa. With a delighted squeal, she flung it open.

"A gold locket, how lovely! Thank you, Papa." She handed the box to Lucy, who withdrew the treasure and clasped it around Louisa's neck.

"And for my darling Amelia, already a young woman." He walked over to the dressing table and held out a box to his daughter. "This belonged to your mother. I think you should have it now."

Amelia opened the box and gasped. Sophie's mouth dropped open. It was a string of the most perfect pearls she had ever seen. Lord Bradbury removed the strand from the case and clasped it around Amelia's neck.

"You are as lovely as she was," he said huskily, a slight catch in his voice. "Take care of them, my girl."

"I will, Papa," she replied, embracing her father tightly despite her ribbon of roses and masses of carefully arranged curls.

Watching them together, Sophie blinked back sudden tears. She was never particularly close to her papa. Harriet, with her love of books and natural intelligence, was his decided favorite. Sophie had been taken under Mama's wing and groomed from birth for one thing and one thing only—marriage. Watching the viscount and Amelia together, a sudden pang of longing tore through her heart. If only she could have enjoyed the closeness of Papa's company. But it was as if he and Mama had split the sisters between them in terms of childrearing and care.

Lucy tapped Louisa on the shoulder, breaking through the heavy rush of emotions that flooded the room. "Come, Louisa, we should go to the schoolroom and await our dinner. Lord Bradbury," she said, bobbing a curtsy. "Amelia, I know you shall do splendidly tonight."

Amelia waved a queenly hand at audience. "Thank you. I shall tell you both about it later tonight."

Sophie hesitated. Should she leave, too, and give Lord Bradbury a few moments' privacy with his daughter? Or should she guide Amelia down to the drawing room? She set the hairbrush she had been clutching on the dressing table and gathered her skirts to go.

"Amelia, I would like a moment with Miss Handley." Lord Bradbury's voice held no trace of its former huskiness. "We shall meet you in the drawing room directly."

Sophie swallowed nervously. Perhaps she had done such a good job that her presence was no longer necessary tonight. If that were true, then 'twould be a bit of a relief. She was terribly nervous about the evening herself. It would be much nicer to be gossiping in the schoolroom with Lucy and Louisa, though she would still need to meet Mrs. Cantrill eventually.

Amelia nodded at her father and threw a grateful smile at Sophie. When she left her bedroom, Lord Bradbury closed the door behind her. Sophie fought a rising tide of panic. Whatever was his lordship about, that they needed such seclusion?

"Miss Handley, there is no need to look so alarmed, I assure you." He smiled casually. "I just wanted to thank you for all you have done for Amelia this week. She has really come into her own. She is, in fact, a young lady. And I know this transformation can only be credited to your handiwork."

Sophie took a step backward. They needed more distance between them. Whenever his lordship came into a room, he seemed to fill it up, or lay claim to all of the air. She schooled herself, forcing silent, deep breaths. 'Twould be beyond silly to faint just now. "You're most welcome, sir. Though I must disagree. It is not by my work alone. Lucy Williams has been a good governess, as well. And we were given quite wonderful raw material to work with, you know."

A smile hovered around his firm lips. "Thank you for the compliment to my daughter. I do think highly of both of my girls."

Were they done? Could she finally leave, and breathe normally once more? No, Lord Bradbury was speaking again.

"This is yours." He held out another box, a long rectangular one.

"Oh, no, sir." Sophie waved the box away. Why, even the case looked expensive and fine. Surely his lordship had spent a fortune on this evening already.

"I must insist," he replied, snapping the box open. Sophie gasped as the candlelight refracted off the diamond bracelet inside, casting prisms of rainbows around the room. "Your wrist, if you please."

Sophie's mouth went dry, and she gingerly extended her right arm. With a businesslike air, he clasped the bracelet around her gloved wrist, holding it up to the candlelight. "Very pretty," he murmured. Then he shot a piercing glance at Sophie from under his brows. "I have excellent taste in all things, you know."

Sophie nodded. She could barely swallow, her emotions too jumbled to allow her to utter a single sound.

"Shall we go?" The viscount tucked the box back into his evening-coat pocket, and offered Sophie his elbow.

"Y-yes." Sophie placed her fingers into the crook of his arm and gathered her skirts. As they left the room and descended the stairs, it was as though he was leading her into another world—an entirely foreign place where she didn't quite understand the language.

She was not at all sure she liked it.

Chapter Ten

Amelia was waiting for them in the drawing room, her eyes wide and her cheeks drained of all color. Sophie released Lord Bradbury's arm and hurried over to her, enveloping her in a warm embrace. "Darling, don't worry! Everything will be perfect. You'll see."

"I'm just so terribly nervous. Papa, what time is it?" Amelia fidgeted with her skirts, shaking them out to make them appear fuller.

"We have a few moments until the guests will begin to arrive," his lordship replied, flicking a glance over at the ormolu clock on the mantelpiece. "Compose yourself, my dear. You are your mother's daughter, and she instinctively knew how to manage any sort of party." He gave his daughter a reassuring pat on the shoulder.

Lord Bradbury's attention and care to his daughter was really quite nice to see. Whereas many fathers would simply ignore their daughters' nervousness, he was good enough to stop and offer the kind of heartening advice that was so crucial to one's confidence. Sophie raised her hand to her hair, carefully smoothing it down, catching a glimpse of the diamond bracelet as it sparkled boldly on her wrist. And yet, he was so overbearing in other respects. Truly, it was difficult to read the man at all.

A loud knock sounded on the door, and Amelia hastened to her place in the entrance of the drawing room. Lord Bradbury confidently strode over beside her. Where should she stand? As both a servant and Amelia's right hand for the evening, surely she should not stand in the receiving line. Both Amelia and Lord Bradbury seemed to have forgotten her altogether, in fact. They were both paying rapt attention to the cacophony of voices in the hallway as guests were divested of cloaks, overcoats and hats.

Sophie took a few steps backward. Perhaps now was the best time to hurry to the kitchen and make sure everything was running smoothly for supper. Yes, that was the best thing to do. That way Amelia could receive her guests and Sophie could make a subdued appearance later in the evening. She turned and headed toward the door opposite the drawing room.

"Miss Handley? Where are you going?" Lord Bradbury barked. Honestly, the man must have eyes in the back of his head.

"I was going to check on the supper," she replied, her voice shakier than she intended.

"You will stay here with us to receive the guests," he ordered, his voice as sharp as a flint.

"Of course, your lordship." Sophie bobbed a brief curtsy at his back. He hadn't even deigned to turn around when issuing his orders.

She crossed the room and stood between his lordship and Amelia, who linked her arm tightly with Sophie's. Now there was no escape. And goodness, how closely Lord Bradbury stood to her! She would not be able to take a decent breath, not until the evening was over and she had retired to her room.

The guests began milling into the drawing room, one after the other. Only a dozen in all—Sophie had counted and recounted the guest list in the days leading up to the event. And because she was included, there was going to be an odd number at dinner unless Mrs. Cantrill arrived with her son. Then there would be an even sixteen. Had they remembered to lay sixteen places? Sophie half turned to go check, but was held in place by Amelia's tight grip.

"Lieutenant Cantrill," Lord Bradbury's voice boomed in her ear. She snapped her attention around to her faux beau as he bowed gallantly before Amelia. How handsome he was tonight, resplendent in sober evening dress. Having never seen him in anything but the simple garb he wore to visit the veterans or to attend church, he was quite a sight to behold. She dimpled at him and curtsied. He gazed directly into her eyes—what magnificent, soulful eyes he had! Sophie blinked rapidly.

Time to begin the farce. As if she weren't nervous enough.

"Lord Bradbury, Miss Bradbury, Miss Handley." He bowed to each in turn. "Allow me to present my mother, Mrs. Moriah Cantrill."

Mrs. Cantrill swept in, her head held at a regal angle. Yes, she was definitely Charlie's mother. They looked as alike as two peas in a pod. Except Mrs. Cantrill's thin cheeks did not possess the same dimples as her son's.

In fact, though she resembled him physically, she had much less of his look of intelligence and wit about her, and much more of haughtiness.

As Sophie curtsied, she glanced over Mrs. Cantrill's gown. It was of an excellent cut, and beautifully draped, but rather too ornate for a simple reception in Bath.

As she raised her eyes to Mrs. Cantrill's gaze, a slight shiver ran down her spine. Mrs. Cantrill was assessing her, too. Charlie must've told her. Would she see through their farce? Mrs. Cantrill's keen eyes took in all that Sophie was wearing, and focused on the diamond bracelet. She held out Sophie's wrist, allowing the jewels to catch the firelight.

"Lovely. Wherever did you find such a beautiful adornment?"

Charlie turned back from his conversation with Lord Bradbury, watching Sophie with something altogether unreadable yet intense in his expression.

Sophie looked around. How best to carry off the situation? Lord Bradbury looked faintly amused, while Amelia looked mildly interested.

"Oh, this? Thank you, Mrs. Cantrill. It is rather sweet. It's—a present from a friend." Sophie laughed airily.

"We trotted out all our finery tonight, Mrs. Cantrill." Lord Bradbury offered the older woman his arm. "Come, let me show you my latest acquisition. A fine piece of art—have you ever seen such a lovely ormolu clock?" With that, he steered her toward the mantelpiece, leaving Sophie alone with Charlie and Amelia.

Amelia looked expectantly up at Sophie, but she had no more words to carry off the social niceties. Charlie knew she was penniless, and that such a bauble would likely have been seized by the duns during her father's bankruptcy so many years before. He was a bright lad, and would put two and two together. Would he think it untoward if Lord Bradbury leant her some jewelry for the occasion? After all, she was only borrowing it. She darted a glance at him. There was no telling what he was thinking. His face was clouded over, and his eyes were dark blanks.

He bowed at the two ladies and retired to the opposite end of the room, chatting with a group of men who were clustered around the divan. Well, that was that. She would likely not have a moment to speak to Charlie alone this evening. There were too many people about, and too much to do. With a shrug, she turned toward her charge.

"You should begin circulating, making polite conversation with your guests," she whispered.

Amelia nodded but stayed rooted to the spot. Sophie patted her shoulder and turned her toward the side of the room, where a sweet-faced old dowager reclined in a velvet chair. "Go on, ask Mrs. White about her dogs. I've seen her out walking them through the Crescent and the park. She adores them like children, and once you set her going, you shan't have to say a word," Sophie encouraged.

With a reluctant sigh, Amelia did as Sophie bid her. And that gave Sophie the perfect opportunity to slip, unnoticed, from the drawing room. She hastened to the dining room and made a careful count. Yes, sixteen shining places were laid on the polished mahogany table. Servants bustled around, making the few final touches that would make the party entirely comfortable and luxurious.

Sophie leaned against the wall. She filled her lungs with air and slowly exhaled. Everything was going to be fine. So far, Amelia was doing quite well. And Lord Bradbury had distracted Mrs. Cantrill perfectly. There was no need—just yet, anyway—for Mrs. Cantrill to doubt the veracity of her courtship with Charlie. Only one problem stood in her way—Charlie's dark, unreadable expression.

It wasn't jealousy, was it? No, of course not. Likely he saw the bracelet and assumed the worst. Thought of her as frivolous and silly all over again. And why not? She darted a glance at her wrist. Why, this one bracelet could keep two veterans' families in great comfort. Or it could feed dozens of hungry children. She resisted an urge to unclasp it and fling it across the room.

She was caught, straddling two worlds she didn't comprehend, though she knew both well. Poverty and wealth. Servitude and privilege. As a servant, she belonged to neither. Too well-borne and well-paid to be poor, and yet too humble to pretend to be anything but a helper to The Honorable Amelia Bradbury. In all honesty, she didn't know which world she really wanted.

Charlie's dark, forbidding face crossed her mind.

No, she did know.

But that path—given what the man thought of her— was likely closed to her forever.

Bradbury was up to something. Charlie toyed with his empty glass. Since he didn't drink after dinner, there was very little to do at these functions but watch as the men enjoyed their port. And Bradbury had the smug, satisfied air of a cat who'd gotten the cream—or at least, knew the cream was close at hand.

The ladies had already retreated to the drawing room, led by Amelia, who had been subtly prompted by Sophie. All through dinner, Charlie had watched Sophie as she guided her young charge through the complicated rituals of Society. Nary a gaffe had been made, a rarity for a young girl's debut.

Mother's expression throughout the meal had mellowed and softened, and when they left the room, she had claimed Sophie's arm. The faux courtship was now, as far as Mother was concerned, a reality. She liked Sophie, he could tell. Now, all that remained was to see if Mother would try to coax him back to Brightgate again.

But there was the matter of that bracelet. The way Sophie had blushed when Mother mentioned it did not bode well. He flicked a glance over at Lord Bradbury. Had he given the bracelet to Sophie? And if so, what were his intentions?

"A pretty young gel, what, Bradbury?" one of the older men at the end of the table said with an appreciative chuckle. Charlie strained his ears.

"Whom are you speaking of, Whitlock? My daughter Amelia?" Bradbury leaned forward, an amused grin crooking the corner of his mouth.

"Ah, I was speaking of the blonde chit—your daughter's gel. Susan? Sally? Blast, what was her name?" Whitlock poured more brandy into his glass with a steady hand.

"Sophie. My daughter's seamstress." Bradbury lolled back in his chair.

"Rather decorative, what? Sir Hugh's daughter, I presume?" Whitlock replied.

"She is rather decorative, and a huge help to my daughter. Practically arranged this evening herself, you know." Bradbury was holding something back. You could see it in his elaborately nonchalant expression.

"Well, to the manor born, and all that." Whitlock smiled. "Now, I meant nothing against Amelia, you understand. But one can't pay elaborate compliments to one's host's daughter," he explained with a laugh.

"No offense taken, I assure you. And I agree—Miss Sophie is very—ahem—ornamental to have about the house." Bradbury tipped his glass at Whitlock with a sly grin, and both men chuckled.

Something gnawed at Charlie's gut—a primal urge he hadn't felt in years. He clenched his fist under the table. So Bradbury thought Sophie decorative, did he? Had he given Sophie that bracelet as a token of his esteem? If so, what had prompted her to accept? Surely she understood what accepting such an expensive gift signified.

His jaw clenched. He'd like to wipe that smug look off his lordship's face with one quick jab. The way his lordship spoke, as though Sophie were an object to be attained—no different from that ridiculous ormolu clock he had brayed about to Mother. His heart surged with a feeling of protection for Sophie. She was his best friend's sister now, for all intents and purposes, and he needed to watch over her. For Brookes's sake. Not for any other reason.

As the men joined the women in the drawing room, Charlie sought out Sophie and remained stuck, like a stubborn burr, to her side. They talked of everything and nothing. He made more polite chatter in that night than he had in years. But it didn't matter. He was staking out his territory, and that was that. Several times Bradbury looked their way, his brow lifted, and Charlie was hard-pressed not to raise his brows in return.

As the guests began to depart, Sophie wandered over to the fireplace, standing before the blaze. He followed, drawing closer to her magnificent form than he had dared before.

"Charlie, are you angry at me? Honestly, I can't read your expression. Your mother—she believes our courtship to be real, does she not?" Sophie whispered.

"No, I am not angry." He stared into the fire as though he could find the key to his jumbled emotions in its flames. "Who gave you the bracelet?" It slipped out before he could stop it.

"I am borrowing it. It is no gift," she said. "I don't own anything fine enough for an evening like this."

Something in his heart unclenched. "You look lovely." And she did. She looked, well, more than lovely. She looked like the kind of young lady a fellow would be elated to court.

She blushed so deeply he could see her color rise in the firelight. "Thank you."

The drawing room was nearly deserted; it was time for him to go. Bradbury was glancing his way, sizing him up as he would over a game of chess—or even a pair of dueling pistols. "Thank you for a pleasant evening, Miss Handley," he said, projecting his voice a bit. "Shall I come to call on you Thursday when you are off work?"

She looked up at him, startled confusion darkening her eyes. "Um, yes. Of course, Lieutenant." Then she darted a glance over at his mother, and held out her hand. "Until then."

He bowed over her winking diamond bracelet, triumph making the blood rush to his face. He paid his respects to Amelia Bradbury and smiled cordially at his lordship before bundling his mother off into the carriage they had hired for the night.

Well, nearly a smile. Perhaps more like a slight smirk.

"Sophie is a lovely girl, Charles." Mother settled against the cushions with a satisfied smile.

"I agree, Mother. Tonight—she was incomparable."

"You've chosen well." Mother's tone was more relaxed than it had been in ages. Charlie smiled in the gathering darkness.

"Yes. Yes, I have." If he closed his eyes for a moment, he could just imagine that the courtship wasn't false, and that Sophie Handley really was his intended.

Chapter Eleven

Sophie yawned openly. With only the last few servants milling about, cleaning up the remainder of the dinner party mess, it was a luxury she could at last give in to. Amelia had already retired upstairs about half an hour before, to gossip with Louisa and Lucy. Sophie had remained behind to help put the house back in order, but also to sort out her jumbled emotions. Really, the entire evening had been one long turn on the torture rack, as far as she was concerned.

She prided herself as a master of the art of flirtation. In fact, there were few young women in Derbyshire as talented in that particular form of expression as she. And something had transpired tonight. Rivalry had run high between Charlie and Lord Bradbury throughout supper and afterward. And Charlie had made a point to announce that he would call on her on Thursday. Loud enough for his lordship to hear. Weren't they supposed to keep their faux courtship a secret? Only his mother was supposed to know. It was, after all, a ruse to keep her happy during her trip to Bath, a ruse that would be dropped the moment she left for Brightgate.

In proclaiming his intentions so loudly, Charlie ran the risk of piquing his lordship's attention. And if his lordship knew she was engaged—even falsely—then he might dismiss her. Many young women lost their posts the minute they announced an impending marriage. It wasn't a pretty fact of life, but it was a true one. And in mentioning his intentions, he ran the risk of making a faux courtship seem like a real engagement, which could lead to all sorts of problems and difficulties.

Charlie understood these things, surely. Didn't he?

She bent to pick up a spent cigar butt that had missed its target, the ash tray, by at least a few feet. My, how nice it would be to retire upstairs, cozy in bed with a hot brick at her tired and throbbing feet.

"Miss Handley?" A cultured baritone voice boomed behind her.

Startled, she dropped the butt on the Aubusson carpet and turned to face her employer.

"Taking up a new habit?" he inquired, nodding at the remnants of the cigar.

She chuckled appreciatively. "Oh, no, your lordship." She dusted her hands on her skirt. "Merely trying to clean up."

"Leave that for the other servants," he replied tersely. His mouth was stretched into a taut line. "I should like to speak to you in my study before you retire."

Oh, goodness. Here it was. She was going to be sacked, just because her faux courtship had been brought to his lordship's attention. She followed her employer down the interminable hallway, past all the doors painted just alike, and into his study, where a fire crackled in the grate. He patted a leather chair with his large hand, and took his seat behind the desk.

She sank into the chair as bidden, her heart in her throat. How it would hurt to leave Louisa and Amelia and Lucy. They were all becoming sisters to her. Replacing the void that Harriet had left when she married—not that Hattie had intended to abandon her. That's just the way marriage worked.

His lordship stared at her, his dark eyes unfathomable. Really, it was most unnerving. Despite her best efforts, she twitched in her chair. Would this interview never begin?

"What, exactly, is your connection to young Lieutenant Cantrill?" His lordship's voice was smooth as silk.

"He is a good friend of my family, your lordship. His best friend, Captain Brookes, is married to my sister Harriet." Surely that would stave off all further questions. It was rather like being in the Old Bailey, only she wasn't sure what crime she was accused of committing.

"Ah, yes. I know John Brookes. He's a good man." Lord Bradbury turned his head, staring off into the fire. "Is there any other connection I should know about?"

She swallowed. Would he simply come out with it and sack her? Or must she hang by her fingertips a bit longer? She racked her brain for an excuse that was both reasonable and true. "I am helping Lieutenant Cantrill with his work with the veterans' widows. My sister is funding quite a bit of their welfare, and I am acting as her liaison while I am employed in Bath."

A muscle twitched in his lordship's jawline. "I see." Those terse two words, ground out from clenched teeth, did not offer much comfort.

She sat quietly, hardly daring to draw breath. Her fate seemed to hang in the balance. A wrong word here or there, and she might lose her position. But his lordship said nothing—merely stared into the fire with a moody expression on his face.

The tension was like a bow string stretched too tautly. Surely she would snap if she had to stay here much longer. The best thing to do was to assume control of the situation, and make a graceful exit. She rose, fumbling with her bracelet.

"Thank you so much for the loan of this bracelet, your lordship." She extended the bauble toward him, hoping he wouldn't notice the way her hand shook. "It was the perfect match for this gown."

He turned, staring at her with those same dark, unreadable eyes. He waved one large hand idly in the air, as though swatting at a fly. "Keep it. I purchased it expressly for you, Miss Handley."

"Oh, no. I couldn't." She still clutched the bracelet in midair. "It's far too expensive a gift to keep."

The corner of his mouth quirked down, and a dangerous spark lit his eyes. "I can afford it, I assure you."

"I am not sure I can," she whispered.

"What does that mean?" For once, she had his full attention. He was poised, like a cat ready to jump on a plump and unsuspecting mouse.

"An expensive gift like this could carry a higher burden than I am able to pay." It was difficult to explain. Surely he took her meaning. It could mean her position, her reputation, or even Charlie Cantrill. Not that she was really engaged to him. But she could not have him thinking ill of her for accepting such an expensive gift.

"You told Mrs. Cantrill it was a present from a friend. And it is. I want you to keep it." He pushed his chair away from his desk and rose.

Sophie's mouth went dry. What was he about? She placed the bracelet on his desk and took a step backward. "I couldn't think of anything else to say when she asked me about it. 'Twas the first explanation that came to mind. I meant nothing by it."

"Will you accept it as a gift if I tell you that I am indebted to you? All of your efforts to help Amelia paid off handsomely tonight. She was flawless, and the evening went off without a single problem. I must say, I was more than impressed." He came around the side of the desk, a changed expression altering his face. For the first time ever he was open and friendly, without a trace of his former feral grace, his eyes unclouded.

"Thank you." She glanced away. His pure regard was almost as troubling as his usual inscrutable expression. Could she leave now, without seeming ungracious? Fatigue settled over her like a heavy cloak. Her eyes felt as though sand had been blown into them.

"Miss Handley," he replied, his voice free of its usual silky tone. "I would take it very much as an honor if you would accept this little gift. Seeing my Amelia so confident, so proud tonight—it was quite astonishing. And I owe you something for your efforts." He scooped it up and handed it to her. "Accept this trinket as a token of my gratitude for all your hard work."

His tender affection for Amelia was genuine. Her mind flashed back to the moments before the soiree, when he gifted Amelia with her mother's pearls. He truly adored his daughters and would likely be grateful to anyone who helped them succeed in Society. With a nod, she took the diamond bracelet, which was warm to the touch—even through her glove. Perhaps the interview was finally over.

"Now, then. We understand each other." He smiled as though immensely satisfied. "Go on to bed, Miss Handley. You must be exhausted. When you awaken tomorrow, I am sure Amelia will want to see you. She has much to plan for the upcoming Season."

"Of course." She bobbed a curtsy. "Thank you so much, Lord Bradbury."

He waved a careless hand. "Think nothing of it. Off with you, now."

She couldn't suppress the wide grin that broke across her face. Why, it was as if she finally understood her employer, and he understood her. The faint thread of darkness that always wove through their conversations had vanished. It seemed she had a true ally and friend in his lordship.

She mounted the stairs, her legs heavy as lead. Perhaps she could sneak past the girls' rooms and retire without having to speak to anyone. It would be so nice to sort through the evening's images in her mind. Usually, after an event like this, she loved to stay up and talk about it with Harriet. But tonight she couldn't wait to be on her own.

She changed into the nightgown that had been thoughtfully laid out on her bed by one of the servants, and brushed her hair with long, steady strokes. She tucked the diamond bracelet into a box on her dressing table. She would never wear it in public, of course,

but it was rather nice to know that such a pretty object
was hers.

Satisfied, she looked in the mirror. She would have to
pay Aunt Katherine a call soon. The older lady wanted
to know all about Amelia's debut, and had made Sophie promise to spill the details as soon as she could.
Perhaps she could call on Auntie tomorrow, after her
tasks were done. A good "chin-wag," as the old lady
termed it, would be just the thing.

Mother sailed into the sitting room the next day,
barely acknowledging Mrs. Pierce, who answered her
authoritative knock as quickly as her arthritic knees
would allow.

"Charles, my son! Guess what I've done. I've written your uncle Arthur and told him all about you and
Sophie. You always were his favorite, you know."

Charlie dropped his Bible, his morning's meditation
shattered. Warning bells clanged in his mind. "What
did you tell him, Mother?"

"Merely that you've found a nice young gel and will
probably wed her soon." She swatted him on the shoulder in a rare, playful gesture. "Uncle Arthur is a veteran,
too. I knew my brother would be pleased to hear about
how far you've come since returning from Waterloo."

"Mother, there is no guarantee we will get married."
His heart thumped painfully against his ribs. "We've
only been…courting."

"Well, I am sure that an engagement isn't far off. I
saw the way she looked at you." Mother removed her
gloves and untied her bonnet. "I am sure that by the

time the letter reaches your uncle in Italy, you will be betrothed and ready to set about reading the banns."

Mother's brother was a shadowy figure from his past, someone she spoke of often, but whom Charlie had only met once. Perhaps it would be possible to remedy her mistake without too much trouble.

"Mother, have you told anyone else?"

"Well, I told the Pooles about Sophie, of course. They were very put out to not be invited to the viscount's, you know."

Charlie groaned. "Why did you do that? The Pooles? You might have well announced it in the middle of the Circus."

"They are my hosts, Charles," she reminded him severely. "Anything of import, I should share with them. And my son finding a suitable young lady is decidedly important."

Charlie rumpled his hair with his one good hand. "Mother," he replied in a serious tone of voice, "we've only been seeing each other for a few weeks. If anyone gets the wrong impression, then the social consequences could be dire."

"I'll say it again, my son—you will be engaged to Sophie Handley in a matter of weeks. Now, what really remains is the question of your future. Obviously you will not continue to live…here…" Mother waved her hand around his small sitting room. "This is no place to bring a bride and no place to raise a family. We shall write to your brother directly, and he will help you secure a home in Brightgate—"

Charlie shoved his chair away from the table, counting to ten as he had taught himself to school his sudden and fearsome temper. Sophie had suggested the false courtship as a way to help him out—as a way, in fact, to keep him in Bath. And here Mother was, running with it, putting Sophie in potentially dire social consequences. Whatever could he do to save the young lady who had, in her turn, tried to save him?

He turned on his heel, ignoring his mother's questions and exclamations, and rushed up the stairs to his bedroom, where he slammed the door. At last, peace and privacy. He needed time to think. He had always let his family order him about. The only way he had found any freedom was in joining the military—nearly being killed at Waterloo. Then refusing to return home and electing to stay on in Bath. It was only in putting real physical distance between himself and his family members that he was able to enjoy freedom.

Now what could he do? He needed to find a way to control the situation without flames running rampant. If only someone could help him. He couldn't confide in anyone, for Mother would be furious if she knew the courtship wasn't true. And Brookes and Harriet were too far away to help. Besides, they would likely shy away from the notion of a false engagement, no matter how noble the intention was. In fact, Brookes would likely plant him a facer if he knew what Charlie was about.

No—he needed to speak with Sophie. Together, they would find a way to get out of this situation without causing the social downfall of every person involved. He checked his pocket watch. He could take Mother to tea at Aunt Katherine's to stall her. In fact, Aunt Katherine might be able to help, as well. She was kind and empathetic and knew the histories of everyone involved. Plus, she loved meddling in other people's affairs. He could harness her love of sticking her nose into other people's business and use it to his own advantage—and Sophie's, of course.

That was the only answer. And they must get started without delay. He hurled open his bedroom door and hastened back down the stairs.

"Mother, I've a surprise for you. We're headed to tea at Katherine Crossley's."

Chapter Twelve

The visit to Aunt Katherine's would have to be delayed until later in the afternoon. From the moment she had set foot in her workroom that morning, Sophie had been inundated with tasks from his lordship. He had even asked her if she would be willing to mend a waistcoat that had been torn slightly by the laundress. She had never sewn anything for his lordship before, so the task was slightly daunting. She craned her neck and moved closer to the light, making tiny invisible stitches in the silk lining of the garment. It was a beautifully made waistcoat, finely tailored. Sewing men's clothing was much more precise—there was far less room for the imagination. On the other hand, one did have a duty to one's employer.

Sophie held the waistcoat up and gave it a little shake. A few more carefully placed stitches, and she would be done. Then she still needed to talk with Amelia about the month's social calendar—her upcoming dances, her dinner parties and a hundred other gatherings that would require a special wardrobe.

A knock sounded on the door. Another servant, Nancy, bobbed a curtsy from the doorway.

"Miss Handley, his lordship would like to know if you will be done with the waistcoat in time for supper tonight."

"I will." Sophie tied a minuscule knot in her thread and snipped it with a pair of scissors. "In fact, I am done now."

"Very good." Nancy took the waistcoat, draping it over her arm. "He also wanted to know what your afternoon schedule is like."

Sophie grabbed her sewing basket, tucking her scissors and thread away. Then she poked her needle into her pincushion. "Well, I had planned to spend an hour discussing Miss Amelia's upcoming Season."

"And after that?" Nancy looked at her expectantly. "Were you expecting to do anything else?"

Sophie rubbed a weary hand over her eyes. "I would like to take tea at my friend Mrs. Katherine Crossley's house, but I can delay that if his lordship requires my attention."

Nancy smirked. "I think his lordship thought you had a gentleman caller coming by this afternoon."

Oh, of course. Charlie Cantrill. Heat flooded her face, and she was unable to meet Nancy's gaze. "No. He will call on me on Thursday, when it is time for the veterans' meeting."

Nancy's smug expression deepened, and she left without another word. Botheration, was everyone keeping tabs on her relationship with Charlie? After all, this was supposed to be a simple act of kindness to keep him in Bath. Now it was gathering speed, and even the other servants were privy to it. She rolled her eyes and rested her head against the cushion. If only Lord Bradbury had been more discreet when he sent Nancy up to see her. Having another servant question her about her plans concerning a young man was beyond embarrassing.

Oh, well. Nothing could be done about it now. She needed to retrieve Amelia from the schoolroom so they could begin their discussion. The sooner she finished her tasks, the sooner she could go see Aunt Katherine. And really, conversation with the down-to-earth old woman would be quite refreshing after all the confusion and anxiety she had endured over the past few days.

She rose and hurried down the hall, where she claimed Amelia from Lucy. They enjoyed an hour of pouring over invitations, deciding which gowns would do for which occasion. Sophie drew up a list of what she still needed to do for the Season—which gowns required modifications or trimming. They agreed upon a new design for a riding habit. Her sartorial future decided, Amelia skipped off to enjoy tea, and Sophie rushed out of the house for Aunt Katherine's. If she hung about too long, someone might put her back to work.

It was a fine day, and the ten-minute walk to Aunt Katherine's was just the thing she needed to boost her flagging spirits. For once, it wasn't raining. A mild sun broke through the clouds and brightened the colorful gardens as they began to bloom. Why, it even smelled like spring—the fresh scent of flowers and earth sweetened the breeze as it ruffled her curls.

She knocked on Aunt Katherine's door, and Knowles ushered her in. How good it was to be among familiar faces that reminded her of home and Harriet. She practically ran into the library and crushed Aunt Katherine in a warm embrace.

"Goodness, child, I am so glad to see you." Aunt Katherine patted the seat beside her on the settee. "I can't say I've always thought so. When you threw John over, I should have liked to scratch your eyes out."

Harsh words indeed, but said in such a loving and warm tone that Sophie could only laugh. "I wouldn't have blamed you, Auntie dear. But it all worked out for the best, didn't it?"

"Tut, tut. It worked out very well for John and Harriet. But now I wonder—how did it work for you?" The old lady's piercing gaze searched hers.

"Very well. I like what I am doing. I like being useful. I feel myself growing, if that's the right word."

Auntie rang for the tea. "Don't ask me about the correct words. That is your sister's job, finding the proper expression for every occasion."

Sophie smiled. "True. Oh, Auntie, the dinner party went so beautifully." Settling back in her chair, Sophie described the event to the last detail, enjoying the brightened interest in Aunt Katherine's expression.

"It sounds like you did very well by young Amelia. What a brilliant debut for such a well-connected young lady. She will be able to make a most eligible match when she has her first London Season next year. Will you go with the family to London?"

"I don't know." Aunt Katherine had such a way of winnowing out secrets. She pounced on the one subject Sophie thought she could avoid—the future. But now, looking at Auntie's kindly, wrinkled face, she felt compelled to tell the truth about everything—her sham courtship and Lord Bradbury's puzzling attentions.

They were interrupted by the arrival of tea, and Sophie took the few extra moments to gather her composure. She must be honest and open with Auntie—because the wise old woman could help her sort through her jumbled emotions, much in the same clear-eyed way Harriet used to.

"Auntie, I made a blunder. A stupid blunder, which could cost me dearly. I dreamed up the idea of a faux courtship with Charlie, so his mother would stop pestering him to return to Brightgate." Now she had Aunt Katherine's full attention. The old woman had even put aside her interminable knitting once she began to speak. "And I am not sure what Lord Bradbury's intentions are, but—he gave me a diamond bracelet." The words tumbled out in a rush.

"Well, really." Aunt Katherine's gaze was bright, and she smiled. "Now this is all quite exciting. So you have two young men interested in you?"

"Yes. No. Not really. I don't know." Sophie placed her teacup on the mahogany side table. "My courtship with Charlie is merely a ruse, and it's possible that I received the diamond bracelet as a simple thank-you gift, as Lord Bradbury implied. On the other hand, the two of them were squaring off like two rams at the dinner party."

Aunt Katherine laughed and clapped her hands. "How delightful."

"Not really. Oh, Auntie, I am so confused. I don't know what to do. I was trying to help Charlie, but I made such a cake of myself."

"How so? It seems to me you have done beautifully.

You were trying to help a friend, were you not? And so what if Bradbury gave you a diamond bracelet? The man can well afford a diamond carriage, from what I hear."

Sophie massaged her temples. Her head was beginning to pound. And she wasn't making her meaning clear.

"I just—I just don't know. It all seems to be wrong, somehow. Just when I think I have Lord Bradbury or Charlie figured out, they begin behaving in a different manner. It's all so confusing."

Aunt Katherine clasped Sophie's hand. "The most important thing for you to determine is how you feel. Let's begin with Charlie. Now, you threw my John over when he returned from Waterloo with a missing leg. Do Charlie's injuries offend your sensibilities?"

Sophie paused. How to explain the difference between the two situations without hurting Auntie's feelings? Drawing a shaky breath, she began, "Well, it was not so much that John's injury offended me. It was more than that. You see, Auntie, when he came back from the war, he had changed altogether. He was a different person."

Aunt Katherine nodded, her keen eyes resting on Sophie's face. "Go on."

"But I didn't know Charlie before the war. As I know him now, well, that's the only way I have known him. So his injury is merely a part of him. Does that make sense?"

The old woman folded her hands in her lap. "I believe so. Do you love him? Or do you love Lord Bradbury?"

Sophie paused once more. It was too soon to know

for sure, wasn't it? She enjoyed Charlie's company, esteemed him for the work he did—she liked him very much indeed when his guard came down, and he permitted himself to joke about.

But love? After her experiences with John Brookes and Lieutenant Marable, she was reluctant to admit to love, or even permit herself to fall in love.

"I esteem Charlie greatly, but I don't love him—why, I hardly know him." It was difficult to say those words. Something inside her resisted them.

"And what of Bradbury?" Aunt Katherine patted her back with a gentle hand.

Sophie heaved a great sigh. "I am hoping that, in time, I can have his recommendation so I may start my own couturier. That is what I want—I want to become more than just a flighty young woman—a flibbertigibbet."

Aunt Katherine leveled the same assessing gaze on Sophie that she had before, and cocked her head to one side, causing her corkscrew curls to shake.

"A diamond bracelet, even from someone as wealthy as Bradbury, is a very extravagant gift. You should know that his lordship may have designs on you, too, pretty little Sophie."

"Surely not, Auntie. I'm just a lady's maid to him. But then—it's hard to tell what his designs may be. He's so secretive, Auntie."

"Well, if he offered for you, would you have him?"

Sophie paused. She loved Amelia and Louisa like sisters. It would be wonderful to stay with them forever, watching them mature into women with families of their own. If she married his lordship, she would never worry about money again.

But she disliked the cold and calculating way he assessed her, the way he ordered her about. Would a life with Louisa and Amelia be worth it?

"I couldn't say," she replied flatly. "I don't love him, but I love his daughters."

Aunt Katherine sat back, appearing well pleased. "I shall help you, Sophie. But you must trust me."

Sophie shrugged, gazing at the old woman in wonderment. "Help me? How?"

At that moment, Knowles entered after making a discreet scratch on the door. "Lieutenant Cantrill and Mrs. Moriah Cantrill, Mrs. Crossley."

Mother had done nothing but prattle on the way over to Aunt Katherine's, wearing Charlie's nerves to a frayed edge. What a relief to enter Aunt Katherine's salon, to be braced by the old woman's indomitable spirit. But wait— Charlie stopped short in the doorway. Sophie was there. The very woman his mother had been chattering on about for the entire morning was now before him, as radiant as the morning sunshine. She was confiding in Aunt Katherine; he could tell by the way they sat closely together, bent forward like two willow branches on opposite settees. But whatever the confidences were, they fled as Sophie sprang into social action. Charlie held out his hand. Hers betrayed not a tremble. She was so very good at handling the social niceties with grace and poise.

She really was made for Society, that was certain. His heart gave an extra beat.

"Mrs. Crossley, I believe you met my mother some years ago in Bath," he began, attempting to rise to the occasion as Sophie had done.

"Mrs. Crossley, so good to see you again," Mother effused, before turning to exclaim over Sophie's gown and her hair. Then she immediately launched into a recounting of the evening for Aunt Katherine's benefit. "If only you could have been there, Mrs. Crossley," she breathed. "It was a brilliant occasion, and Miss Bradbury handled herself so well. Of course—" she turned a dazzling smile in Sophie's direction "—she owes it all to her tutor. Miss Handley was exquisite."

Sophie returned the smile. "Thank you, ma'am."

Mother rubbed her hands together briskly. "Now, Mrs. Crossley, I am sure you enjoy hearing the latest news as much as I do. So I shall not hesitate to inform you that my son and Miss Handley have been courting. Is that not famous? I am beside myself with delight."

Out of the corner of his eye, Charlie caught a glimpse of Sophie as she started in her chair. Color bloomed in her cheeks, making her look like a rose in full blush. But she said nothing. Only the corners of her mouth turned downward slightly. She appeared not to feel Charlie's gaze upon her.

Aunt Katherine pursed her lips in an amused fashion. Her eyes twinkled merrily. "Was it supposed to be a secret courtship?"

"Charlie mentioned that they had been keeping it quiet," Mother replied with a chuckle, "but I am too delighted to keep the matter to myself. I have already written my brother, Arthur, about it. Do you remember Arthur, Mrs. Crossley? He, too, is a veteran."

"Of course I do. He settled somewhere abroad, did he not?" Aunt Katherine asked the question in a polite tone, but kept her eyes fastened on Charlie. Under such close regard, his face began to heat. Dash it all, he was tired of Mother and of any more talk. He stood so quickly that his chair scraped across the floor with a teeth-jarring sound.

Mother ignored him. "Yes, he settled in Italy. He's made a fortune in shipping. Vinegars, wines and all sorts of similar goods."

Charlie strolled over to Sophie's chair. They needed to formulate a plan. "Would you like to take a walk in Aunt Katherine's garden?"

She looked up at him, an expression of gratitude in her china-blue eyes. "Yes. I should like that very much." She rose and tucked her arm into the crook of his right arm.

"You two children run along," Aunt Katherine warbled. "It is too fine a day to spend indoors. Mrs. Cantrill and I shall have a nice chin-wag while you enjoy the splendors of my garden."

Mother smiled too brightly and shooed them toward the double glass doors with a wave of her gloved hands.

Once out on the veranda, Charlie took a deep breath of the balmy spring air. Gathering his courage, he turned to Sophie. "I'm sorry. My mother is an incorrigible gossip. I should have known she would take our ruse and run with it."

Sophie patted his arm. "Honestly, Charlie. It's all right. I am not offended that anyone would think our courtship was real."

His heart beat faster. Really? Was that so? Not that

it mattered, of course. She was merely being polite. Still, every sense he had strained against reason, and he crushed a desire to gather her in his arms and kiss her breathless.

Calm yourself, man. He exhaled slowly, and turned her down the garden path. He had not felt that way about a woman for years. Not since his broken engagement to Beth Gaskell. He needed to clear his mind and focus on the matter at hand.

"She's told members of my family, and even a few friends. She's coming perilously close to calling it an engagement. I am a career soldier, but I confess I have no idea how to handle this particular battle. I don't know how to extricate you without damaging your reputation."

"Remember who I am? What I am? Fickle and flighty Sophie." She gave a bitter laugh that wrenched his stomach. "If it comes to that, no one will think anything of it if I break our engagement."

"I don't think of you that way," he muttered. It was the truth. He hated for her to think poorly of herself, when he had seen so much good in her.

She paused and turned toward him, her bright blue eyes glowing. "Don't you?"

"Not at all. I admire you greatly." It was difficult to say the words, but something told him she needed to hear it.

She reached up and pecked his cheek with her soft lips, leaving a burning mark behind. "Oh, Charlie," she whispered. "That means more to me than all the diamond bracelets in the world."

The kiss, hastily given, and her words, breathlessly

uttered, rendered him slightly dizzy. He closed his eyes, willing himself to stop being such a fool. Sophie was merely being generous and sweet; it was beyond ridiculous to infer that she offered more than friendship.

He strolled around the garden with Sophie on his arm until Aunt Katherine shooed them back inside for tea. As he held the door open for Sophie, he made a silent vow. She would never regret this decision to help him. He would make sure that Sophie's kindness would not go unrewarded or forgotten.

Some way, he would repay her.

Chapter Thirteen

Did her feet ever touch the ground over the next few days? It was hard to tell. Charlie's good opinion of her mattered more than she dared admit. Her hands flew through her daily tasks. She pin tucked, she pleated, she embroidered as though every stitch would somehow solve all their problems. Somehow, some way, it would all work out. Harriet had always admonished her to put her faith in God, and she finally did so—wholeheartedly. With His blessing, she was earning her own way in the world. She was earning the esteem of good men. She no longer thought herself a flirt and a careless coquette. She was becoming someone deeper and more profound with each passing day.

Today was Thursday, and she dressed for her day off with special care. She was off to the veterans' meeting this morning, which, of course, meant that she was to see Charlie. He would, in fact, be waiting for her outside the kitchen door in a matter of moments.

Not that she was leaping at the chance to see him—no, she wouldn't go that far. But she did enjoy his company tremendously. She tied her bonnet ribbons in a jaunty bow under her chin and hummed a snippet of her favorite waltz. How wonderful everything was. How she loved everyone this morning!

Her bedchamber door opened, and Lucy came into the room. "You are disgustingly cheerful," she announced, and flopped down on the bed.

"Why shouldn't I be? It's a beautiful day. And you? Why are you so glum? After all, you will have a chance to see your ensign." Sophie pinched her cheeks, accentuating her already high color.

"Yes, I do get to see Rowland. But every moment with him is agony. I want so much to tell him everything I am feeling—how much I adore him, how I would do anything for him—and yet I cannot." Lucy picked at the coverlet, her face a mask of pain.

"Oh, Lucy." Sophie swooped down and crushed her in a smothering embrace. "If you are in love, everything works itself out."

"Are you in love?" Lucy interrupted. "The way you've been acting, I assume Cantrill proposed? Has he given you a ring? Are you planning the banns?"

"Well, no." And what was all her good cheer for, then? She wasn't in love with him. Surely she wasn't.

Sophie shrugged. "We admire each other greatly. But our courtship is not real. I'm just…enjoying matters while I can."

"If you think that's wise, then you are a fool." Lucy sighed. "Sophie, not everything is as wonderful or as set as you seem to feel at this moment. For some of us, the path to true love is very rocky indeed."

Sophie wrapped her arm around Lucy's shoulders

and held her close. "Enjoy what time you have with the ensign, then," she whispered. "Savor the moment."

"Very well." Lucy rose. "Come, we will be late. I am sure the lieutenant is waiting for us."

He was. There was something very sweet and poignant about the way he stood patiently beside the kitchen door, toeing at a rock with his boot. Sophie's heart gave a lurch when he spied them and straightened. She gave him her most alluring smile, and was rewarded with his heightened color and stammered greeting. What was happening between them? Giddiness seized hold and she paused for a few moments before taking his hand. This wasn't love. Was it?

They set off down the street, passing the garden that had burst into bloom, Lucy on his right arm and Sophie gently holding his mutilated left elbow. It felt good to be gripping him so close to where he was injured—as though her very touch could heal years of suffering. "How does your mother fare?" she asked in an undertone meant only for his ears.

"Very well, thank you. She elected not to accompany us this morning. She is staying in at the Pooles'." His clipped response signaled something. Likely they had argued that morning. Mrs. Cantrill was not fond of Charlie's work with the veterans' fund. Sophie squeezed his elbow, communicating that she understood.

Lucy jumped into the conversation, asking Charlie more about Ensign Rowland's injury and his experience during the war. Sophie tuned out their voices, happy to simply walk beside Charlie on this fine spring day. As they neared the church, she said a silent prayer of thanks. What a marvelous Season this was turning out to be.

As they entered the narthex, Lucy went off in search of Ensign Rowland, her novel tucked under one arm. Charlie and Sophie paused, alone for the first time since their moment in the garden a few days before. She breathed deeply. He smelled of fresh linen and saddle leather—clean scents that reminded her of happier times on the estate, before it was taken away.

"What shall I do today?" She turned her face up to his.

He leaned closer, and the heat from his body began to make her feel dizzy. Goodness, how attractive he was. Would he kiss her? She pursed her lips and closed her eyes in anticipation.

"Would you—would you talk to Widow Adams today and see how she fares? I am worried about her. I've heard rumors that she cannot afford to feed herself or her grandchild," Charlie whispered.

Sophie opened her eyes slowly. Charlie had taken a step backward, and was looking over the gathering crowd with a businesslike air. The moment was gone. It was time to get to work. Well, of course—she was acting like a perfect goose. Their courtship wasn't even real, after all.

"Yes, of course." She untied her bonnet strings. "Anything else?"

"Try to engage Mrs. Baker in conversation. See if she has need of anything. She is so quiet that I worry about her. Her husband was with me at the farmhouse during the battle. A good fellow, and a brave one." With that, Charlie turned on his heel and joined the mass of men who gathered near the altar.

She cast her bonnet and shawl aside and looked around. Lucy was sitting in a side pew, reading to Ensign Rowland. The young lad was listening with such an intent expression on his face. Was it adoration? Or merely gratitude? 'Twas hard to tell. She gathered her wits and drifted toward a group of widows who had congregated at the back of the church. Some were sewing, others knitted. It was such a cozy, domestic scene that her heart warmed at the sight of them.

They looked up at her and smiled as she drew close. She returned their greetings heartily and hugged a few ragamuffin children. Her heart surged with love. If only she could spend her life working to help these women, right beside Charlie. What they needed was so simple: food, shelter and clothing. Her mind flashed back to Lord Bradbury's house. The rolls upon rolls of fabric in her workroom. The breakfast table laden with sausages and eggs every morning, regardless of the number of people who came to dine. The diamond bracelet he gifted so carelessly.

The diamond bracelet. She sank onto a pew. Surely that one bauble, as she had thought before, could feed many of these women for a good year. Harriet need not be the only woman gifting money to the veterans' fund. The bracelet was hers, wasn't it? She could do with it as she saw fit.

He was in grave danger of falling head over heels in love with Sophie Handley if he wasn't careful.

Charlie rubbed the stubble of his cheek with his hand.

The spot where she had kissed him still burned, the imprint of her lips tingling as though it had just happened. The looks she had cast his way, the heavenly blue of her eyes, the dimpled sweetness of her smile—honestly, she was enough to make a man dizzy. And yet, it was all a ruse. An act, merely for his benefit. She was, after all, the daughter of an actress. She was playing her part to perfection, simply to help him out.

If only he could break through to the real Sophie. That moment in the garden, when she had kissed him because he told her she wasn't a flighty miss—surely that girl was the real Sophie Handley. If only she would stay around forever. He liked that young lady immensely. Why, he could even dream of sharing his home and his life's work with that young lady. If only there were a way to strip all the layers aside and meet each other on the same level, they could at last finish this strange dance they'd begun upon her arrival in Bath.

He turned and spoke to the reverend, and grew comfortably engaged in his work. The morning passed swiftly, and before he knew it, everyone was gathering their things to return home. It was time to escort Lucy and Sophie back to Lord Bradbury's home. He scanned the crowd, but could not spot either young lady. Ensign Rowland exited out the side door, and Lucy was nowhere near him. So where could they be?

He combed through the narthex, but they weren't there. Had they left without him? Surely not.

As he rounded the corner of the vestibule, hushed female voices caught his ear. Lucy and Sophie were engaged in some private conversation, but he couldn't discern the words. As he neared the two girls, huddled over each other, whispering in rapid undertones, a chill ran down his spine. Were they speaking of him? Perhaps he had tipped his hand, and Sophie guessed that he was becoming too fond of her. He'd feel like a proper fool then.

He coughed and cleared his throat, and the whispering in the corridor stopped. "Miss Handley? Miss Williams?" he called. "It is time to return to Lord Bradbury's house."

"Here we are," Sophie announced, coming round the corridor. "Lucy and I were just having a chat about the ensign before we left."

"Were you?" A muscle twitched in his jaw. Well, perhaps that was true—maybe Miss Williams was informing Sophie of his progress, and they had stopped to whisper together so as not to hurt the lad's feelings. But if that was so, then why was Sophie's face so flushed with rosy color? Lucy looked as troubled as she had sounded, her face dark with worry. He patted her arm. "Never mind, Miss Williams," he said in a hearty tone. "The ensign appreciates your help and has shown marked improvement. And I appreciate all you are doing, too." A distinct prickle of unease worked its way down his spine. They weren't telling him the whole truth of their conversation, but there was no way to demand candor and honesty without sounding like a wounded bull or a candidate for Bedlam. So he merely offered each woman an elbow, and walked them back to Lord Bradbury's house.

At the back porch, Miss Williams dipped a curtsy and let herself inside, leaving Sophie and Charlie alone. She smiled up at him, flashing those dimples that made his breath catch a little in his throat. "Well, Lieutenant, I had a lovely morning. Thank you for taking us. Lucy and I have made great plans."

"Plans?" Perhaps they had some idea of what they wanted to do for young Rowland. But still—the whispered conversation in the corridor, Lucy's troubled gaze—none of it made sense. He was a trained tactician, and earned his bread by gauging unfamiliar situations and making the right call for attack. But put him next to a pretty woman, and he had no idea what he was about.

"Yes. I can't tell you yet, as I am still working on the details." Sophie bounced on her heels, her eyes dancing. "But I think you will approve."

He bowed, raising an eyebrow. "If you say so." He hated to sound so unsure. After all, he was a man. No—he was a soldier. He straightened. "I had better be going."

"Of course." Sophie's glee dimmed, and she gave him her hand with an uncertain air. "Shall I see you soon?"

"I am certain we will meet soon." He clasped her hand briefly, then released it. "Good day."

"Good day." With one last quizzical look over her shoulder, Sophie went inside Lord Bradbury's grand townhome.

Charlie heaved a huge sigh and quit the kitchen garden, rounding the side of the house. As luck would have it, his lordship was alighting from a carriage as he passed.

"What ho, Cantrill?" he called. "What are you about, poking around the back of my house?"

"Merely returning Miss Handley to you safe and sound," he replied tersely. He was in no mood for polite banter.

"Ah, I thank you for that. She is a rare jewel." Bradbury looked at him sharply. "May I ask why you borrow her quite as often as you do? You made a show of announcing your intention to call at dinner the other night."

"We are merely family friends." Charlie shrugged. "I am keeping an eye on her while she is in Bath."

"Are you really?" Lord Bradbury smiled, a stealthy grin that raised Charlie's hackles. "I just came from the club. Had a nice long chat with Bradford Poole. He seems to think there is far more to your relationship than friendly feelings. Is that so?"

What could he say? If he told Bradbury of their false courtship, Sophie could lose her position. Bradbury had said as much. Yet he ran the risk of calling Bradford Poole a liar, after his own mother had informed Poole of the courtship.

What a mess. Like sinking into the mire at Waterloo, more or less.

"Not at all, I assure your lordship. If we become engaged at any point I shall be sure to inform you."

"Excellent. See that you do." Lord Bradbury cocked his head to one side. "I have designs on the young lady myself. Gave her a nice little bracelet to pique her interest. Not anything too elaborate, but a pretty girl deserves a few pretty baubles. So—if you are leaving the field, bear in mind that I might take your place. I bid you good day."

With that, Lord Bradbury entered his house and shut

the door with a decisive click, leaving Charlie on the lawn—impotent and enraged. So Lord Bradbury had given Sophie the bracelet? And Sophie had lied about it, to both himself and to his mother.

He stalked through the streets of Bath toward Beau Street, wishing for an umbrella so he could stab at bits of garbage that whirled about and collected in the gutter. Anything to relieve his rage. Was he livid with Lord Bradbury and his sly grin and worldly ways? Or was he furious with Sophie for lying?

Neither. He was just bitterly disappointed. He thought Sophie had changed from the girl who cast John Brookes over. She seemed so mature, so thoughtful since her arrival in Bath. But was all of that a mere facade? His anger ebbed, and he wiped a weary hand over his brow.

There was nothing to do but wait. He was shackled to Sophie, for better or worse, for the next few days. He mounted the steps of his flat, ready to have a few moments of quiet reflection and a pot full of bracingly hot tea.

But instead of these comforts, Moriah Cantrill met him inside with a letter—sent via express post, if he could judge by the markings. "Do open it, Charles," Mother commanded. "It is from your uncle Arthur."

Chapter Fourteen

Sophie weighed the diamond bracelet in the palm of her hand.

She could sell it and get money to help the widows in Bath. She had given much thought to it since yesterday. With the proceeds from its sale, she could buy enough fabric and notions to help clothe all the women in the group, and their children, too. She could devise a sort of sewing circle among the women, everyone sharing in the work. In no time, all the women and children could have new dresses. She might even devise a few patterns—something simple that would maximize the use of the fabric and make the dresses quicker to sew. The threadbare garments the widows wore could be a thing of the past.

If she only sold her diamond bracelet.

And yet—

She stared into the fiery sparkle the diamonds cast in the morning light. It was very hard indeed to give up such a beautiful thing. She'd never owned anything like it in her born days. When Papa was rich, she was too young for jewels. Only Mama had them, and meant to keep them for Harriet and for Sophie. But then, Mama's jewel case was the first thing the duns seized after Papa died. She clasped it around her wrist once more. The bracelet was heavy and warm against her skin. It slid up her arm and caught just before her elbow. She held her arm up, watching the diamonds cast prisms around the room. Could she really give it up?

How astonishing that Lord Bradbury could afford to give such a jewel away like candy. And how equally astonishing that just one of those could clothe a group of fifteen individuals for a Season.

"'If thou wilt be perfect, go and sell what thou hast, and give to the poor...'" Sophie whispered. She had no need of the bracelet. It could help many people in desperate circumstances. She unclasped it and tucked it into her handkerchief, then placed the bundle gently inside her reticule. There was a pawnshop in Lower Bristol Road. She could certainly sell the bracelet there. There were also jewelers. Where should she go to sell it? And how quickly could she get there?

Louisa and Amelia were in the schoolroom with Lucy. They would likely be occupied until luncheon. She had nothing to do this morning except darn a few stockings, and that could be accomplished quickly. If she hurried to the pawnbrokers, no one would ever need to know that she had gone. It was just a few minutes away.

She rushed to her wardrobe and pulled out her bonnet and pelisse. If she hesitated for even a moment, she might change her mind.

She dashed downstairs and through the back door of the kitchen, scurrying toward the bend in the road that connected Windsor to Bristol. She could be there in fifteen minutes if she hurried. Holding on to her bonnet with one hand, she hastened her steps.

This had nothing whatever to do with Charlie Cantrill. Once his mother departed and their faux courtship finally ended, then she would no longer seek his approval. Right? His puzzling demeanor certainly had *not* kept her up all night, wondering what was bothering him. He might be handsome in a forbidding sort of way, and he might have wonderfully muscled arms, but he was nothing to her. Nothing at all.

In truth, the bracelet was something of a fetter. It linked her to Lord Bradbury in a way she didn't exactly like. And the sooner that fetter was broken, the better. This experiment would benefit so many people, and it was good training for when she had her own dress shop. She could see how well she would do at supervising the cutting and stitching of many gowns at once. It was quite exciting.

She rounded the corner and found the pawnshop. It was a pleasant-looking building with a cheerful window box full of daisies. Gathering her courage, she opened the door and stepped hesitantly inside.

The shopkeeper was consulting with a young dandy, who appeared to be selling a pair of cufflinks. Sophie squinted at them. Yes, they were very fine. Had to be rubies and gold. It was impossible not to overhear their conversation, but Sophie kept her head discreetly turned to one side. She feigned interest in a pair of ornate silver candlesticks as she waited for them to finish their transaction.

"What can you give me for them?" The young man drummed his fingers nervously on the countertop.

The shopkeeper held them up to the light. "A few hundred?"

The young man cleared his throat. "Can you make it four?" His voice was husky and low.

"Yes, but let me warn you. It's young bucks like you who keep me in business. Stay out of the gaming hells and you will have no need to sell anything." The shopkeeper counted out the money and handed it to his customer, who sighed audibly.

"Obliged to you," he replied. Spying Sophie, he swept a low bow. "Miss." He departed, slamming the door behind him.

"How can I help you, miss?" The shopkeeper turned to her with a friendly smile.

"I have a bracelet to sell." She opened her reticule and withdrew the handkerchief. Then she parted the fine linen fabric, revealing the sparkling jewels.

"Are you sure?" the man replied incredulously. "That is an exceptional bracelet." He turned it over carefully, examining it closely. Then he pulled out a magnifying glass and looked at it again.

"Yes, I am quite determined. How much can you give me for it?"

The shopkeeper glanced up at her. "Are you in debt?"

"Goodness, no." Sophie smiled.

"Are you selling it for a friend?"

"No. It was given to me, but I can use the money better elsewhere." She briefly described her intention to clothe the widows of Waterloo. "So, you see, the brace-

let can do more good for these women than it could ever
do merely decorating my wrist."

He pursed his lips. "Very well. I must say I admire
you. Most young ladies would rather keep the bracelet than sell it for anything. I can give you one thousand for it."

Sophie gasped. "Are you sure?"

He nodded. "Quite."

She accepted the money with trembling fingers and
left the shop in haste. The shopkeeper might reconsider
and decide he was giving her too much. She fairly flew
down the street, holding her reticule tightly against her
chest. This was more than she bargained for. Here was
the start of an entirely new fund, one that could clothe
all the widows and their children—not just for a Season, but for a year.

Rounding the corner of Upper Bristol, she collided
with a man and fell. He grasped her elbows and steadied her just before her knee struck the cobblestones.

"Sophie."

She glanced up, still clutching her reticule.

Charlie Cantrill. Of course. She had a way of bumping into him whenever she was trying to complete a
task on her own.

"Sir," she panted. "I had no idea you were there. I
beg your pardon."

"It's all right," he responded, letting go of her as
abruptly as he would a snake. "I was coming to see you.
What are you doing here? I expected to call on you at
Lord Bradbury's."

She couldn't shake the feeling that she had received
pilfered goods. Her face heated to her hairline and she

could only stammer. "It—it was s-such a pretty day…"
She had to get control of herself. Clearing her throat,
she tried again. "What did you need to see me about?"
Was he going to offer an explanation for his strange
behavior yesterday?

"I've had a letter from Uncle Arthur. He's making me
his heir, if we wed. And Mother wants us all to journey
to Brightgate together."

She was hiding something. That much was certain.
As she turned away from him briefly, Charlie bent
and retrieved a piece of paper that had fluttered to the
ground when they collided. He tucked it into his jacket
pocket and looked at her expectantly.

She was blushing, her cheeks a pretty shade of pink.
"So, our faux courtship has gotten rather…out of hand."

He nodded, tightening his mouth into a grim line.
"It would appear so."

Her face, normally so open and so inviting, was like
a window with the curtains drawn. He could discern
none of her thoughts or feelings. It was rather disconcerting, to tell the truth. "What do we do now?" she
asked, her voice shaking.

He passed his hand over his brow. "I don't know
what to do." The words rushed out of him like water
in a stream. "This courtship was supposed to fix one
problem. Instead, it's created a host of others. I have
no idea how to proceed. I am a career soldier, Sophie.
And I have no idea which direction to go."

"Why does your mother want us to journey to Brightgate?" She placed her hand on his arm.

He coughed, spluttering out the words. "For...the... wedding."

Her complexion turned a deeper shade of pink. "Isn't that rather hasty? We aren't even engaged yet."

"For the time being, Mother wants you to meet my family."

She shook her head. "I am not sure I could get away. Amelia's Season will start in earnest in a few weeks, and I am expected to be on hand." She pursed her lips. "Although, Lord Bradbury has made it quite clear that if I become engaged, I will be relieved of my position in his household."

Charlie's head snapped up. "I surmised as much." She was in as untenable a position as he. Worse, even. She stood to lose everything. He clenched his teeth together.

Her lips were trembling. Despite his best efforts, his heart softened. He could not bear to see a woman cry, even if he were completely unsure of said woman's motives. "Oh, Charlie, what are we to do?"

"Don't cry," he admonished her. "We will think of something."

"If I go with you to Brightgate, I will lose my job. If I don't, then you will lose your inheritance," she replied in that same trembling tone, unshed tears darkening her eyes to sapphire. "It's a terrible situation with no escape."

"What if you came with me to Brightgate?" he reasoned. "Perhaps his lordship could be persuaded to let you stay on. I could speak to him. I will ask him to release you for just a fortnight, and then you would return."

"But then our arrangement would be made public. He would know we were courting, and that your mother expects us to wed. Otherwise, there would be no reason for us to go together. And it would be quite indecent for me to travel with you if we weren't betrothed." Tears spilled over and ran down her cheeks.

Against his better judgment, he reached out and traced the path of her tears with his thumb. "Don't cry," he pleaded in a husky tone. She was entrancing him, and he was helpless against it. At any moment, he would promise her anything. Beauty was always his weakness, and beauty in distress was irresistible.

There had to be some way she could journey with him to Brightgate without causing any commotion. They could leave their engagement unannounced. Once in his brother's home, without the distractions of Bath, he could reason with his family. Find some way to make everyone happy. And then Sophie could return to her position, just as she needed to...

Aunt Katherine.

Aunt Katherine would arrange matters with Lord Bradbury, and the Cantrills would not even be a part of the equation. If they happened to journey at the same time—or close to it—then no one need be any the wiser. Of course. Unbidden, a grin broke across his face.

"I have the answer. If Aunt Katherine journeyed with you, then you could go as her companion. You are relatives, after all." Hastily, he explained the rest of his strategy to her.

"But once we are in Brightgate, everyone will expect us to be engaged." Her brows drew together in confusion. "I only see how this gets me there and back without losing my position. I don't see how this benefits *you,* Charlie. You still have to find a way to make your uncle happy so you can be his heir."

"I don't care overmuch for being an heir," he responded. "I still want to live simply, and I still want to continue my work in Bath. If I were my uncle's beneficiary, I would give almost all of it away. This ruse merely buys us time. Time for me to reason with my uncle, and time for you to be away from work for a while. You've been quite busy—surely a respite is in order?"

"I suppose." She rubbed her temples. "I must go back to Lord Bradbury's, Charlie. Louisa and Amelia may notice I am gone, and I don't want to get into trouble."

"Of course." He offered her his arm. "Come along."

On the way back to Lord Bradbury's, Sophie was silent. Her normally effervescent manner was dulled, and the spark was dimmed from her expression. It was most unusual for her to be so solemn. He patted her hand in what he hoped was a reassuring manner. "Don't fret, Sophie. It will all work out fine. I will speak to Aunt Katherine and we will arrange matters so that your position with his lordship is secured."

She shook her head. "That's not what I am worried about."

"What is troubling you, then?"

"I don't know. I wish my life were simple. I wish I could just help others, as you do. It seems like every time I take a step to help someone, all I do is muddy the water." She paused and turned toward him. "Oh, Charlie, I am sorry that I caused you so much trouble.

I was honestly trying to help. Whatever you think of me, I think of you as a friend."

He blinked. Her candor never failed to knock him back a few paces. "Think nothing of it," he responded. "You are a good friend."

Tears filled her eyes again, and she blinked rapidly. "I must go." She waved her hand toward Lord Bradbury's home. "Luncheon will be served soon. Will you let me know how things progress? How shall I know when Aunt Katherine has spoken to his lordship?"

"I will have her send word. I will try not to contact you, to avoid raising his lordship's suspicions." He bowed over her hand. "I shall see you soon."

She bobbed a quick curtsy and rushed toward the rear of the townhome, clutching the reticule closely. As he turned to go, the rustle of paper in his pocket stopped him. He drew it out and unfolded it.

A receipt from a pawnbroker. For a diamond bracelet. His eyes widened at the sum listed.

Whatever was Sophie about? What game was she playing? Was she an innocent girl and a good friend? Or was she a siren luring men to their doom? Could she use her pretty face and easily shed tears to get exactly what she wanted?

Whoever she was, he intended to find out. Away from Lord Bradbury and Bath, he would at last find out who Sophie Handley was—and what kind of woman she really was, under this facade of beauty and grace.

Chapter Fifteen

Sophie smoothed her hands over her gown, a creation of taffeta embroidered with tiny purple roses. The fabric was discarded with a shrug by young Amelia, so Sophie had quickly saved it for a gown of her own. And now, as she surveyed her reflection in the mirror, she was heartily glad she'd done so. One wanted to look one's best when meeting the prospective in-laws.

She crossed the floor of her room and peered out the window into the yard below. The inn bustled with activity. Every moment, it seemed, a new traveling coach pulled up or another one took off. Brightgate wasn't as busy as Bath, of course, but it buzzed with more energy than Tansley. And even after her few months in Bath, she still wasn't accustomed to the sight of so much activity.

How had she come to be here, after all? The past week had whirled by in a blur. Aunt Katherine, in her usual imperious way, had secured the trip for Sophie, without Sophie being privy to the conversation she had with Lord Bradbury. In fact, it was Amelia and Louisa who broke the news, as they rushed into the sewing room crying one afternoon. Amelia was particularly upset, for she was to attend her first dance at the Assembly Rooms that week, and was distraught that Sophie would not be there to guide her. Instead, Lucy had been pressed into service as a chaperone, borrowing a pale pink satin gown of Sophie's for the occasion.

A knock sounded on the door. "My dear, are you ready? The carriage is waiting."

Sophie turned from the window. "Come in, Auntie."

Aunt Katherine opened the door, resplendent in a rich gown of deep purple velvet. "My dear, you look lovely. The Cantrills will be quite besotted with you." She came in and kissed Sophie on the cheek. "Well, shall we go?"

"No." Sophie sighed. "I am not ready. In truth, Auntie, I am afraid."

"Afraid?" The old woman sank onto the window seat. "Of what, may I ask? Surely there are no ghosts or monsters at the Cantrill home."

Sophie managed a weak smile. "I must disagree. There is the specter of our faux courtship, and of course, the monstrous lie we have concocted to fool his relations. How on earth am I to behave tonight?"

"You must behave, first and foremost, in a manner that is a credit to yourself and your family." Aunt Katherine patted Sophie's shoulder, her many rings glistening in the late-afternoon light. "I have enjoyed watching this false wooing from afar, so to speak. It's all very exciting and glamorous for an old woman like me. On the other hand, I worry about you, just as I would worry about one of my own. What of your heart, Sophie? Is helping Charlie enough for you?"

Sophie bowed her head. "I want only the best for Charlie. He is a good man." That was all she could manage. For weeks now she suspected her feelings for him might be deepening, but it was so difficult to know one's own mind.

"Then show him the real Sophie while you are in Brightgate. You have such a gift for inspiring love and warmth in others, my dear. You make it easy for us to love you. Even I, stubborn old woman that I am, was determined to hate you for throwing John over. And I couldn't. You are just too sweet." Aunt Katherine gave her a stinging peck on the cheek. "You must know that above all else, Charlie is determined to be right. He needs to feel that he is always correct, and that explains his confusion with you. Away from the distractions of Bath, you have the freedom to make of this whatever you wish. And I shall cheer you on. I vow everything will turn out well."

"Do you really think so, Auntie?" The pressure of Auntie's hand felt good. It was almost as nice as being at home with Harriet, when their problems were simple. They needed food and shelter back then. Now things were so much more complicated. False entanglements, diamond bracelets, viscounts and veterans—how deeply troubling everything seemed.

"I do." She rose, beckoning Sophie with an imperious gesture. "Come, Moriah Cantrill is waiting. And so is Robert and so is Charlie. Show the Cantrills what a lovely creature they are getting for an in-law."

The carriage ride from the inn to the Cantrill home was short—too short. It would have been nice to have more time to prepare. And yet there was nothing to be done. The sooner she met her faux in-laws, the better. At least it meant one more hurdle she had cleared. No matter what Auntie thought, she would never prove anything to Charlie Cantrill. That stern expression, those dark eyes…she gave an inward sigh. If only she could prove herself to him. Being his…wife—she could hardly bring herself to think the word—was a mere dream that would never come true.

The carriage pulled up next to a lovely home done in the Georgian manner, all redbrick and symmetrical windows with white sashes. The front door was painted a glistening snowy white, framed by a Palladian window and side lights that reflected candlelight from indoors. It was quite a massive square block of a home—a bit on the new side, with none of the weathered beauty of Brookes Park or the stately grandeur of Lord Bradbury's townhome.

"My goodness," Sophie breathed, as she stepped out of the carriage.

"Yes, Sir George did quite well as a merchant. They built this home not long before his death. This was their third home in nearly a decade. Moriah wanted bigger and better homes, so they kept rebuilding and tearing down. She finally commissioned this one from a London architect," Aunt Katherine said, gazing up at the windows.

The door opened and a servant appeared. "Come, let us go inside before they send the entire household out to greet us," Aunt Katherine muttered.

Sophie laughed, tilting her head up toward the second story. One of the windows opened and a handsome face, remarkably like Charlie's, but more florid and less serious, ducked out.

"Are you my new sister-in-law?" he called.

"Not at all," she called back. "I am merely being courted."

Aunt Katherine beamed. "Robert Cantrill, do stop monkeying about and come down to greet your guests as a gentleman should." She turned to Sophie. "The hold you have over men is quite remarkable," she whispered. "I like basking in your glow."

Sophie's cheeks heated. Here she was, calling up to Charlie's brother like a hoyden, when she was supposed to be making a good impression. Surely she was off on the wrong foot already.

Robert disappeared from the upstairs window and reappeared at the front door as they finished winding their way up to the house from the curbstone. "I must say, my brother knows how to choose them." Robert welcomed Aunt Katherine with a kiss and then drew Sophie inside. "Though what you see in my brother's ascetic nature is beyond me."

"I adore Charles for his simplicity. I only wish I were as good as him." She looked Robert straight in the eyes. It was the truth, after all.

He threw back his head and laughed. "Well, if you can entice that hermit back out of his cave and have him rejoin Society, I shall be indebted to you forever."

Something was a little off. Surely brothers, just like sisters, enjoyed teasing each other now and then. But there was an edge to Robert's banter that seemed mean—as though he *enjoyed* saying hurtful things about his brother. And when he kissed her hand, his lips lingered longer than she felt was appropriate. Thank goodness Aunt Katherine was nearby. She wasn't sure she liked Robert at all.

He ushered them into a drawing room decorated in exceedingly good taste, and went to fetch his brother and mother. Sophie glanced at the paintings on the wall—portraits, mostly. She walked over to one and peered closely up at it. No resemblance to Charlie stared back at her. How very strange. She turned back toward Aunt Katherine. "This room is lovely but lifeless," she whispered.

"Moriah has professional assistance with her decoration," Aunt Katherine murmured back. "She has retained the services of several impoverished members of the gentry to help her."

Impoverished gentry. Just like her family.

The door opened, and with a rush of gratitude, Sophie spied Charlie. He had a shuttered look on his face. No light shone from his eyes. He looked absolutely miserable. He wandered in behind his mother and brother, bowing to Aunt Katherine.

Sophie walked over to him, her arms outstretched. "Charlie."

He clasped her hands in his good one. "Sophie."

"I was just asking this lovely creature what she saw in the likes of you," Robert said with a laugh. "She said she adores you for your simplicity."

"I do," Sophie retorted, schooling her tone so it remained light and breezy. "I find Charlie the most attractive man in Bath, because he cares so much for the welfare of others." If she kept her tone bantering, perhaps Robert would get the message and leave Charlie alone.

Charlie stared deeply at her, a spark of life lighting the depths of his brown eyes.

Mrs. Cantrill sank onto the settee, next to Aunt Katherine. "Of course, when they wed, they will soon rejoin Society. They would never raise a family in that dank apartment of Charlie's in Bath."

When they wed? Mrs. Cantrill was assuming quite a bit, wasn't she? Once more, Sophie felt the urge to defend Charlie against his own family. "I would live in a mud hut in Timbuktu with Charlie if he so ordered it," she replied with a saucy grin.

"Ah! Young love," Aunt Katherine warbled, breaking into the conversation. "When I married Mr. Crossley, I was quite prepared to cross the world with him on his merchant ships. We old women forget how love overrides comfort when you are young and besotted."

Sophie cast a grateful look at Aunt Katherine, then turned to Charlie. "Shall we take a turn about the room?"

"While we plan your futures, of course," Aunt Katherine added.

Charlie offered her his good arm, and she squeezed his elbow as they began strolling around the perimeter of the room.

"Handsome portraits, but I don't see a likeness." She waved her hand at the walls.

"They are none of them family members," he murmured in an undertone and shrugged. "My mother bought them all at a country home that was in the process of being dunned."

Just like her home had been. "Oh."

"They lend a certain cachet." He cast his voice in perfect imitation of his mother.

Sophie giggled. "We can make up stories about these people if you wish. Perhaps that old man over there collected fine teacups."

Charlie smiled for the first time in ages and entered the spirit of the game. "Very well. Then his wife was that sour-looking woman over there, and she never approved of his hobby."

"So she smashed the teacups—"

"And he tore her favorite tapestry to bits," Charlie finished. She laughed, her heart aglow. Charlie could be very jolly company when he wanted to be. If only he would enjoy life more—allow himself to love and be loved.

"All right, you two, that's enough giggling for now," Robert interrupted. "Miss Sophie, do you play?" He indicated the pianoforte with one hand.

"Not very well. Harriet practiced more than I did," she admitted. "But I will try."

She selected a simple country tune and began playing note by note. "My, it's been years since I've played."

"You are doing quite well." Robert applauded. "Will you sing, too?"

"Only if I must," she rejoined with a laugh.

Charlie had no idea Sophie could play and sing, but she did both with such effortless enjoyment that it was impossible not to be fascinated. Robert sat next to her on the bench, turning the pages for her. So he stood and leaned against the instrument, feasting upon her with his eyes. Away from Bath, she was delightful, with none of the complexities that her association with Lord Bradbury roused. And her simple defenses of him against his brother and mother were also charming. It was difficult indeed not to be completely besotted with her.

Robert was. He was oozing confidence, trying to woo her in the same way he had tried to win over every girl Charlie had ever shown an interest in. Some brothers were physically competitive, but not Robert and he. Instead, Robert tried to assert his authority by winning over every female Charlie ever came into contact with. It was a ridiculous rivalry, and one he had lost interest in long ago. And yet, when Robert scooted closer to Sophie on the bench and she backed away, triumph surged in his breast. She liked him better than Robert. It was as simple as that.

She finished her song and looked up at him. "I shall play one especially for you, Charlie," she said with a small smile. Then she launched into a plaintive, captivating little tune that bewitched him.

"Lully?" he responded.

She nodded.

As she sat there, playing and smiling, he watched her. That indefinable feeling that lingered in the back of his mind, and in the depths of his heart, now rose to the surface. What would it be like to be married to Sophie Handley? To have a beautiful, enchanting woman by his side for the rest of his life? Someone to defend, and someone to defend him. A real helpmate.

Aunt Katherine called over to Robert, who bowed and quit the bench. Now was Charlie's opportunity.

He sank down beside her in the spot Robert had just vacated.

"Your brother is rather pushy," she whispered.

"Elder brothers. What can I say?" He gave a bitter laugh.

"I like younger brothers better."

He said nothing, but warmed himself in the glow of their companionship. Was this the missing piece in his life? Everything in his life was so staid and orderly—but lonesome. Would welcoming Sophie in give him that final feeling of peace he so desired?

"Sophie, thank you so much for coming to my rescue." He was fighting a rising feeling of panic, as though if he didn't say the right thing at the right moment, Sophie would vanish from his life forever.

"Aunt Katherine arranged it. Just as you said she would. I can hardly believe I am here myself." She trilled her fingertips over the keys.

"I haven't been a very good friend to you." Dash it all. What was he trying to say? Why would the feeling not subside?

"Oh, Charlie." She gave him a sweet smile as the song trailed to an end. "I understand. Really I do. Families are very complicated. I love Harriet, but we have had a mixed-up life together. And most of my family members don't even speak to us. So I do understand how you feel."

"I don't want to be alone." The words fell from his lips before he could stop them.

She merely turned and regarded him with those large, china-blue eyes. She was waiting patiently for him to continue babbling.

"Sophie—" He broke off. The feeling of panic was overtaking him completely. It was like fading in and out of consciousness on the battlefield as his men carried him into the farmhouse at La Sainte Haye. He had control no longer. "Thank you."

Her eyes were fathomless pools of blue. "You are welcome, Charlie."

That wasn't the conversation he meant to have. His feelings about her were still so uncertain. And yet, away from all the false trappings of Bath, he was seeing the real Sophie. He liked what he saw. No, that didn't do justice to how he felt. He loved her. And like a fool, burned too many times to count, he was going to place his hand too close to a candle flame. His heart was thumping so heavily against his rib cage, surely she could see it through the fine lawn of his shirt.

"Sophie. I—I ask you this not because of any entailment from my uncle, but from a deep and abiding feeling that will not be denied…" He trailed off, taking her hands from the piano keys and clasping them in his good hand. "If what you think of me is true…" Dash it all, he was babbling again like an idiot. "Will you marry me?"

Was that a hesitation? Her eyes lowered for a moment, and he was that she would refuse. Most kindly, of course.

He bowed his head, steeling himself for the inevitable refusal.

But it never came. Instead, Sophie's clear voice whispered, "Yes, Charlie. I will."

Chapter Sixteen

Everything had changed, and yet on the surface, nothing was different. Moriah Cantrill, Sophie's future mother-in-law, was effusive in her congratulations and reminded them all that she had predicted that Sophie's courtship would, in time, lead to a betrothal. Aunt Katherine had beamed over the assembled company, warbling her best wishes and pressing Sophie's hand so hard, her rings left imprints on Sophie's palm. And Robert had kissed her cheek, his eyes flashing with something that wasn't entirely pleasant.

But after the congratulations and celebration of the engagement were over, it was as if the faux part of the courtship simply never existed. As far as Charlie's relatives knew, their affection had always been genuine. And so their engagement, sealed with a diamond ring that had belonged to Charlie's grandmother, seemed not entirely remarkable, but planned.

She had accepted him with such speed it left her dizzy. She wanted, more than anything, to marry Charlie and spend the rest of her life with him. Why? She loved him. He was as essential to her being as air and water. He gave her a purpose beyond mere existence.

And now, as she strolled down the village streets on Charlie's good arm, she had been dropped into a world of plans and dreams for the future. Aunt Katherine and Mrs. Cantrill waited for them back at the house, but Charlie had insisted on going out for an airing with Sophie. What a relief to finally be alone with him, after two days of endless wedding talk with family.

"Would you like to live in Brightgate?" Charlie asked her. "Robert says there are a few lovely estates for rent out in the country."

"What of your work with the veterans?" She paused, turning to look at him. "Won't we continue to work with the widows' fund?"

"You would do that—with me?" His voice held an incredulous tone. "I thought perhaps you would rather establish a home out in the country, something more in keeping with your previous style of living."

"My previous style of living was in a poky old cottage in Tansley Village," she reminded him with a laugh. "We had a chimney that smoked and a garden that could only grow potatoes."

He smiled. Charlie's smiles were becoming more plentiful now that they were engaged in truth, and it warmed her heart to see his sweet, crooked grin. "I meant the style of life you were used to as Sir Hugh's daughter. Or even as Lord Bradbury's seamstress."

"Oh, Charlie." She reached up and pecked him on the cheek. "Those ways of life seem so distant now. Why, I can hardly remember life with Papa. And though I will miss Amelia and Louisa, my tenure at Lord Bradbury's has not given me a taste for the finer things in life."

"Then…you would be happy to settle in Bath?" He was blushing a deep shade of red. It was entirely captivating.

"'Whither thou goest, I will go,'" she whispered, tucking her arm under his.

They rounded the bend of the road, and the Cantrill home, squat and square and prosperous, loomed in the distance.

"There's bound to be a fight about it, you know," Charlie muttered. "Mother and Robert have very little patience for my work in Bath."

"Don't bother your head with what they think," Sophie admonished him. "After all, your work benefits many people. Surely that must mean something to them."

"It does not." He sounded so defeated. Tired, almost.

"Well, I should like to talk to you about the fund," Sophie replied. Perhaps her plan to clothe the widows in Bath would make him brighten up. After all, she had never told him about selling the bracelet. "I have a few ideas about the widows that I have been mulling over for some time."

"Can we talk about it this evening, after supper?" Charlie replied distantly. "We're almost there, and I have to get into the proper frame of mind to see my family. It requires work, you know, to remain pleasant around them when they are so against everything I say and do."

"Of course, darling," Sophie murmured. It felt wonderful to call him darling. Her reward was the deep shade of red that flushed across his handsome face.

As they entered the house together, the sound of Aunt Katherine's warble and Moriah Cantrill's quavering soprano practically reverberated off the walls. "Oh, dear, more wedding plans," Sophie sighed. "And I haven't even written to Hattie yet."

Charlie shrugged out of his cloak and removed his hat, dropping both on the hall tree.

"Is that you, Charlie? You must come and give your opinion on this estate at once," his mother commanded shrilly. "Robert has found a perfectly lovely place in Derbyshire for you, and yet Mrs. Crossley says you must stay in Bath."

With a roll of his eyes and a sigh, Charlie walked down the hallway to the parlor.

Sophie removed her bonnet, taking her own time about it. There was certainly no rush to enter the fray and have to choose sides in the great Bath versus Derbyshire debate.

"Sophie, if you don't mind, I wish a word with you in my study."

Sophie jumped at the sound of Robert's oily tones, and then pretended a laugh. "Oh, dear, you caught me off guard."

"Beg pardon," he replied smoothly. "But I have a need to speak with you privately."

"I—uh—" Surely there was some escape. She didn't exactly relish the thought of being alone with Robert, and she missed the warmth and security of Charlie's presence. "I believe I am wanted in the parlor. Wedding plans, you know."

"Oh, but this will only take a moment." Robert linked his arm through hers, propelling her into the book-lined room. He pushed the door closed but didn't latch it, then indicated a chair by his desk. "Come, sit."

"Was there something you needed from me, Robert?" Perhaps they could hurry things up a bit. And then she could seek the safety of Charlie's protection in the parlor.

He leaned back in his chair, surveying her as he would a fleck of dust on the carpet. "Your position in the Viscount Bradbury's household is rather…unique, is it not?"

This line of questioning, so abrupt, was rather unsettling. "I don't think it's very strange. His lordship wants the very best for his daughters, including a personal seamstress at their beck and call."

"But his lordship gifted you with a very expensive bracelet. Is that true?"

"Yes." She fought the bile rising in her throat. How did he know this about her? And why did it seem so distasteful when he said it aloud?

"But according to the investigator I hired to look into your past, you sold the bracelet at a pawnshop in Bath. Why not keep it? Such a bauble from his lordship is quite a feather in your cap." He shrugged and looked at his fingernails, picking at one cuticle. "Have you any vices you must maintain that require a good deal of money? Perhaps, like your mother, you are addicted to laudanum."

She shoved her chair back and rose. "It's not like that. I assure you, Robert."

"Miss Handley, you must understand my position as

head of this family and as the manager of my family's estate. My brother has been most unlucky in his choice of young women. The first woman he chose threw him over the moment he returned from the war. And since then, his ascetic lifestyle has made most decent women turn away from him."

"What has that to do with me?" Her voice was trembling violently, and she cleared her throat to steady it. "Why I sold the bracelet is no concern of yours. But I don't like your insinuations. I am your brother's betrothed, after all."

"I am only protecting my brother's interests. He's soft-headed when it comes to women, especially pretty ones. Our family is wealthy beyond measure. I can't simply allow Charlie to marry anyone he chooses. Besides, his marriage was a condition of my mother's, and not of mine. I'd rather he come home and get to work than marry anyone, especially anyone with such a troubling past." Robert's tone remained even and reasonable, his face impassive.

Red spots appeared before Sophie's eyes. She was trembling so, she had to grasp the back of a chair to keep from falling over. "You think so little of your brother, to say nothing of me."

"I have more experience of the world." Robert shrugged. "I am more jaded. As soon as I set eyes on you—beautiful, charming, graceful—I had to hire a thief-taker to find out more about you. So, unless you break off the engagement, I will cut my brother off entirely. He won't have a farthing left. And I will make sure Uncle Arthur knows about this, as well. I'll tell my mother about my findings also. Some of them—

particularly about your family background—are really rather colorful."

If she broke things off with Charlie, he would be spared. He could not hope to do the work he started in Bath without his family backing him. Why, that was the whole reason for this farce to begin with. "I just want him to be happy. I believe in his work, even if others don't."

Robert shook his head. "If you believe in him so much, then you will let him go. The whole marriage rubbish was my mother's idea. But I am the head of this family. And I work very hard to maintain our fortunes, and have spent years trying to make my brother realize his responsibilities. If he marries you, I will make sure he stays in Brightgate, and his deplorable work for those miscreants will cease."

Sophie grew cold all over, and suppressed a shudder that ran through her body. So that was it, then. Their engagement was over. Charlie could not continue his life's purpose unless she broke their betrothal. And she could not help him unless she let him go.

Tears stung the back of her eyes, but she lifted her chin and looked directly at Robert. "Very well. I will break our engagement. I—I can't now. Give me some time. I need to…" Her lips trembled violently, and she bit them to keep from bursting into tears. "I need to compose myself."

"I'd rather the thing was done quickly," he responded with a listless wave of his hand. "As soon as possible."

"May I go now?" If she was going to break down and cry, she needed to do so in the privacy of her own room.

"Fine, yes, do run along. But you must break things

off soon. I prefer by tomorrow." He turned his chair toward the window, completely oblivious to her inner turmoil.

She turned and ran blindly from the room and out of the house, tears streaming down her face. It was but a few short streets over to the inn, and she could bury her face in her pillow and weep until she had no more tears. It was the right decision, for both of them.

But oh, how it hurt.

Something was amiss. Robert appeared in the parlor, his sharpest elder-brother-knows-best look in his eyes, to inform them that Sophie had a headache and had returned to the inn to rest. Aunt Katherine rose at once, demanding to go back to the inn, as well. "Tut, tut, my poor Sophie," she clucked. "I must go to her and see that she has a handkerchief wrung in cologne for her forehead. The best thing for a headache, my dears. I shall see you tomorrow. Adieu."

After Aunt Katherine left, a strange hush fell over the parlor, broken only by the ticking of the clock on the mantelpiece. Robert paced the floor as Mother sat, looking at fashion plates with an absorbed yet contented look on her face. Something had happened to Sophie. Her sudden disappearance was too odd. But what had transpired?

Charlie could stand the tension no longer. "Out with it, man," he snapped at Robert.

Robert gave him a smug grin and halted his pacing. "Right away, sir."

"What, might I ask, is wrong with you? You've been looking like a cat that's got in the cream ever since you entered the room." Charlie eyed him, irritation mounting in his chest.

"Boys—temper," Mother admonished absently, staring at one fashion plate through her lorgnette.

Robert shook his head, the smug grin still crooking the corner of his mouth. "I should have known, Charlie. Your taste in women is as bad as ever. In fact, beauty blinds you in a way that I find fascinating. Fortunately, I came to your rescue before you made yourself a fool again."

Mother dropped her lorgnette. "Whatever do you mean, Robert?"

Charlie's heart pounded in his ears so loudly he could barely discern Mother's response. "What game are you playing at, Robert?"

"Spot the fortune hunter, little brother," Robert replied. "Miss Sophie Handley is the daughter of an actress, one Cecile Varnay—"

"But her father was Sir Hugh Handley," Mother broke in. "Surely that connection is worth preserving."

"Sir Hugh died penniless, and the girls were thrown out of the ancestral home. None of the Handleys will speak to them," Robert informed her. "I hired a thief-taker to find out everything about Sophie Handley's past. It's all rather extraordinary."

"Everyone knows about the Handleys," Charlie responded, tightening his mouth grimly. "She has sought a position in service. Doesn't that make it obvious that her family connections no longer serve her well?"

"Ah, yes, her position in service. Rather unusual, that. Does no one else find it odd that Lord Bradbury has employed such a pretty seamstress to live in his household and obey his every whim?"

Charlie curled his hand into a fist. "What are you insinuating?"

Mother rose from the settee, her face an ashen shade of gray. "Yes, Robert, I must protest. You are making some rather bold insinuations. After all, it is well-known that Lord Bradbury spoils his daughters dreadfully. It is not unusual that he would employ someone to cater to their needs."

"Oh, Lord Bradbury spoils everyone. Including his servants. He bestowed a rather valuable diamond bracelet on Sophie, Mother—which she kept and then later pawned in Bath." Robert rolled his eyes. "Once again, Charlie has picked a woman who is destined to make him a laughingstock. First Beth Gaskell. Now Sophie Handley."

Mother grasped the chain on which her lorgnette hung. "Charlie—is this true? She said that bracelet was a gift from a dear friend."

"Oh, it was a gift from a dear friend," Robert interrupted. "Just rather later than we all suspected."

"You aren't telling me anything I don't know already," Charlie ground out between clenched teeth. His anger ran so high, a whistling sound rang through his ears. "I knew about her family and I knew about the bracelet. What of it?"

"What of it?" Mother gasped. "Charlie, if it's true— if she truly accepted such a gift from Lord Bradbury and then pawned it—why, that's simply unacceptable."

"It seems like nothing connected to me is welcome within this family," Charlie spat. "My work with the poor is ridiculed, my aspirations for my future mocked. And now you insult my fiancée. Perhaps it is time I begin asking whether I want to be a member of this family or not." At the moment, a life without family members sounded inviting.

"Oh, Charlie." Tears streaked down Mother's face. "How could you say such a thing?"

"Well, what do you propose? You can't marry a fortune hunter. I won't allow it." Robert stalked over to Mother and laid his hands protectively on her shoulders.

"I am not making a single move until I talk with Sophie," Charlie retorted. "She may not even want to be a member of this esteemed family after what you likely said to her, Robert. Headache, indeed. I knew you were up to something the moment you entered the room."

"I was merely protecting our interests—and yours. I would think you would thank me."

"Remind me to thank you properly later, when our mother isn't present," Charlie replied, jabbing his finger at Robert's arrogant smile.

"Oh, boys," Mother wept. "Do stop arguing. This is dreadful. A brilliant match, dashed to pieces."

"Nothing is dashed to pieces." Charlie turned swiftly toward the door. He needed to see Sophie—talk to her, see her face once more. Robert's accusations had charred something sacred. He needed to gaze into her clear blue eyes again, to convince himself that he was right and his brother was wrong.

"Guard your pocketbook, brother," Robert called after him as he raced out the door.

Chapter Seventeen

"Tut, tut. No more crying. My cologne remedy is a proven cure for the worst of headaches." Aunt Katherine pressed the cold, damp handkerchief against Sophie's temple.

Tears oozed out of the corner of Sophie's eye, but she said nothing. Trying to explain Robert's behavior to anyone at that moment was a task she could not face. Better to have Aunt Katherine believe a lie. She simply could not bring herself to tell the old woman the truth.

Her heart ached for Charlie. Why did he not come? Had Robert told him nothing? The moments ticked by in agonizing silence, broken only by Aunt Katherine's occasional murmured platitudes.

Surely Charlie would never believe Robert. He had been dreadfully wronged by Beth Gaskell, but that was years ago. And Sophie had spent every moment trying to prove her good intentions to him ever since she started helping with the widows' fund in Bath.

"Now why all these tears? Tell me, pretty Sophie." Aunt Katherine removed the cloth and looked deeply into Sophie's eyes. Her wrinkled, kindly old face glowed with a fondness that made Sophie's heart ache. Aunt Katherine loved her, even if others didn't. "You are giving this old woman quite a turn. I have never seen you so upset. Usually you have such a lovely, sunshiny way about you."

Sophie sighed. Perhaps she could talk around the matter, without breaking down completely. "That dratted diamond bracelet has caused me no end of trouble," she whispered.

"Why do you say that?" Aunt Katherine replied, folding the handkerchief and placing it in her lap.

"Because it is a driving wedge. It has separated me from what I want."

"And what is that?"

"Peace of mind. Simplicity. Goodness." They were mere concepts, of course. But they all meant one thing to her—Charlie Cantrill. Her lips trembled, and she bit down to keep them still.

Aunt Katherine's brow furrowed. "I don't understand you. Speak sense, my girl."

"I can't, Auntie. Everything is topsy-turvy." Homesickness washed over her like a wave, leaving an empty feeling in the pit of her stomach. "Oh, I miss Hattie. I wish she was here."

A knock sounded on the door, and a servant poked her head in. "There's a Lieutenant Cantrill here to meet Miss Handley. He's down in the parlor, waiting."

"I'll be right down," Sophie replied. She sat up, trembling all over. Goodness, how dizzy and out of sorts she felt.

"Are you sure, my dear?" Aunt Katherine asked as the door closed behind the servant. "You look dreadfully pale. I can go downstairs and tell Charlie to come back tomorrow, after you've had a decent rest."

"No. I must go." Sophie rose on unsteady legs. She would keep her promise to Robert so Charlie could continue his life's mission. "I must see Charlie."

She walked down the stairs slowly. Her legs might give out if she rushed. She opened the door to the parlor and saw him—tall, proud, untouchable. His brown eyes had darkened to black, and he was as pale as death. The stubble of his beard stood out in dark relief. He looked haunted—and hunted.

"Robert spoke to you." It wasn't a question, merely a statement of fact.

"He did." She sank onto a chair. Her legs would no longer support her.

"I know about everything. Your family, your mother's past." He was staring at her, his gaze burning her skin, but she could not raise her eyes to his. If she looked at him, her resolve would crumble. And that would mean the end of her noble decision.

"Yes."

"I know about the bracelet. I know that you pawned it. I saw the receipt the day I ran into you in the street." His voice had a catch in it. "I've known for some time that Lord Bradbury admired you. I don't know why you accepted the gift. I don't know why you sold it. But, Sophie—none of that matters. I would defy all my family's objections if you will be mine."

Her heart surged with bitter triumph. Despite everything, he loved her. And least she had that. But still, she had to free him. She had to free them both. It was the only way.

"I cannot, Charlie."

"Why?" Charlie grasped her shoulder with his good hand, bending down to peer in her face. "Because of how Robert treated you? Oh, Sophie, don't listen to him. He's a blackguard, a ne'er-do-well—"

"He's your brother." The words fell like shards of ice from her lips. "You cannot outrun your family. I know that only too well."

"What are you saying?" His hand tightened on her shoulder, as though he was afraid she was going to disappear.

"I am releasing you from our engagement. I'm releasing you from everything associated with me. The faux courtship, the trip here to Brightgate—all of it was a miserable farce."

"It wasn't." He knelt on the floor in front of her, compelling her to look him in the face. She turned her head to one side. "Surely you must see that."

The situation was becoming unbearable. Another moment of him kneeling before her, so sweet and tender, his handsome face clouded with fury and love, and all hope would be lost. She would succumb, and they would spend the rest of their lives rejected and mocked by the Cantrill clan, just as the Handleys had rejected and mocked her family.

There was but one way to end things forever. It was hateful, but it would work. She could pretend to be as flighty and fast as Robert believed her to be—as Charlie had believed her to be when she first met him. She must manipulate the flaw in his character—the need to be right, to always be right. It was the only way to rescue them both.

She was the daughter of celebrated actress Cecile Varnay, after all.

Sophie inhaled deeply. "I've changed my mind, that's all," she replied, forcing a light and breezy tone into her voice. "I don't want to spend the rest of my life working for the poor or living in poky old Brightgate. I love the glitter of Society, and I want to spend the rest of my days in Bath, working for Lord Bradbury."

"This is very sudden." His voice was a low growl that caused the hairs on the back of her neck to stand up. "This doesn't sound like you at all, Sophie." He leaned toward her, and traced her jawline with the tip of his finger. "Only today you told me, 'whither thou goest, I will go.'"

She could not suppress the shiver that ran through her at his touch, and her shoulders jerked. "I—I was joking," she breathed. "La, how you take on so. I vow, you are so easy to fool."

"Either I am easy to fool, or you are a consummate actress," he snapped. "I do not believe this charade, Sophie. I only wonder why you are acting in this manner."

To save us both.

"I suppose I finally saw what Beth Gaskell saw upon your return." It was so hard to say the words. She forced them out between clenched teeth. "And I thought I could stomach your defects, but I find I cannot. Robert merely made it easier for me to say goodbye."

He sucked in his breath as though she had punched him in the stomach. A terrible silence descended over the parlor. Sophie's heart pounded in her ears. What a cruel, wicked thing to say. She never would have done it—but she needed to. Surely he would go now and leave her in peace.

"Very well, Miss Handley." He rose, and a draft of cool air replaced the warmth of his body, leaving Sophie sick and cold. "Our engagement has ended. I trust I can still depend upon you to help with the widows' fund? You are, after all, your sister's liaison."

"Oh, I can't be bothered with that." She waved her hand listlessly. "I shall be too busy with Lord Bradbury's family. I will write to Harriet and ask her to make other arrangements."

"See that you do." His voice was laced with polite warning. He was leaving, his boots thudding across the parlor floor. "I should hate to ever see you again."

The door slammed shut, rattling the pictures on the wall. Sophie laid her head against the back of the chair. She was too heartsick to cry anymore. She only felt an icy sense of dread and loneliness, a feeling that would probably never go away.

In a moment, she would go upstairs and tell Aunt Katherine that she was ready to return to Bath. She'd have to field the old lady's prying questions. She'd have to pack. She'd have to endure the several days' coach ride back to Bath, for Aunt Katherine traveled at a leisurely pace that set one's very nerves on edge.

But at the end of her journey—what then? Sophie closed her eyes, conjuring the sweet faces of Amelia and Louisa. She would have those dear girls. And she would have Lucy. If she couldn't have Harriet, at least Lucy was a good second. She'd nurse her wounds privately and pour everything she had into those trusted friendships.

And perhaps she could give her money to the widows in Bath without ever letting anyone know where it came from. Yes, that was the best thing to do.

She rose from the chair. There was no use feeling sorry for herself. After all, she had shoved Charlie away. He had come to her full of tenderness and love, ready to cast his family aside for her sake. What she did, she did for him, though he must never know it.

With leaden feet, she crossed the parlor and trudged up the stairs.

"So?" Robert was waiting for him, lurking on the landing as Charlie strode in. "Did she deny everything?"

Charlie was in no mood for Robert and his mocking ways. In fact, Robert was the cause of all this misery. "I'll thank you to get out of my way."

"So, then, will we be welcoming this fast piece into the bosom of our family? Will the Cantrill fortune be spent faster than I can make it on a blonde chit with blue eyes?" Robert shook his head. "I expected better of you, brother."

"Our engagement is over." Charlie shouldered past his brother and mounted the second flight of stairs.

"What a relief." Robert followed close on his heels. "Now perhaps you will see reason and come to live in Brightgate. I cannot manage all the family's wealth on my own, you know. It's time for you to take an active role."

Charlie paused, turning on his brother. "Aren't you afraid that I am not competent to manage anything? After all, you pointed out that I cannot seem to find a decent woman to share my life with. Surely you cannot entrust me with the finer details of estate management."

Robert turned a mottled shade of violet. It was not a pretty sight. "No— I never meant that—"

"Oh, dear brother, you inferred it. And that's fine with me. I couldn't be trusted with the management of the Cantrill family fortune. I'm merely a career soldier, after all. And I even blundered at that, losing my arm and fainting for the length of the battle at La Sainte Haye." Charlie finished mounting the stairs and stared deeply down at his brother's furious expression. "So I shall do what is best for the family. I'll return to Bath and continue my work with the poor. It seems to be the only thing I am capable of."

"Charlie—" Robert's smooth, oily voice held a pleading tone. "Please, see reason. You cannot go on living the way you do in Bath. It's simply not acceptable. Stay here in Brightgate, live in luxury. Help me with the estate. It's really what you should be doing."

"On the contrary. I refuse to apologize for my work with the veterans any longer. It's the only thing that gives my life a purpose. And now that my future happiness with Sophie Handley has been wrecked, it's the only solace I shall have. So cut off my income, Robert. Shame me as much as you wish. If I can't have the woman I want, I shall at least live the life I want." He slapped the banister with his hand. "I leave for Bath within the hour. Break the news to Mother. I am done with the lot of you."

True to his word, within the appointed hour, Charlie left his family home in Brightgate without a single look back. Mother's tearful pleadings still rang in his ears. But he was right. He was sure of it.

He relaxed his rigid back against the carriage seat. He would return and continue his work with the veterans, without interference from his family, for the foreseeable future. He was liberated—and at the same moment, as alone and solitary as he had ever been.

His mind flashed back to Sophie's resolute profile, her pale cheeks and proud tilt of her head. She was the only thing he was uncertain of. Had she really changed her mind about him? Or had she cast him aside in a kind of noble martyrdom? He had thought she'd changed over the months she had been in Bath. She'd grown more serious, more compassionate, and warmer. And yet, today her behavior had been so flippant that it left a sour taste in his mouth. Her reference to Beth Gaskell had been the very last straw.

He would bide his time. The answer lay in patience. He would give them both time to recover.

And then he would find a way to see the real Sophie Handley.

Chapter Eighteen

"So what of your lieutenant?" Lucy tossed the book she had been reading aside and looked up at Sophie, who was embroidering one of Amelia's gowns as she sat tucked up on the settee. "You've been home from Brightgate for nearly a week now, and I haven't heard a word about him."

"Hush." Sophie flicked a glance at the closed door of her bedroom. "No one knows I journeyed there to meet his family."

"Don't be silly," Lucy responded, propping herself up on her elbows. "No one can hear us. So, how did the matter play out?"

Sophie sat for a moment, concentrating on a stitch. How much of the entire sordid tale did she dare admit? The wound was too fresh, too raw to gossip and pick over with Lucy. So she chose not to tell the whole story. "Suffice it to say, I did my part. As far as Charlie's family could discern, our courtship was real. And we broke the matter off before the farce went too far."

"Ah, so if things went splendidly, why are you so pale and miserable? And why are you losing weight? I saw you pinning up one of your dresses the other day to disguise how thin you've gotten."

"Now you are the one being silly." Sophie tugged at the thread. "I have no idea what you are talking about."

"You love Charlie Cantrill," Lucy said. "So why not marry him? Did you not find a way to entice him to make the faux courtship a real engagement? I vow— my wonder at your powers of flirtation is woefully deflated."

"Stop." Tears clouded her vision. She could no longer discern the fine lawn she had been embroidering. She took a deep breath.

"Oh." Lucy clasped her hands around her knees. "Something went wrong."

"I don't wish to speak of it." If she were to keep her countenance, then she had to change the subject. There had to be a fresh topic of conversation, something that would captivate Lucy and keep her from prattling on about Charlie. "How is Ensign Rowland?"

Lucy's eyes sparkled, and she smiled broadly. "Oh, Sophie. He is the most amazing man. We've met each other every week while you were gone. And did you know—" Lucy launched into a narrative centered around the ensign, not stopping for breath as she cataloged his many finer points.

Thank goodness. That gave Sophie time to recover her sensibilities. She took another fortifying breath and turned her thoughts back to her stitching. There was no need to wonder about Charlie Cantrill. From what she could gather from snippets of gossip from Lucy, he had returned to Bath and to the veterans' club shortly before she came home. He was working with his usual fire and energy. But that's all she really knew. Lucy paid heed only to her beloved Rowland, and sketched just the briefest description for Sophie when she came home on Thursdays.

And that was as it should be. Charlie Cantrill was none of her business, after all.

A soft knock sounded on the door. "I'll go," Sophie declared, giving the dress a shake. "It's probably Amelia, come to see her gown before she goes to bed."

She opened the door, but it was not Amelia's smiling face that greeted her. Instead, Lord Bradbury stood before her, a drink in one hand.

Lucy scurried up from her position on the floor, and they both bobbed him a curtsy. "Your lordship."

"Miss Williams, I wish to see Miss Handley. Alone." Lord Bradbury strode into the room. Sophie had not seen him since her return from Brightgate. He had been attending some business in London, and had only just arrived that very day, according to the housekeeper.

"Yes, of course. Good night, Sophie." Lucy scooted past them both, cutting her eyes curiously at Sophie as she passed by. She closed the door very softly behind her.

"Mind if I sit down?" Lord Bradbury indicated the settee with a wave of his hand.

"Not at all, sir." Sophie hastily removed her sewing basket and pincushion from the seat. "I was merely working on a dress for Amelia. A little embroidery to make it look very fine."

He lowered himself onto the settee and took a long sip of amber liquid. "You take good care of my daughter."

"I love them both." It was the simple truth. Coming back to those girls had really been her saving grace. Why, when she was in their company, the pain of losing Charlie numbed to a dull ache.

"And they love you." He stared moodily down into his glass.

They sat together as Lord Bradbury drank, silence settling over them. Why had Lord Bradbury come up at this time of night? He had found out about her engagement in Brightgate. He knew she'd lied. Was he going to sack her, after all? She snuck a glance at him from under her lashes. If he was angry, he was hiding it well. He merely looked deep in thought.

"You are probably wondering why I am here," he finally responded, as though reading her thoughts. "You should know that I have heard what happened in Brightgate. I was not entirely pleased that you went to see the Cantrill family. As you know, I cannot keep a married servant around. It was rather duplicitous of you, Sophie."

She swallowed. He knew the truth. And moreover, he had never called her by her first name before. It sounded very strange coming from him.

"I'm sorry," she murmured. Her imminent departure was certain.

"Everything is fine now." He looked into his empty glass. "You aren't marrying him."

"No." The word fell heavily from her lips. "How did you come to know?" She could have bitten her tongue out the moment she said it. It was really none of her business to question his lordship. And as long as she was keeping her job, what did it matter?

As long as she *was* keeping it…

"Someone hired by the Cantrills was poking around the household staff, asking questions about you," he replied. "So I hired him to do a little counter-espionage, as you might say. I know everything that happened in Brightgate."

"I see." Of course. That made complete sense.

"So now I must ask—what do you want, Sophie?" He placed the glass on her side table and leaned forward. "Your engagement is broken. Surely you don't want to spend the rest of your days sewing for my two girls. A bright young thing like you? You must have some ambition."

"Well…" He hadn't fired her yet. Perhaps, if she played along with his game as politely as possible, he would forget how she lied so she could go to Brightgate and help Charlie. "I love sewing for Amelia and Louisa and would gladly do so for the rest of my days. They are such sweet darlings."

"Go on," he responded, examining her with a grave air.

"But if the day comes when they no longer need my services exclusively, I should like to become a professional modiste. I would love to have my own shop."

"Here in Bath?"

"Yes, Bath is lovely. There's a bustle of activity, but it's still delightful and quaint. I fear I would become lost in London."

"My thoughts, too. That's why I stayed here after my wife died. A good place to make a home for my daughters."

She gave him what she hoped was a warm smile,

though her nerves were still a jumble. "You are a good father."

"Yes, well." He became brusque and businesslike, rubbing his hands together. "I need your assistance tomorrow, Miss Handley. If you will accompany me, there are a few things I should like to show you in Bath. Be ready at half-past noon."

"Of course." Her eyebrows drew together in confusion. "Is it something for the girls?"

"No." He rose from the settee. "Something for myself. As I have said, I have excellent taste in all things, but I will defer to your judgment."

The next day, Sophie was ready at the precisely appointed time. She selected a simple afternoon dress of fawn silk and a spencer jacket. Lord Bradbury had not said where they were going, so she needed to be practically dressed for anything while still looking presentable.

"Ah, yes," his lordship called as he entered the vestibule. "You look quite nice. A trifle plain, perhaps."

"I wasn't sure—" she began, flustered. She should have chosen something more elaborate, more in keeping with being in the company of a viscount.

"Not at all, my dear." He withdrew a strand of pearls from his pocket. "I was merely commenting that your gown will make a fitting frame for these."

Sophie sucked in her breath. They were absolutely incredible. "Oh, no." She backed up a pace. "The bracelet was enough."

"And yet you sold it, you minx," he replied with a

laugh. "Come, don't dissemble. Let me see how my taste in pearls has held out over the years."

She could not refuse without making a scene, or offending him. And her position in the household was still rather tenuous after he found out the truth about Brightgate. It would do no good to offend his lordship. So she submitted as he clasped the smooth baubles around her neck. She managed a tight smile as he raked his eyes over her form.

"Perfect," he muttered. "As though you were made for them. Now promise me you won't sell these, no matter how much blunt you need. If you ever want for anything, you have only to ask me."

Her face heated, and drops of perspiration broke out on her forehead. "How did you know I sold the bracelet?" Was he furious with her? His face wore the same impassive and urbane expression as always.

"The same detective who was vetting you out for the Cantrills, of course," he replied. He took her by the arm and steered her toward the waiting carriage outside. "I bought it back, by the way."

He boosted her inside the carriage and rapped on the window.

"Where are we going?" The pearls hung around her neck like a noose. And she didn't like his bantering tone. She preferred matters to be completely neutral between them, except when he spoke of his daughters. That he did with such warmth, it did her heart good. But when he started flirting with her—well, she had no idea how to react.

"I want to show you a nice little property I am thinking of purchasing," he responded in an easy tone. "We'll drive by, as it is currently occupied. You may see it from the outside. And then there's another place I should like for you to see when we are done there."

He was bringing her along for advice on properties? How strange. She sat against the seat, trying to stay calm and collected. After all, Lord Bradbury wasn't acting in a menacing way. Overly familiar, perhaps, but not menacing.

The carriage paused before a little, blond stone building near High Street. It had lovely, large windows that faced the front squarely. Shoppers bustled in and out of its two French doors.

"Now what do you think of that?" He pointed out the building with a flick of his head. "It's a millinery shop now, but I think it would work well for a modiste. Those windows would allow for ample display of gowns."

"It's—very nice." She lifted her brows and turned toward his lordship. "Are you buying it?"

"I own the building already," he responded. "But I can find a new place for the tenant if you like it. Personally, I feel it is exactly the right location for a modiste. Lots of foot traffic, you know. Even on a weekday like this, it's a-buzz with activity."

"I can see what you are saying. But—I am not sure I understand why you need my opinion."

"For your shop, Sophie, my dear. Let me be perfectly plain. I shall set you up as a modiste in this very location, if that's what you wish." He rapped on the window, and the carriage turned away from the curbstone, plunging back into the midday traffic.

"But Amelia and Louisa will need me for a long time yet." Her brow furrowed in confusion. Was he simply buying her off with the pearls and the modiste shop because he was going to sack her? A way of pensioning her?

"My daughters will continue to be dressed by you," he stated flatly. "They love you too much for me to let you go completely. But on the other hand, you can share your talents with all of Bath this way—gain a respectable following, fame and status. It is my way of saying thank you."

"Oh." That knocked the wind out of her sails. She had no idea what to say. "Thank you, my lord." Her life-long dream was finally coming true—what meant everything to her was accomplished with such ease by him.

The carriage drew to a stop before a large, imposing townhome on a tony side street. "Come, take a look inside."

He clasped her hand firmly in his, leading her up the front staircase. She was so used to going in back entrances, it felt uncomfortable to walk up to the front door. His lordship fumbled with some keys and finally swung the door open, revealing a lovely vestibule with a curving mahogany staircase.

Two rooms branched off on either side of the staircase, each fitted with moldings as far as the eye could see. But everywhere she looked, the townhome was empty. Not a stick of furniture or scrap of carpet marred the varnished surfaces.

"Are you thinking of leaving the Crescent?" She could hide her confusion no longer.

He threw his head back and closed the door behind them. "Little Sophie, you are a delight. No, of course not. The girls and I will remain at our townhome. This is for you—if you want it. If it's not what you desire, I have a few others in mind. I liked this one for its location. Close by your shop, and close enough to the Crescent that I shan't take long to reach here."

She sank onto the staircase, eyeing him warily, her breath coming faster. "I don't understand you, Lord Bradbury. Why are you giving me this house?"

"Sweetheart." He sank down beside her and took her hands in his. They were large and warm and trapped her completely. She could not tug away. "You must know by now that I care deeply for you. I adore you. I can think of nothing else but you. And so, now that your ridiculous courtship with Cantrill has ended, I am making my intentions known."

"Are you proposing?" She choked out the words.

"Darling, you know I cannot marry you, as your family situation precludes marriage." He clasped her hands more tightly, and his voice became low and tender. "But no harm would come to you, I swear it. You would be under my protection forever. As a viscount, I cannot marry where I choose, but I can love where I choose. And I choose you, my dearest." He kissed her forehead gently.

"You cannot marry me?"

"No." He shook his head with a rueful air. "Your status in Society is at best questionable, my darling. But that doesn't change my opinion or feelings about you. You have captivated me since the moment I laid eyes on you. It may not be what we wish it to be, but this arrangement is as close to heaven on earth as I can make it."

Two paths were before her, as clearly marked as bridle trails in the park. She could say yes. She could become his mistress and live a life of ease and luxury. She would become a renowned modiste. Every need cared for. Every want catered to. She could still see Amelia and Louisa.

But she would be his. She would belong to Lord Bradbury, just like these empty buildings. She would be an empty shell, cared for and pampered, but bereft and alone.

On the other hand, she could not stay in Bath if she said no. Refusing his lordship was a sure ticket home on the next Yellow Bounder.

Tears filled her eyes. How buffeted she felt, like a ship on a stormy sea. Tossed about with no anchor.

No anchor...

No anchor...

"Darling, are you ill?" Lord Bradbury caught her in his arms.

"No. Yes. I don't know. I haven't had anything to eat today." It was ridiculous, but the only excuse she could offer.

"Let us go home, then," he replied. "You shall rest this afternoon, and have some dinner. When you feel a little better, we will talk over the future."

He half led, half carried her back out to the carriage, under the frank appraisal of the coachman and footmen. Sophie burned with shame from her head to her feet.

Inside the carriage, Lord Bradbury tucked her up beside him, stroking her curls and murmuring words in a soft undertone. But she couldn't hear him. She couldn't see anything. All she saw was Charlie Cantrill, his ashen face and stooped shoulders when she bade him goodbye.

Chapter Nineteen

Sophie took another fortifying sip of tea. Lord Bradbury had insisted on sending a repast up to her room as she reclined in bed. The servants had eyed her with repressed interest, and Nancy had even been so bold as to wink at Sophie as she brought the tea tray. There was no use denying what had happened. Everyone surely knew that Lord Bradbury had a more than professional interest in her.

Even Lucy, stalwart trusted friend Lucy, was in on the gossip. She perched on the foot of Sophie's bed, her best schoolmarm expression pasted on her face.

"You look rather mutinous, Sophie. I fear that doesn't portend well for Lord Bradbury."

"Would you have me stay in Bath and be his mistress?" Sophie snapped.

Lucy tilted her head to one side. "Well, he would protect you. And you would be set for life. He's very generous—the way he treats his daughters, the high pay he lavishes on all the servants—he would never be stingy or mean."

"He offered to set me up as a modiste. With my own townhome," Sophie admitted.

"You see? You would never have a care in the world. And just think, Sophie. After turning down two marriage proposals and losing out with Charlie Cantrill, this may well be the best offer you will ever have. So why do you look like a thundercloud? Surely this is a wonderful bit of luck. You have nothing to lose by becoming his mistress."

"I would lose my self-respect. I would lose everything. My life would be just like that vacant townhome he showed me today—beautiful but empty. I don't love him. And I won't debase myself by entering into a relationship with him that cannot be sanctified."

"But what of Louisa and Amelia? You could become like a second mother to both of them. They adore you so."

"I love them, too, but I cannot be a second mother to those girls when I am a courtesan to their father." Honestly, Lucy's practicality and pragmatism was wearing. She had hoped Lucy would see her side of the story, and help her figure out what to do next. Now she was utterly alone, trying to pick her way out of the mire.

"How are you going to tell Lord Bradbury no?" Lucy regarded her with frank interest. "I would never, ever want to defy that man. He's generous, but I think he would be a terrible adversary. Isn't he coming up to see you this evening? What do you propose to do?"

Sophie twirled a lock of hair around her finger. The thought of defying Lord Bradbury was not at all pleasant. And yet, neither was spending the rest of her life as his mistress. She would not continue to be placed in positions she did not want. The whole business of dealing with men was exhausting, come to think of it. They all wanted something from her, and snuck around behind her back spying on her, and insulted her family, too—her good, hardworking family that had never, ever done anything to harm anyone.

Harriet. She wanted to go home to Hattie.

"I'm leaving." She set her teacup down with a determined clink on the side table and pushed her coverlet aside.

"Where are you going?" Lucy stared at her, open-mouthed.

"I'm going home to Tansley, where I belong. I'm leaving right now, through the back door. And don't you breathe a word of this to Lord Bradbury." She scurried about, changing out of her chemise and into a dark wool riding habit. "I'll take one small bag with me so I can travel quickly. You can have the rest of my clothes." She opened a carpet bag and tossed a few garments inside.

Lucy leaped from the bed and knelt beside her on the floor. "Sophie, are you mad? There is no way for you to travel alone. Have a little sense. At least stay the night and start fresh in the morning."

"I have my own money. I shall hire a Yellow Bounder and leave right away." That was the beauty of having a bit of money. She was her own person, beholden to no one.

"If you do that, I shall tell Lord Bradbury. Right now." Lucy stood and walked over to the door. "It's simply not safe for any young woman to travel alone."

"Botheration, are you on his side or mine?" Sophie snapped.

"Neither. But I would never forgive myself if you were harmed, Sophie." Lucy's hand rested on the doorknob.

Sophie sat back on her heels. "Stop. Don't tell him. I shall think of another way." She paused for a moment, racking her brain for a solution. Aunt Katherine, of course. Auntie would send her home without delay. And she would be safe in the Crossley traveling Berlin. "I shall leave right away and go see Aunt Katherine, and she and I will arrange my travel together."

Lucy removed her hand from the doorknob. "That's more sensible. She will travel with you, or send a servant."

Sophie resumed her packing. Goodness, it would never do to have Auntie come along. "She'll have to send a servant," she muttered. "I refuse to travel at her poky pace."

She tucked her hairbrush and hairpins inside the bag and cinched it. There was no more room to pack anything else, and besides, she wanted to leave as much of her life in Bath behind as she could. "Will you find a way to tell Louisa and Amelia that I am all right, and that I send my love? Without alerting Lord Bradbury, of course."

Lucy nodded, her brows drawing together. "I don't relish the task, but I will."

As she closed the drawer of her dressing table, a small leather bag caught her eye. She reopened the drawer and withdrew the leather pouch. Inside was her thousand pound treasure for pawning the bracelet. She weighed it in one hand and looked at Lucy.

"I pawned the bracelet Lord Bradbury gave me."

Lucy nodded. "Yes, I know."

Did everyone know? Good gracious, she had no privacy at all. "Do you think the money I received from pawning the bracelet is mine?"

"Are you asking on moral grounds? Do you mean, should you return the money to Lord Bradbury?"

"Precisely. He bought the bracelet back. Perhaps I should repay him."

Lucy paused for a moment, giving the matter some thought. "Why did you sell the bracelet, Sophie? For material gain?"

"No. I sold it because it seemed like such a fetter. Even then I was being tied to Lord Bradbury in a way I disliked. I was going to use the funds to make clothes for the widows and children of the veterans' fund. I never had a chance to do so."

"Oh, Sophie." Lucy came over and folded her in a warm embrace. "Of course it's yours. I would keep it and do whatever you want with it. Lord Bradbury has plenty of money, and besides, he gave that gift to you. It's yours to keep."

"Then this is what I want you to do." Despite everything, she wanted to give Charlie the money for the widows in Bath. He had opened her eyes to a reality that she never knew existed. And she could never turn her back on it again. "After I am gone—several days after I am gone, in fact—I want you to take the money to Charlie and say it is an anonymous gift for the widows. Then, if you don't mind, try working with the women to create a sort of sewing class or ladies' group, one that would allow its members to sew dresses for each other."

Lucy accepted the leather pouch from Sophie and

opened it. "My goodness, there is enough money in here to feed and clothe several families for a year or more. Sophie, are you sure you want me to do this without telling Charlie anything?"

"Do not tell him it came from me." She hefted her valise in one hand. "When I came to Bath I had every intention of striking out on my own. And over these few months, I have failed at every turn. I failed with Charlie, and now with Lord Bradbury. I haven't even begun to shepherd Amelia through the rigors of a London Season. And I never had a chance to do anything for the widows." She patted Lucy on the shoulder and crossed to the door. "Perhaps if I stay far removed from it, the widows of Waterloo will become a success."

"Sophie, don't feel that way. None of this is your fault." Lucy turned and watched her go, her eyes sparkling with unshed tears.

Sophie blew her a kiss. "I shall write when I get settled at Brookes Park."

And with that, Sophie fled down the stairs and through the kitchen, which was blessedly empty, as most of the servants were employed with serving supper to Lord Bradbury and his daughters. As she opened the back door, a gust of warm August wind ruffled her hair. It felt good to set foot on the porch and stomp out of the yard—every footstep forward was a step toward freedom.

Even though the moment was thrilling and liberating and exhilarating in an odd sort of way, her heart beat heavily in her chest. She was leaving Bath for good. There would be no more gossip about the fund, no chance to overhear any tidbits about Charlie from

Lucy when she returned from reading to the ensign every Thursday afternoon. And even the slightest opportunity of seeing Charlie in the bustling, crowded streets was now over. She was headed home. She was a failure in everything, but she was, at least, still her own person.

It was rather a cold comfort, but it was all she had.

Sophie had stopped coming to the Veterans' Club meetings. In fact, she seemed to have vanished from Bath altogether. Any possible sight of her blonde curls and graceful figure at St. Swithins or out on the street simply disappeared. Her friend Lucy still came to the meetings, but was so wrapped up in Ensign Rowland that she barely spoke two words to Charlie.

What was wrong with Sophie? Had she fallen ill?

He could ask Aunt Katherine, but how much of the tale did she know? Did Sophie tell her that his family had behaved in an infamous manner? And if so, how would the old woman feel about the matter? After all, she and Sophie were now related. Any slight on Sophie could be construed as a slight on Auntie.

He could barely discern anything the reverend was saying, but whatever it was, the veterans agreed with him. They sat in the pews, nodding in agreement as the reverend continued his lecture.

He really should be paying attention. This was his purpose in life. Not Sophie Handley.

"We must all work together for the common good," the reverend said, breaking through the haze of Charlie's jumbled thoughts. "As a band of brothers, we must stand together and help one another through these difficult times. No matter what others may say, we are one."

The veterans nodded and harrumphed their agreement.

Solidarity. It's what he tried to offer Sophie. He would have gladly stood with her in defiance of all his family. Why then, did she push him away? For she had. The love that shone in her eyes during those few blissful days in Brightgate—that was not the work of an actress.

He scanned the crowd once more, but Sophie's bright golden head did not appear among the women working in the back of the church. He would go to Aunt Katherine this afternoon and talk with her. Surely Auntie would help him. Surely she knew where Sophie had gone.

A hand tugged at his elbow. Charlie spun around. But it was only Miss Williams standing before him. He fought to maintain a placid countenance. "Miss Williams. How do you do?"

"May I speak with you privately for a moment, Lieutenant?" A frown furrowed her brow.

"Yes, of course." He led her to a small cloakroom off the altar area. It was empty save for a few robes and one rickety wooden chair. "Please, sit."

"No, thank you. I would rather stand." She turned to face him squarely. "I am going expressly against the wishes of my dearest friend by doing this, but I must be completely honest with you. I have a feeling it's the only way to save you both." She extended her hand, which grasped a small leather pouch. "This is for the widows of Waterloo. From Sophie."

He took the leather pouch and ripped it open. There

was money in there—a huge amount of blunt. He looked up at Miss Williams, his eyebrows raised in question.

"Sophie sold the bracelet Lord Bradbury gave her. It was her intention to use the funds to help clothe the widows and children in Bath. As you can see, it was a dream that could have come to fruition, except she left Bath in haste."

"She has gone?" All the air was sucked out of his lungs. It must be true, for Miss Williams's face betrayed no sign of jest. Yet hearing it from Miss Williams was unbearable. "Where is she?"

"She left for Tansley Village three days ago. She wanted me to wait to give you this money until she was settled there, and she wanted me to give it to you anonymously. But I cannot do so. You must know the truth. I do not know what transpired in Brightgate, but I have some idea that it happened as a result of that bloody bracelet. And I cannot have you thinking ill of Sophie any longer, though it pains me to break my promise to her."

"I don't think ill of her. She pushed me away." Just a few short months ago, he never would have admitted something like that to anyone. But he was hanging by his fingertips to a cliff. Unless he was completely honest, he might plummet into the depths.

Miss Williams grasped his hand and pressed the money into it. "Then you should go after her."

Something didn't fit. She was holding back. "Why did Sophie leave so quickly?"

"Lord Bradbury made her an offer—not of marriage, but of a different kind." She gave a discreet cough, and her cheeks pinkened in the dim light of the cloakroom. "Sophie refused, and fled to Tansley that very evening."

"He made her an offer...?"

"Lord Bradbury was going to set her up as a modiste, with her own townhome and everything." Miss Williams sighed. "Really, it was impractical of her to refuse. Especially such a powerful man. But you know our Sophie, she would never do anything of the sort, no matter how ridiculous it was to refuse. She went to see her Aunt Katherine and arrange her passage home. She was going to take a Yellow Bounder, but I made her see reason in that, at least."

Charlie's fingers curled into a fist around the leather pouch. He swallowed several times before he could speak again. "Thank you for telling me everything, Miss Williams. I am most indebted to you. And now I shall leave you. I have business I must attend to without delay."

"Of course." She released his hand. "Where are you going?"

"I am going to track down that blackguard, of course."

She grinned. "Godspeed, Lieutenant."

Chapter Twenty

'Twas nearly time for luncheon, so that surely meant Lord Bradbury would be at the club. Charlie elbowed his way through the streets of Bath, the late August breeze ruffling the tails of his coat. His darling Sophie, a mistress for Lord Bradbury? How insulting, how cowardly an offer she had been made. And coming so close on the heels of his family's infamous behavior— no wonder she fled to the comfort of Tansley. He didn't blame her. Not one bit.

And of course, there was the little matter of the money she had gifted to the widows of Waterloo. She had taken a gift meant to signify something untoward, and was turning it into a gift of Christian love for others. And at every turn, she had been insulted and accused. The question was no longer whether or not he would go to see her in Tansley. The question was, would Sophie deign to see him when he arrived?

He took the stairs up to his club two at a time and burst the doors open, not waiting for the butler. He left his hat and glove on, for he had no time to waste. There sat Bradbury, in the dining room, a dinner of cold chicken on his plate. If he was melancholy over Sophie's departure, it hadn't affected his appetite.

"Bradbury. A word, if you please." Charlie took off his hat and flung it into the empty chair beside Lord Bradbury.

"Of course. Sit down. You look fit to be tied." Lord Bradbury's eyebrows were raised in mild surprise. "How might I assist you, Cantrill?"

"I suppose you know by now that Sophie is gone." He bit out the words, an angry flush making his cheeks grow hot.

"Yes. Gone to her family in Tansley. What of it?" Lord Bradbury set down his fork and took a sip of wine.

"She left for one reason and one reason only. You made her an improper offer. How dare you, sir?"

"Now, Cantrill. Before you begin sermonizing at me, do remember that the offer I made Sophie was in good faith. I could not, in fine conscience, make her an offer of marriage. She has not the background I desire in a second wife." Lord Bradbury took another sip of wine and set his glass aside. "And what business is it of yours, pray tell? I thought you quit the field long ago."

"We were engaged," Charlie ground out through clenched teeth.

"Were you? Sophie never said." Lord Bradbury chuckled, the sound raising Charlie's hackles. How dare his lordship laugh at his most private—and treasured— moments? "What happened, then? Why did you leave the field to me and my improper advances?"

"Sophie broke it off. I know not why."

"It probably had something to do with the young pup who was questioning my staff on behalf of your brother,

Robert. Ah, you see, Cantrill? Your family is just as cautious as I am. Even though Sophie is the daughter of Sir Hugh Handley, her mother's side of the family gives one pause. So why are you angry with me? It seems of the two of us, I was the most honest. I was very clear on what I could and could not offer Sophie. And there was no sneaking around on my part."

It was unnerving to be thus spoken to by such a blackguard. Surely Charlie was in the right. After all, he wanted to marry Sophie. What Lord Bradbury proposed was shocking, abominable even.

"How do you know Sophie is in Tansley?" Better to direct Lord Bradbury away from his diatribe about his honesty. And Charlie did have a sneaking suspicion there was a smidgen of truth to what he was saying.

Lord Bradbury picked up his fork and began toying with the haricots verts on his plate. "I came up to see Sophie one night, to get her answer. She was not there. And Miss Williams—my daughters' governess, a good friend of Sophie's—told me what had happened." He sighed. "My daughters feel her loss most keenly. They loved her so much. Sophie had the gift of making people love her."

Even sour, heartbroken and maimed lieutenants.

"Are you going to go after her?" Lord Bradbury looked at Charlie, the light of challenge sparking his glance. "If she said yes to you once, there is every chance that she might say yes again."

"Aren't you going to seek her out?" It was best to know if one was going to be paired in a duel, after all.

"No." Lord Bradbury set down his fork and pushed his chair away from the table. "I know when to cut my losses. It's what makes me such a formidable faro player. There are plenty of delectable young things out there who would be only too happy to become my mistress. That need shall be filled with no trouble." He paused and then smiled at Charlie, the corner of his mouth twisting down. "But I must say, were I a younger man—one not so concerned with Society—I would toss my cares aside and follow that gel. She is an Incomparable. Truly lovely. Very much like my first wife."

Charlie swallowed. He came here in anger, ready to challenge Lord Bradbury to a duel. Ready to upbraid, to subdue, to shame. And now—he felt no anger. Only shame; shame at himself for being so weak, shame at mankind for being so concerned with the proprieties that Sophie's spirit was crushed.

"If you wish to follow my advice, young man," his lordship continued, fitting his fingertips together, "you would go after pretty Sophie. After all, what care do you have for Society? Aren't you so immersed in your aid to the veterans' fund that you ignore every ball and soiree? What have you to go home to every night? What will happen to you when you grow old? I have my daughters to keep me busy and young at heart. Whom do you have to love?"

"It's odious to be given advice from a blackguard like you," Charlie muttered. His lordship had struck a nerve, though Charlie hated to admit it, even to himself.

Lord Bradbury threw his head back and barked with laughter. The sunlight streaming in through the open windows caught the graying hair at his temples, gilding them to silver. "You are fortunate I am so graceful in defeat, Lieutenant."

Charlie said nothing, but stared at his opponent, his spirit decidedly vanquished. What his lordship said was true. And though he was still a rogue for trying to co-erce Sophie into becoming his mistress, at least he was honest about his intentions. Honesty was as much of a virtue as austerity at times.

"I have no idea how to proceed," he finally admit-ted. "But I agree with you that Sophie is worth follow-ing." He rose, grabbing his hat from the chair. "I bid you good day, your lordship."

"I wish you luck, Lieutenant," Lord Bradbury re-plied in a cordial tone. "Though I hate to admit it, I am jealous of you."

Charlie left the club and trudged down the steps, the very steps he had taken two at a time just minutes ago. All the anger had flowed out of him, leaving nothing but a tired sensation of confusion in its place. If he went to Tansley, would Sophie even speak to him again? Likely Brookes would plant him a facer. And Harriet—the look she would have in her large dark eyes. He shut off his thoughts with a snap.

He retraced his steps to St. Swithins, as the chimes in the belfry tolled the hour. He must make amends some-how. He entered the hushed sanctuary and ran headlong into Reverend Stephens, colliding with him violently.

"Lieutenant? Are you quite all right?"

"No, Reverend. My apologies. I am…very distracted today." Charlie put out his good hand to steady the older man, and attempted a twisted smile. "I am wandering about in a daze, so it seems."

"I noticed you were quite moved by something Miss Williams spoke to you about," the reverend replied, concern wrinkling his brow. "Would you like to talk about it?"

Charlie shook his head. He couldn't yet put into words all the feelings that were roiling inside of him at the moment. He could only force out three sensible words: "I am flawed."

"We are all flawed, Lieutenant. It is what makes us human."

"No, mine goes beyond a mere human flaw. I desire to be right all the time. I hunger after righteousness the way a starving man craves bread. I wear my austerity as a debutante flaunts a new gown. It's a terrible weakness in me, sir...I don't deserve Sophie Handley." The words rushed out of him like water flowing down a swift-moving stream.

"I see." The reverend fell silent, as though he were considering Charlie's predicament. The moment stretched on so long that Charlie's nerves, already frayed, snapped.

"Help me, Reverend, please." He had never begged for anything. Never demeaned himself before. Now he was pleading for the answers to save his very life.

Reverend Stephens laid his hands on Charlie's shoulders. At his touch, a strange feeling of peace passed over Charlie. It was as though he were listening to a beloved father. "My dear son, you must first be at peace with yourself before you can love another. You must forgive yourself your failings. Forgive others for failing you. We are none of us perfect. But we can strive to become better people, as God wants us to be."

"Thank you, Reverend." Charlie drew a deep breath. "I understand—or at least, I think I do."

"Don't be so hard on yourself, Lieutenant. Remember, 'be ye kind one to another, tenderhearted, forgiving one another, even as God for Christ's sake hath forgiven you.'" With a final pat on Charlie's shoulders, the reverend departed, exiting through the narthex.

Charlie stood in the stillness of the church, allowing peace to flow through his body.

Forgiveness. It was something he had never attempted. And yet, it was essential—not just for his well-being, but as the only way he could win his beloved.

His soldierly instincts returned, and purpose and determination filled his being. He had a plan. Now he needed only to execute it.

The handsome stone facade of Brookes Park could barely be picked out on the horizon. Sophie's heart leaped with joy. Soon she would be embracing her beloved sister. Soon she would be kissing her beloved housekeeper Rose's wrinkled old cheek. She hadn't realized how much she missed her tiny family while she was in Bath. She had been so consumed with fittings for Amelia and the widows of Waterloo and later, of course, the myriad details of her doomed love affairs, that she had forgotten how sweet her home life had been. Though Harriet wrote regularly, it was not the same as being home.

The past few days had sped by in a whirlwind, on the road with an elderly servant of Aunt Katherine's. For Auntie had provided the Berlin and wished her Godspeed, approving of Sophie's plan to return to Tansley without asking for more information about her hasty flight. Instead, she had merely nodded her gray corkscrew curls under their little lace cap, and gave a ring of her bell to summon Knowles. Auntie's wise old eyes had seen all, discerned all, without Sophie having to breathe a word.

God bless Aunt Katherine.

It seemed an eternity until they entered the half circle that delineated the driveway at Brookes Park. No one was standing outside to meet her. As she planned it. She wanted no one to be alerted to her travel, for she didn't want to have to explain, in a letter, why she was leaving Bath. That conversation was best held face-to-face, with a bracing cup of tea, a soft settee and a closed door.

As the carriage slowed to a halt, she nodded to the elderly servant, Hannah, who had accompanied her on the journey, and let herself out. She bounced down onto the gravel with a satisfying crunch. The footman scurried around to help her, but she waved him away.

"I can manage on my own, thank you. You may put the horses away in the stable, and be sure to come into the kitchen for some refreshments. Make sure Hannah understands that she is to come along."

"Very good, miss." The footman bowed respectfully.

Sophie mounted the front steps with pride. She was going in the front door, not slinking around the back. She hadn't gone through a front door since that awful day when Lord Bradbury took her to see her new townhome.

She pounded on the door. "Hattie? Brookes? Anyone home?" she called.

The door jerked open, showing Stoames's kindly, wrinkled face. "Miss Sophie?" the batman asked, his grizzled brows drawing together in surprised confusion. "Is it really you? Bless my boots, it does me good to see you."

"Stoames!" She enfolded him in a hug. "I am so glad to see you. Where is my sister?"

"She and the captain are working in the library," Stoames replied, patting her shoulder. "I'll go and tell them you are here."

"No, don't tell them, Stoames. I want to surprise them." She shrugged out of her pelisse and untied her bonnet, then shook out her skirts.

"That you will. We had no idea you were coming. Mrs. Brookes will be so happy to see you. She's missed you something dreadful." He took her pelisse and bonnet in his weathered hands and waved her down the hall.

She turned to go, but had one more question. "And Rose? How is Rose doing?"

Stoames's weather-beaten face turned a dark shade of red. How extraordinary—who knew an old soldier could still blush? "Mrs. Rose fares well. We—uh—she and I are thinking of getting married."

"How marvelous!" Sophie rushed forward and hugged Stoames once more, knocking him back a pace. "Darling Stoames, was it the scones that did it? Rose is an incomparable cook."

He rubbed his grizzled head with his hand, and shrugged his shoulders playfully. "That was my main consideration, Miss Sophie."

She laughed. How good it was to be home. Funny to think of Brookes Park as home. It had been many things to her over the years—a possibility, a prize to be won, a lost cause—but now it was really and truly a home.

Hattie must have worked her magic. Wherever her sister went, comfort and serenity took hold.

She walked down the hallway to the door of the library, which was half-open. She pressed the door slightly to widen it without alerting the occupants to her presence. Ah yes, there was Brookes, his handsome head bent over a ledger, his quill scratching along the page. Harriet sat across from him, in a smaller, more ladylike desk, scribbling something on a sheet of foolscap. Sophie's heart lurched, and she pressed her quivering lips together. She had a sudden and foolish desire to cry, and it would never do to burst into tears just now.

She stared intently at her sister's glossy brown hair, parted exactly down the middle and looped around her ears. The same hairstyle…and yet something was different. She ran her eyes over Harriet, trying to assess the difference. Yes, something had changed. For one thing, Harriet looked softer, rounder even.

Sophie stepped into the room, her boots making nary a sound on the heavy Oriental rug. Then she cleared her throat.

"My, my, Hattie! You've gotten positively plump!"

Chapter Twenty-One

"Sophie? Sophie, my dear—is that really you?" Hattie dropped her pen and stood, her face draining of all its color. Brookes also cast aside his quill and rose, his face breaking into a surprised grin.

"Sophie, bless your heart. We had no idea you were coming home." He walked around his desk, with that same loping stride he had adapted long ago for his wooden leg, and enveloped her in a warm hug. Then he turned to Harriet and extended his hand to her protectively. "Harriet, are you all right?"

"Yes, of course!" She ran her hand over her middle and then clutched Brookes's hand as she came out from behind her desk. "Oh, Sophie. My dear, I have missed you so." Harriet embraced Sophie, but something—a large, round ball, it felt like—wedged between them in the embrace.

Sophie took a step backward, holding onto Harriet's shoulders. "Goodness, Hattie. Is Rose's cooking agreeing with you a bit too much? Or is there something you wish to tell me?"

Harriet smiled her beautiful, quiet smile, and cast

her eyes downward. "I am expecting. The baby should come sometime after the New Year."

Sophie's heart glowed. How many wonderful things had happened in the short time she was in Bath? And now she was here to watch them all come to fruition. "Harriet, Brookes, I am so happy for you both! This is a cause for great rejoicing."

Brookes motioned her over to a leather chair. "Sophie, did you travel alone? Why is no one with you? And how did you come here without letting us know? I would have sent our carriage for you, anytime you desired a trip home." His dark voice betrayed a concerned tone.

"Well…" Sophie hesitated. With Harriet's delicate condition, and her own dawning fatigue, she had no desire to discuss the unfortunate reasons for her visit. She cast a pleading look at Harriet, who nodded briskly.

"Brookes," she chided. "Sophie's worn out. And after days and days of pub food, I am sure she is ready for a decent meal." Harriet leaned over and rang the bell. "There will be plenty of time for discussions after my poor sister has recovered from her journey."

Brookes nodded, and then looked over at Harriet. Something flashed between them—a look, an understanding. Then he added, "I'll just go see to the horses. Give you time to settle in, Sophie. I'll see you two ladies again at supper." He bent down and planted a kiss on top of Harriet's head, and then patted Sophie's shoulder as he departed.

Bunting, Brookes Park's butler, entered just as his master was leaving. "Did you need something, Mrs. Brookes?"

"Yes, Bunting. A lavish tea tray, with every good nibble Rose can conjure. And don't tell Rose that Miss Sophie is home yet. I want to surprise her in a little while."

Bunting's broad face betrayed the hint of a smile. "Very good, ma'am."

After the door closed softly behind him, Harriet turned to Sophie, her dark blue eyes wide. "Now that you know my news, shall I hear yours?"

The dam was indeed in danger of breaking again. Sophie took a deep breath to calm her nerves. "So much to tell, sister. I don't know where to begin."

"Why don't you begin by telling me if anyone accompanied you? And how you happened to come here?"

"Aunt Katherine arranged my travel. She saw to everything, and sent Hannah along as my duenna. She would have sent word ahead, Hattie, but I swore her to secrecy."

Harriet nodded. "Auntie is quite good at arranging last-minute flights from Bath. You recall—it was she who helped me to come home quickly after Mama fell so ill."

Sophie's heart lurched, and tears stung her eyes. "Of course, I remember." Oh, botheration, the tears would not be checked. "My Hattie, what a muddle. And I hate to cry about it. I don't want to cry about it. But if I tell you everything that's happened—" she broke off to give a mighty sniff "—then I'll start blubbering."

"Wait until the tea arrives," Harriet warned sagely. "It's much easier to talk about bad news when you've had a bite to eat."

"Now you sound like Rose." Sophie couldn't hold

back her laughter, but it quickly dissolved into a watery sob.

"Rose is very wise," Harriet replied quietly. "Now, did you know that Rose and Stoames are engaged?"

"Yes, Stoames showed me in. How fantastic! And a little scandalous, too."

"Yes. You can imagine how the sheep and the cows are gossiping about it." Harriet laughed.

"I forgot. Tansley isn't exactly a beacon for Society, is it? How refreshing," Sophie replied. Bunting knocked discreetly on the door and entered, bearing a tray of delectable goodies and a steaming hot pot of tea. Sophie breathed in deeply. While it was true that Lord Bradbury's cook was quite good, nothing ever compared to Rose's light hand with scones.

Harriet busied herself with pouring the tea and filling a small plate with tempting foods. She admonished Sophie that the tea was too hot to drink, and Sophie could not suppress a smile. Harriet would always be the older sister, perennially ordering her about. Keeping her safe from harm. Why, if Harriet had come to Bath, she would have prevented everything that had befallen Sophie.

They ate and drank in sisterly comfort, Sophie taking strength from Harriet's calming presence and from Rose's excellent cooking. They chatted about the farm and the mill, about Harriet's plans for the baby's room, and about the romance that had blossomed between Stoames and Rose.

It was a long, languorous August afternoon, already beginning to feel like autumn. In the distance, cattle lowed. Servants bustled past the library door as they attended to the business of running Brookes Park. Such a peaceful place. No one wanted anything of her. No one expected anything of her. How easy it would be to fall back into her old lazy, selfish ways.

"Harriet, I want to confess," she began quietly.

"Dear Sophie, you may tell me anything." Harriet leaned forward and patted her knee with a gentle touch.

Once she began speaking, all of the words flowed out of her—halting at first, and then gathering momentum. She told Harriet everything—her love for Amelia and Louisa, her comradeship with Lucy, her work with the widows and her plan to clothe them all with the funds from the pawned bracelet. She poured out her love for Charlie Cantrill, her disgust at his family's behavior, her disappointment at Lord Bradbury's improper advances.

Harriet's eyebrows raised until they disappeared under the wings of her dark hair, and her blue eyes grew wider and more sapphire-tinged as Sophie's story progressed. Sophie explained her flight to Aunt Katherine's, her secret journey in the Crossley Berlin and then her blessed arrival at Brookes Park. Harriet, ever a good listener, simply nodded and prompted with the occasional question, but did not break in until Sophie finished her woeful tale and poured another cup of tea.

"My goodness," was her eventual reaction.

"Precisely." Sophie drank deeply.

"Well, my dear, if John ever hears that Lord Bradbury tried to make you his mistress, he will likely challenge him to a duel." Harriet sighed. "And I shall, of course, have to find a way to make peace between Charlie and John once he hears how terribly you were treated by the Cantrills. Oh, Sophie, this was not what I wished for you at all. I wanted you to enjoy your time in Bath."

"I did enjoy it. I learned so much—if only I could tell you how I've grown, Hattie." She paused. "Can you not prevent Brookes from challenging every man I knew in Bath to a duel? I don't want anything more to do with any of them. I want to stay here and enjoy the peace and solace of Brookes Park for as long as I am able. May I be the maiden aunt to your adorable baby?"

Harriet smiled. "I shall be delighted to have your company during my confinement, and of course, Brookes Park is your home. You can choose one of the suites upstairs, and make it your very own. I shall have to speak to John about the Cantrills and Bradbury. He still has a fearsome temper at times. I will let him know your wishes, my darling."

"Thank you, Hattie. It's so good to be home. Tell me, shall we go to the kitchen now and tease Rose about Stoames?"

Harriet laughed. "I should like nothing better."

The first step began with forgiveness. He could not win Sophie back if he had a heart full of bitterness and hatred. Even so, this was the hardest thing Charlie had ever attempted. He was never this nervous, not even when facing a battle.

He glanced around the Assembly Rooms. The chandeliers glittered, and their guttering flames cast prisms of light around the highly polished floors. He adjusted his cravat. The thing was about to choke him, and the points were so high he could not move his head naturally. This was why he never moved about in Society. It was so deuced uncomfortable.

But all would be well. He would come here to do what he needed to do, and then he would leave. He could almost feel the sweet, late-summer breeze on his face as he left the overcrowded ballroom for the very last time. How wonderful it would feel. Freedom at last.

A crowd of young debutantes parted, and he spotted his quarry. He strode across the ballroom with quick, purposeful steps. The young women, all clad in pastel gowns with varying degrees of modesty, stared at him with frank interest. A redhead turned to a brunette and whispered behind her gloved hand. They nudged each other and giggled.

He ignored the chits and walked straight up to the young lady who had been the cause of so much misery and grief for the past year. Her long, black hair was piled loosely on top of her head, and her gown, a shimmery gold, was cut far too low for decency. He averted his glance, heat flooding his face. Shame filled his soul, for this was the girl who had broken his heart. But here, in the crush of this stuffy ballroom, he saw her for what she really was.

And he forgave her.

"Miss Gaskell, may I have this dance?"

Her chocolate-brown eyes flashed with something like laughter. "Of course, Lieutenant."

He led her out onto the dance floor, wrapping his good arm around her lower back. She grasped his prosthetic hand and took a step back. The strange pull in his gut that had always surged with her touch had completely vanished. Attraction and aversion vanished. She was, simply, a girl he once knew. He looked down at her, a smile touching the corners of his mouth.

"Miss Gaskell, I must ask you something."

She tossed her glossy dark head and gave him a brilliant smile. "Of course, Lieutenant."

"Can you forgive me?"

She paused in the midst of their waltz, stumbling over her slippered feet. He smoothly guided her through the next step, helping her regain her footing.

Her eyebrows drew together in a straight line, and her brilliant smile had faded to an uncertain frown. "I beg your pardon?"

"I asked your forgiveness." He guided her through the next turn by pressing his hand against her back.

"For what? Is this some kind of jest? If so, it is in very poor taste."

"It is no jest." He glanced down at her, then looked back out at the ballroom, steering her through the crowd with expert precision. "When I returned from the war, I was a changed man. Not only physically, but in my mind, my heart, my soul. I was a different man from the one who left for the Peninsula with your miniature in my trunk and your whispered promises in my mind."

"Please, don't." Her eyes were bright with unshed tears.

"Upon my honor, I do not wish to pain you," he continued. "But I have done you a grave disservice, Miss Gaskell. When I returned and I was so very changed from the man you had pledged to marry, I should have given you more time to get to know me again. Or at the very least, I should have set you free without any ill feelings. I did neither." He paused and guided her through a tricky turn, holding her firmly at the small of her back. "And for that, I am truly sorry."

She looked up at him, an uncertain expression still on her face. "Your apology is accepted, Lieutenant. May I ask why you chose this moment, and this place, to speak to me about this matter?"

"I am in love, and the only way I can win the one I love is by righting all of these wrongs. I am starting this journey with you, because my anger at you made me fight my feelings for this lady for far too long. And I am sorry I held bitterness in my heart. I should have understood your perspective."

The music ended with a flourish, and he broke his hold on her to bow. She curtsied deeply, and he averted his glance from her too-low bodice.

"Would you stroll about the room with me?" Beth asked, linking her arm through his.

"Of course," he replied with what he hoped was a gallant air, as his impatience to quit the crowded ballroom mounted. He had planned to have one dance and be off. He led Beth to the perimeter of the room as the musicians began striking up the notes for the next dance.

Beth cleared her throat, an unusual flush creeping over her face as he glanced at her in profile. He had made Miss Elizabeth Gaskell, one of the highest-flying chits in Society, blush. Truly today was an unusual day. One for the betting books, if he still partook in that diversion.

As they neared a secluded part of the ballroom, where only a few straggling servants bustled about carrying trays of food and drinks for the dancers, Beth halted in her tracks and spun around.

"I'm sorry, too," she blurted, her eyes darting left and right as she spoke.

"You are?" He could hardly believe his ears. The spirited, devil-may-care debutante had never apologized to anyone for anything in his recollection.

"Yes." She cleared her throat and spoke more softly. "When you returned, the changes I perceived in you made me feel as though an ocean were between us. And I thought I couldn't marry you because we were no longer the same people. I should have behaved… differently. Can you forgive me?"

As she spoke, peace flooded his soul. Forgive her? Of course he could forgive her. She was, after all, a very young girl, spirited, sometimes unwise in her choices. She had not deliberately set out to harm him, any more than he had deliberately set out to run her off.

"Of course I do. Do you forgive me, Miss Gaskell?"

Her cheeks turned a deeper shade of pink. "I do."

"Thank you." He offered her his arm once more, and they resumed their stroll around the room. "Miss Gaskell, I offer you my very best wishes for the future. But I must depart. This ballroom is playing havoc with my sensibilities."

She laughed, tossing her head once more. "You never did like balls or soirees."

He led her over to a gilt chair and bowed. "No, indeed. But I am very glad I came to this one. Goodbye, Miss Gaskell."

She curtsied deeply and gave a genuine smile, one that warmed the cockles of his heart. "I wish you the best of luck with your young lady, Lieutenant. And I am very glad you came tonight, too. Adieu."

He left the ballroom as quickly as he could navigate through the crush, his light spirits returning as the soft August breeze ruffled his cravat. That was the first step on his journey. He had more to make before he could travel to Tansley and beg Sophie to be his. But it was a journey worth making.

Chapter Twenty-Two

"Honestly, Hattie. Four gowns are not nearly enough for my niece or nephew," Sophie protested, her lap full of fine cambric and flannel. "I shall make at least four more, and then start stitching together nappies."

Harriet shook her head, chuckling softly. "My baby is not one of your fine Bath ladies, Sophie. Really, fewer gowns should be sufficient."

"Are you going to deny me this pleasure?" Sophie held up a length of fabric, measuring it from the tip of her nose to her outstretched hand. "No, indeed. After Rose nearly dissuaded me from making her wedding dress, now you want to keep me from whipping up some delightful baby gowns? Really, I never knew that the Brookes family was such a stingy lot."

Harriet merely smiled and rolled her eyes, then directed her attention back to her manuscript. They sat together in the sitting room of Sophie's suite, the morning sun gilding the cheerful yellow walls. She had been at Brookes Park for less than a week, and already she had become accustomed to the easy pattern of life there. She took on the task of making Harriet's entire layette, with baby clothing and diapers, and had let out several of Harriet's gowns to accommodate her increasing middle. Over Rose's embarrassed protests, she had declared her intention to make the wedding gown for those upcoming nuptials. Oh, it wasn't the daring and lavish kind of stitchery she was used to in Bath, but it was infinitely dearer and cozier.

A knock sounded on the door. "Enter," Sophie and Harriet chorused in unison.

Bunting entered, bearing a letter on a silver tray. "This came for you this morning, Miss Sophie."

She glanced at the handwriting. A letter from Lucy. Nervous excitement coursed through her. She had been too busy to write Lucy, but hoped to hear from her just the same. She snatched the missive off the tray. "Thank you, Bunting."

"Mrs. Brookes, the captain desires for you and for Miss Sophie to join him in his study when you are done with your morning's work."

"Of course, Bunting," Harriet replied. "We shall be down after Sophie has had a chance to read her letter."

He nodded respectfully and bowed as he closed the door.

Sophie broke the seal with shaking fingers.

My dear Sophie,
You can only imagine the hue and cry that your departure has caused in the Bradbury household. Amelia and Louisa broke down into hysterics upon hearing that you had gone, and I had to administer the vinaigrette as Amelia nearly fainted. Lord Bradbury has said nothing about

*your departure, but goes about his business in
the same suave manner that he always does. The
on dit links him to a certain blond soprano who
is as ambitious as she is beautiful.*

*I managed to obey your wishes for a few days,
and then finally told the truth of your departure to
Lieutenant Cantrill. He was furious at Bradbury
and left, I think, to challenge his lordship to a
duel. If anything came of their confrontation I
have not heard it. But the lieutenant has been
absent from all the weekly veterans' meetings,
and I believe he is no longer in Bath.*

*My dearest Sophie, I wish you could return, as
I miss your companionship. Now I have no one
to advise me about the ensign. Would you believe
that we are also meeting on Tuesdays in the park?*

Lucy's letter broke into a rambling paean to the many
virtues of the ensign. With a sigh, Sophie skipped to
the end of the missive.

*If you cannot come to Bath soon, I shall have to
journey to Tansley to see you. My best wishes to
you and your family, darling.
With fondness,
Lucy*

Sophie folded the letter back up and cast it aside.
"Well, it is settled, then. Everyone knows of my flight
from Bath. Even Lieutenant Cantrill."

"Who was the letter from? Was it from Charlie?"

Harriet put her pen down and stacked the sheets of foolscap together in a tidy pile.

"No, it was from Lucy. She has told Charlie of my departure, and she told Louisa and Amelia, as well. Apparently, Lord Bradbury is not suffering from a broken heart. He is already linked to a famous blond soprano." It hurt, a little, to acknowledge this. Not that she wanted him to pine away for her. But it was like an admission of how very little she meant to him that he found a replacement already. She really was as interchangeable as two dolls in a pram, or two empty townhomes on the same street. At least to someone like his lordship.

Harriet was studying her intently, her mouth pursed in a straight line. Her "elder sister" expression, they always called it. "Sophie, dear, do you miss his lordship?"

"Miss him? No. I miss Louisa and Amelia, but I am merely disappointed in Lord Bradbury." It was the truth, after all.

"And Charlie?" Harriet's "elder sister" expression did not waver.

For some strange reason, hearing that dear name expressed by Harriet, who looked much the same as she had back in the old days when Sophie was wavering between Captain Brookes and Lieutenant Marable, was the very last straw. Tears stung the back of her eyes, and she bit her lip. "I love him, but I can never be with him. I promised, after all."

"There, there." Harriet rose with some difficulty and embraced Sophie, patting her back. "Come, let us go speak to John. I have a feeling he will want to know about this."

Of course, Harriet was right. She was, after all, married to the captain, and therefore must know all of his thoughts before they even occurred to him. As the two sisters sat in silence, facing Brookes in his study, Sophie had the uncanny impression that this was how he planned his campaigns.

"Sophie, Harriet has told me some of the adventures you had in Bath, and I must say I am most displeased with the behavior of my fellow man. Cantrill and Bradbury. Two men I thought I knew so well. In fact, I often thought of Charlie as a brother." He fitted his broad fingertips together carefully. "My question to you is simple. As the head of this family, what do you wish me to do about this?"

Sophie swallowed, fighting the rising lump in her throat. "Nothing."

"Nothing?" Brookes shook his head as though he had not heard right. "After one man's family insulted your good name, and after another made you the victim of his untoward advances? Really, Harriet—" he turned to Hattie, his brows drawing together "—talk some sense into your sister."

"We have talked about it," Harriet replied softly. "And I agree with Sophie. Nothing should be done about the matter."

Brookes harrumphed. With marriage and a child on the way, he was growing positively paternal. In no time at all, he would begin beetling his brows and staring at people over the rims of his spectacles. Sophie bit back a sudden smile at that image of Brookes and focused on the matter at hand.

"Both Bradbury and Cantrill behaved in an insulting manner," Brookes continued. "Shouldn't they have some comeuppance?"

"I am turning Lord Bradbury into the villain in my next novel," Harriet interrupted in a helpful tone. "With a different name, of course."

"And what good will that do?" Brookes's gray-green eyes widened in astonishment.

"Literary revenge is the best sort of reprisal," Harriet answered placidly.

Sophie smothered another grin. How marvelous to be back home with Hattie once more. She said a silent prayer of thanks for her sister.

"I am undone." Brookes threw his hands up in the air and leaned back in his chair. "Here I am, ready to seek retribution, and you will allow me to do nothing."

"Brookes, I don't mean to sound ungrateful," Sophie put in. After all, Brookes *was* trying to help. "It's just that nothing will change Lord Bradbury. He is as he always shall be. I am not harmed by his overtures. Especially now that I am back home in Tansley. No one knows about it, and no one shall."

Brookes nodded and appraised her carefully. "And what about Cantrill?"

"She's still in love with him," Harriet broke in.

"Hattie! For goodness' sake." Really, she had no privacy, however well-intentioned her sister's meddling.

"Well, it's true, isn't it?"

Sophie was at the mercy of two pairs of eyes, one dark blue and one gray-green, both watching her with the same interest as a dowager staring at an unruly debutante through a lorgnette. There was no use deceiving anyone, certainly not herself. "Yes, it's true."

"So you see? You can't call Cantrill out. He could well be your future brother-in-law." Harriet shook her finger at Brookes for emphasis.

"I doubt that. Not after all his family had to say. And not after the way I broke things off," Sophie admitted. A miserable, sick feeling was settling in the pit of her stomach.

"Well, time will tell." Harriet gave her a bracing smile and patted her shoulder. "So you see, Brookes, you need not put your pistol or lance skills to the test. No one is in need of a thorough trouncing. At least, not yet."

"Too bad," Brookes replied with a regretful shake of his head. "And I was so looking forward to facing Bradbury's smug grin over the barrel of a pistol."

"And I am heartily glad you are not." Harriet ran her hands over her increasing middle. "Take heart, sister. I have a suspicion that you will get to see your lieutenant someday. And then we will all be able to look back at this moment and chuckle."

Sophie gave them both a smile. She had no wish to argue with Harriet. Let them continue to think that Charlie Cantrill would arrive on a white steed, bearing flowers and a profound apology. She knew better. The familiar pattern her life had taken on at Brookes Park would last until the end of her days.

Charlie knocked on the door of Lord Bradbury's stylish townhome on the Crescent, still riding the tide of goodwill he had experienced the moment he forgave Beth Gaskell. The Bradbury family butler answered the door, his grave expression unchanged as he surveyed the unremarkable cut of Charlie's clothes.

"Sir?"

"My name is Lieutenant Charles Cantrill. I am here to speak with Lord Bradbury, if he is at home."

"I shall see if his lordship is available. Do come in, Lieutenant." The butler led him to a small parlor off the vestibule. It was spotlessly clean and beautifully furnished, if one's taste ran to rich mahogany furniture and paintings of horses, but it appeared never to have been used. Obviously, he was not important enough to warrant one of the grander waiting rooms.

The butler returned with a respectful bow. "His lordship will be with you directly. May I bring you some refreshment?"

"No, thank you. I shan't be here long."

"Very good, Lieutenant." The butler closed the door with a gentle click.

Charlie stood with his hand resting on a small marble statue of a faun, one that probably cost more than the veterans of Bath would ever see in their lifetimes. Strange, the difference between the wealthy and the poor. This small object d'art, which probably escaped his lordship's attention on a daily basis, would feed and clothe a family of four for a year.

Bradbury opened the parlor door, breaking into Charlie's reverie. "Cantrill? To what do I owe the pleasure?"

Charlie bowed. "I've come to offer my thanks to you."

"Thanks to me?" His lordship arched an eyebrow. "Are you jesting?"

"No. Merely trying to right several wrongs. And I began this journey as a result of our conversation at the Club."

Lord Bradbury's lips twisted together in a bemused grin. "Very well. You are welcome. Does this have anything to do with Sophie?"

"Yes. It has everything to do with her. I cannot win her back until I affect some very personal changes in my life. Forgiving others. Letting go of bitterness. That sort of thing." He didn't really like the way Lord Bradbury looked at him, as though he were enjoying some amusement at Charlie's expense. But he was here on a mission and must complete it, no matter how humbling it seemed.

"I see," his lordship replied. Seeing that Charlie hadn't moved, he headed toward the door. "Are we done?"

"Not quite. I wish to beg a favor of you."

"You do?" His lordship broke into a wide, almost feral grin. "And what might that be?"

"You know of Sophie's connections with the Handley family, do you not? How they slighted her poor mother, and how they cut those two young women—Sophie and her sister, Harriet—off without a penny? Seems rather unsporting of them, doesn't it?"

"It does. But then, the Handleys are an old family. Very proud. I am sure when Sir Hugh married an actress, it sent his family into apoplexies."

"It is still unsporting of them, I think. To visit their revenge on his innocent children," Charlie replied with a shrug. "Therefore, I want you to put a stop to it."

Bradbury gave an incredulous snort. "You want me to stop it? How, pray tell?"

"This is precisely why I came to you." Charlie kept his tone even and friendly. "You see, I have few of the connections to the wealthy and powerful that you have. You can block certain measures in the House of Lords, for example. Measures that could benefit the Handley family back in Liverpool. You can put the kind of social pressure on them that would make it very unlikely they would be received in some of the best homes in London and Bath. That sort of thing."

"You want me to blackmail and extort from the Handley clan?" Bradbury chuckled, shaking his head. "I never would have expected that from you, Cantrill."

"Let us be clear—I am not asking you to do anything untoward or illegal," Charlie responded. "But I am asking you to exert a similar kind of pressure on the Handleys that they used on Sir Hugh's daughters, until they relent and stop saying infamous things about Sophie and her family."

"Tit for tat. Interesting. Again, I would not expect that from you, Cantrill. I assumed you were a *turn the other cheek* sort of man."

"I am. That's why I ask you to undertake this for me."

Bradbury threw back his head and laughed, an honest, uproarious sound that echoed through the elegantly appointed parlor. "Tell you what," he replied. "I'll do it. One, out of thankfulness for all Sophie did for my daughters. And two, because I still, in my heart, carry a strong fondness for young Sophie. And three—" his lordship strode toward the door, placing his hand on the knob "—because it amuses me. Who knew you could be so devious, Cantrill?"

"Not devious." He walked over toward the door, standing face-to-face with his lordship. "But as a soldier, I must be a good tactician."

Bradbury laughed again, an appreciative chuckle, and ushered Charlie through the vestibule to the front door. "By Jove, Cantrill, what an entertaining plan. I wish you the best of luck with it. What shall you do next?"

"I leave for Brightgate on the morrow," he replied, stepping out onto the porch. "One last matter to attend to before I strike out for Tansley."

Bradbury nodded, a knowing light sparking his eyes. "I wish you the best of luck. Tell me, if I am able to pull off my part of the plan, may I dance at your wedding?"

Cantrill acknowledged the joke with a tight smile. "You shall. If the lady will have me."

Chapter Twenty-Three

This last visit was, in some ways, harder than the others. After all, Robert and Mother were his family. Despite their faults, he loved them both. And he hated to call them up on the carpet. But it must be done. It was the only way he could finish his journey to forgiveness and pave the way for his marriage to Sophie. If she would even speak to him.

The unremarkable carriage he had hired for his travels drew to a shaky stop before the Cantrill home. Smug, self-satisfied—those were the words that came to mind as he viewed his family home from the curbstone. But even so, it was still capable of providing shelter and comfort. Just like his family.

"You can take the carriage around to the back, Browning, and then apply to the kitchens for some refreshment," Charlie directed. With a respectful tip of his hat, the coachman circled the horses around toward the back of the property. Charlie strode up the drive, his boots crunching on gravel. The place looked deserted. Surely Mother and Robert hadn't gone out of town. That would foil his plans royally.

He knocked thrice upon the door, and Jones, the family butler, answered. Charlie liked Jones. He was the only servant who had stayed on with his mother through the years. Every other servant left after a matter of weeks. In fact, it was not at all unusual for the entire staff to leave as a body, with only Jones remaining to help run the Cantrill home.

"Master Charles? We had no idea you were coming. Madam is paying her calls this morning. But she intends to return before luncheon."

Charlie handed his gloves and hat to Jones. "Not to worry, Jones. I didn't tell anyone I was on my way. Is Robert here?"

Jones nodded. "The master is in his study."

"Thank you. When Mother comes home, tell her to find us there, will you?"

"Of course, sir."

Charlie hastened up the stairs, clenching his fists in anticipation. This was not going to be a pleasant conversation. But he refused to lose his temper. Nothing would stand in the way of forgiveness—and because of forgiveness, his darling Sophie.

"What ho, Robert? May I come in?" Charlie strode in without knocking.

His brother looked up from his ledger, his eyebrows drawn together in wary puzzlement. "Charlie? To what do I owe the pleasure?"

"I've come to talk to you. Brother to brother."

Robert closed the ledger and leaned back in his chair. "Indeed? Does this have anything to do with our last discussion and your hasty flight from Brightgate?"

Charlie nodded pleasantly. "It does."

"Well, then. Do go on." Robert heaved the put-upon sigh of the elder brother.

Charlie took a deep breath. He would not be needled by Robert's air of superiority. Although he could best his brother at fisticuffs, even with one arm missing, violence would serve no purpose.

"I've come to tell you that I am going to marry Sophie, no matter what your objections may be. She is a virtuous, kind and gentle woman and I am lucky to have found her." There. Now let the fireworks begin.

Robert pursed his lips together. "She's a fortune hunter."

"She is not. She pawned that diamond bracelet to give to the widows' fund in Bath."

Robert crowed with laughter. "And you believe that tale? Really, Charlie. Have some sense."

"Not only did I take her at her word, but the funds were deposited with the express intention of clothing all the women and children of the veterans' fund. I've got the money, Robert. It was no mere ruse."

Robert shrugged. "No doubt she has other ill-gotten goods."

"I don't think so," Charlie replied evenly. "She's gone home to her sister in Tansley. But if you are worried about it, then you can cut me off. I would rather have not a single farthing than live without Sophie."

Robert sat quietly, considering his brother for a few moments. "I am tempted to call your bluff, brother."

"It's no bluff. My work with the veterans' fund has taught me one thing—that happiness cannot be bought. Many of those men and women are poor as church mice, and still love each other more than life itself. And many rub along just fine without any money. I would find an occupation and provide for my wife with my own hand."

The door opened and Mother came flying in. "Charles, what is this? Why did you come all this way and not tell us you were arriving? It is most unusual."

"He's come to tell us he will be married to Sophie despite everything," Robert interrupted. "Why, Mother, he even intends…to be poor." He drew the statement out dramatically.

"Oh, Charles, do be sensible." Mother removed her bonnet and pelisse, casting them onto a nearby chair. "Your uncle Arthur was prepared to give you everything should you wed someone…anyone. How could you cast that aside for some romantic notion?"

"I am being sensible. If you have strong objections to my chosen path, then I must sever my ties if I am to marry Sophie. And if Robert is afraid of our fortune, then I can only protect our family by foregoing my income." There, that was as plain and levelheaded as he could explain it.

Mother raised her hand. "Stop it, both of you. No one is taking anyone's fortune, and no one is going to go poor as a result of this. Robert, I must say, I am most unhappy with the way you have handled matters. You should have come to me first. Remember that Sophie Handley is Sir Hugh Handley's daughter. That family connection alone can prove most valuable to us."

"None of the family will acknowledge them," Robert retorted. "Remember, Mother, that I am the head of this household." His face was turning an ugly, mottled shade of purple.

"Ah, but the Handleys will acknowledge Sophie."

Charlie couldn't resist giving his brother a triumphant smile. "I spoke to Lord Bradbury before I came here. He has agreed to exert his influence to heal the breach within the family. So I am sure that the Handleys will, in time, come to recognize both Miss Sophie and Mrs. Brookes as part of their clan."

"There now. You see?" Mother cast her bonnet and pelisse aside and sank into the chair.

"I don't believe it." Robert shook his head. "Why would Bradbury do such a thing?"

"He's grateful to Sophie for guiding Miss Amelia through her first Season. So, in payment for her innate social skills, Bradbury is helping her to regain her place in Society." Charlie gave an elaborate shrug, keeping his expression placid. "Seems most kind of him to me."

"And to me, as well," Mother added. "Now, as to this little matter of Charles's income, I must state emphatically that no son of mine will live in poverty." Charlie opened his mouth to interrupt, but Mother overrode his objection with a curt wave of her hand. "No, indeed. I don't want to hear another word about it."

"What of my work with the veterans? I will not stop working with them, Mother. It is my calling."

"You see?" Robert slapped his hand on his desk for emphasis. "He is deliberately trying to make this family into a laughingstock. I will not stand for it. I told Sophie as much."

"I am doing no such thing." Despite his best efforts, his temper was rising. "When I lay in the farmhouse at La Sainte Haye, I thought I was dying. I prayed to God that if he let me live, I would live in a manner that honors Him." Charlie took a deep, shuddering breath.

It was difficult indeed to talk about those moments, especially to an audience that wasn't exactly sympathetic. "My brothers in arms carried me off the field and to the safety of that house, where I lay bleeding for hours. Had they not disobeyed their orders, and left me on the field, I would have died that day. I owe the men of Waterloo my very life. Surely you would not have me turn my back on them?"

Mother turned to him, her gaze misted with tears. She withdrew a handkerchief from her bodice and dabbed at the corners of her eyes. "My dear boy," she murmured. "Of course I would not have you turn your back on your fellow comrades. But can't we meet in the middle? Could you continue to work with the veterans and yet live in the manner to which we are accustomed?"

"I will not live in luxury while others suffer." It was as simple as that.

"But, Charles," Mother pleaded, dabbing at her eyes again. "Think carefully. You must be able to support a wife and family. You must allow your children to receive a good education, and have decent shelter, clothing and food. While I understand your wishes, surely you see where I am coming from."

He glanced over at Robert, who was—for once in his life—completely and utterly silent. His brother was merely running his thumbnail back and forth over the binding of his ledger. Mother pressed her handkerchief to her lips and said nothing more. Charlie sighed. Was there a way to preserve his integrity and still give his family a comfortable life?

"If I gave up my home in Bath," he began, and then paused.

"Yes?" Mother's tone was hopeful—cheerful, even.

"We would settle where Sophie chooses. Assuming she will even have me after the way my family has treated her."

"Of course." Mother smiled brightly. "Sophie has infinitely good taste. I am sure she will choose something quite stylish."

Stylish? Already he was regretting this compromise. "We will let the lady decide, Mother," he said, a thread of warning running through his voice. "And you, Robert? What say you on the matter?"

"I never knew you almost died," Robert said in a husky tone. His brother's Adam's apple bobbed up and down a few times as he tried to go on. "I mean, I knew you were gravely injured. After all, you lost your arm. I suppose I just never really thought about all you went through. My apologies, brother." Robert turned away from them both. "If you marry Sophie, you will have no objections from me."

Charlie smiled with relief. The long struggle was over. "I forgive you, if you forgive me. In fact, I owe both you and Mother an apology. I have been so blinded by my mission that I haven't taken the time or the effort to explain myself to you. Nor have I been willing, until now, to seek a compromise between our disparate ways of living."

"Oh, my boys, how good it is to hear you both so willing to forgive and forget. Now, Charlie, when are you going to seek Sophie's hand? After all, there is much planning to do. The gown, the wedding supper, the trousseau—surely I must talk to the bride soon."

As she spoke, Charlie's heart hardened in the same way it always had, shutting out her voice and her words. Then he caught his brother's glance across the desk. Robert was staring at Mother, a bemused expression on his face. As their glances caught, Robert chuckled. Charlie couldn't resist joining him. They laughed as they had in the old days, when they were young lads catching frogs in the creek bed, before Society and position and rules had dictated their days.

Their laughter broke down the last bit of a wall around Charlie's heart. He could feel it crash to the ground. That was Mother—always concerned with appearances. And she always would be. Now if he could only make Sophie love them in the way he had learned to—and persuade her to marry into this family.

It had been a white night. Sophie woke, bathed in sweat and tears, from a nightmare. Charlie was dying in the farmhouse, and no one was there to help him. She sat up in bed, her hands trembling, and lit a candle from the tinderbox on her bedside table. It was just a dream. No need to cry. Charlie was alive and well, and probably thanking his lucky stars he had extricated himself from a doomed marriage to her.

Her door opened, and Harriet poked her head around the frame. "Sophie, are you all right? I thought I heard you cry out."

"I had a terrible dream about Charlie." Sophie patted the soft surface of the bed beside her. "Do you mind sitting up with me for a while?"

"Of course not." Harriet lowered herself onto the bed cautiously. "I have many more months to go, and yet I get bigger every day. John will have to widen all the doorways for me to fit through." She pulled Sophie's head onto her shoulder and patted her back. "There now. It was only a dream."

"I know." Sophie wiped the last of the tears away with the back of her hand. "I miss him so, Hattie."

"I understand." Harriet continued soothing her, patting her back in a rhythmic motion. "Have you tried to write to him? Or give him any indication of how you feel?"

"No. I was so hateful to him when we were in Brightgate. It was my intention to send him away, and I did. I was cruel, Hattie. Terribly cruel." Tears spilled down her cheeks anew.

"Surely he understands why you did that. Men can be very acute," Harriet murmured. "I would not give up hope yet."

Sophie gave vent to her bottled emotions, crying as she had not done since Mama died. Everything was such a muddle. And the terrible part was, there was no way to repair the damage she had done. Short of driving back to Bath and flinging herself at him, begging forgiveness, there was nothing she could do. And of course, there was the sneaking suspicion that she would never, ever win him back, no matter what she did. Charlie was nothing if not absolute.

Harriet said no more, but let her cry. Only when her sobs had subsided to the occasional hiccup did she speak again. "Sophie, why do you love the lieutenant so? Why wouldn't you be just as happy with someone else?"

"He opened the world to me." Sophie dried her eyes on the hem of her nightgown. "Until I met him, I was still spoiled and flighty. Mama's death sobered me a good deal, but it wasn't until I knew Charlie and began working with him that I saw real poverty. And I wanted to help. I wanted to be a part of something bigger than myself." She gave a long, shuddering sigh. "He helped me to find God. Because of him, I am a better person."

"It seems to me that is worth fighting for," Harriet said softly. "You shouldn't give up so easily if he had such a profound effect on your life."

"What would you have me do? Rush to Bath and beg his forgiveness?" Really, sometimes Hattie didn't think things through, sensible as she usually was.

"I would at least send a letter," Harriet replied crisply, sitting up straighter and dislodging Sophie from her shoulder. "Tell him how you feel. Did you not aid and abet me in my pursuit of John? Surely I have earned the right to meddle in your affairs."

"Very well." Sophie sighed, pulling the coverlet up higher. Harriet was right. There was probably more dignity in writing, too, since she had more time to consider what she must say. And though writing was never her passion or her interest, she did have a famous novelist for a sister. Surely Hattie could be persuaded to help her put her thoughts on paper. "I shall work on a letter in the morning."

"And you'll post it in the afternoon," Harriet replied in her bossiest tone. "I shall see to it." She heaved herself off the bed with some difficulty.

"I'm sorry I awakened you, Hattie," Sophie said as

she snuggled against the pillows. "Can you go back to sleep?"

"I'll try. I haven't been sleeping well, so you really didn't wake me up. I cannot find a comfortable way to sleep with this large ball I have strapped around my middle." She patted her stomach thoughtfully. "Good night."

"Good night, dearest Hattie." Sophie blew out the candle as her sister left. Now she had to think of the right words to say—words of love and warmth that would ease the pain of her last meeting with Charlie.

It was a formidable task, indeed.

Chapter Twenty-Four

'Twas a mere hour and a half carriage ride to Tansley Village from Brightgate. All one needed to do was begin driving east toward Matlock. If Charlie struck out this morning as he intended, then he would be at Brookes Park in time for luncheon. It was the last leg of his journey, and while it was so close at hand, every moment would be an eternity.

He dressed with haste and packed his few bags while the hired hack was brought around to the front of the house. He extracted the ring Sophie had returned that terrible day at the inn, the ring he had kept in a box in his study for these past few weeks. The jewels flashed in the early morning light, dignified and refined. His grandmother and grandfather had not been as wealthy as his parents, but they spent the money they earned very well. This ring was presented to his grandmother late in life, when his grandfather had sealed a particularly good shipping deal. That accounted for the gem's large size, and the modern style of its setting. It had looked particularly good on Sophie when it was hers. 'Twas time to see it on her hand once more.

He carried his bags down the mahogany staircase and deposited them at the front door.

"Charles? Is that you?" Mother called from the breakfast room.

"It is, Mother. I am about to strike out for Tansley."

"Come in here, my boy. I have something for you."

Charlie resisted the impulse to roll his eyes. Impatience to get on the road fairly sizzled through his being. He had no time for his mother's little anecdotes or words of wisdom. And yet, one still had to respect family.

He entered the breakfast nook and eyed his mother. Her lace cap—a particularly elaborate affair she had purchased in London, all trimmed out with purple roses—bobbed up from her breakfast plate of shirred eggs and bacon.

"This came for you in the post yesterday. I only just saw it." She flicked a letter down the length of the table at him.

Charlie picked it up. The letter crackled. It was written on a strange, brittle paper, rather like woven bits of tree bark. He unfolded it slowly, taking care not to break it. The vellum was covered in a spidery handwriting—so thin he had to squint to read it.

"Is it from your uncle Arthur?" Mother trilled. "I would recognize his ghastly handwriting anywhere."

Charlie's brow lowered as he tried to make out the words. "I think it's from him. I am having a terrible time making sense out of anything he wrote. Can you read it, Mother? Since you are more familiar with his handwriting." He cast the letter back over to her.

Mother pulled out her lorgnette and held it up to the

vellum. "Arthur is doing well," she replied. "Oh, my dear Charlie—he has such news for you!"

"Well, then read it, Mother." Really, this was getting beyond tiresome.

"'My dear nephew,'" Mother read aloud. "'Your mother wrote to me about your work with the veterans of Bath. As a military man myself, and a wounded veteran at that, I applaud your efforts. Originally I was to make you my heir if you wed. But the more I consider the matter, the more convinced I am that you must continue to do your good work without fear of having to earn an independent income or the pressures of providing for a family.'" Mother broke off, pursing her lips. She was drawing it out for dramatic effect. Depend on Mother to go in for drama at just such a crucial moment.

"Go on," Charlie replied tersely. He wasn't enjoying this one bit. His heart pounded in his chest.

"'I am, therefore, providing you with the sum of two thousand pounds per annum so that you may live and marry where you choose while continuing your work with the veterans. I do ask that you write often to me and keep me apprised of your progress. I shall send a letter to my solicitor in Matlock, who will make the funds available to you. God bless you, my nephew. With affection, Uncle Arthur.'"

The life drained out of his legs. He sank into a chair. His mouth hung open—he was gawking, but couldn't help himself. "What does this mean?" he asked gruffly.

"It means, my dear son, that you no longer have to worry about pleasing anyone. Your uncle has made you independent. You may marry Sophie, help the widows, help your veterans, and never have to worry about Robert paying you a farthing." Mother folded the letter crisply and slid it across the polished surface of the table.

Charlie halted its progress with the tips of his fingers. "But why? I don't understand."

"Have you been helping others for so long that you have forgotten what it is like to be blessed yourself? This is your uncle's decision. I knew I was doing the right thing in telling him of your engagement and your work with the soldiers." Mother beamed. "Now run along to Tansley. Your future bride is waiting." She shooed him with a playful wave of her hand.

Charlie rose, shaking his head. "Can this even be legal, Mother? How can I be his beneficiary?"

"He has no wife, no children. We don't share any other brothers and sisters, you know. His great wealth is his to do with as he pleases. And he has decided to settle it on you." Mother straightened her cap and turned her attention back to her cup of tea. "Be gone, Charlie. You are wasting daylight."

"I know I have received a gift, but I don't know how to show my gratitude." Charlie turned toward the door. "Mother, surely you had no idea about this. I feel certain you must be as befuddled as I am."

Mother shrugged. "It's Arthur's money to do with as he sees fit. After all, he has no heirs. And for him to give the money to you because he admires your life's purpose is most gratifying. And of course, it clears the path so you may marry Sophie." Mother smiled brightly. "I have always liked Sophie. Such impeccable breeding. Such a fine old family."

Ah, there was the real Moriah Cantrill. Charlie couldn't suppress the smile that crept across his face.

"Thank you, Mother."

"You are welcome, son. Now, go forth and betroth yourself to a Handley gel."

The miles between Brightgate and Tansley rolled by achingly slow, and Charlie read and reread Uncle Arthur's missive at least a dozen times on the journey. He was able to pick out the words now that Mother had interpreted his uncle's messy, thin handwriting. What she read was true. Uncle Arthur was providing him with a fortune so he could continue his work with the veterans and widows in Bath.

That part of his future was settled. But what lay ahead, he had no clue. The carriage bounced and jolted along the rocky road that led to Tansley, and with each bump Charlie racked his brain for a way to approach Sophie. Would she be willing to receive him, or would she send him away without deigning to say even a simple good afternoon?

Really, charging into battle was more certain than this morning would be. At least one knew what to expect in battle. His mind drifted back to La Sainte Haye—the stench of gunpowder, the groans of the injured, the screaming horses. And then—blackness. So often, he had been ashamed of the fact that he had fainted from his injury. Was he less of a man because he had given way to unconsciousness? Should he have been left to die there on the battlefield? Why did his men save him, only to return to the battle and die themselves?

Whatever God's reason for sparing him, Charlie was

determined to continue living in a manner that both glorified Him and helped Charlie's comrades. And now, thanks to Uncle Arthur, he could continue doing so. But that life seemed quite austere and cheerless and cold without the prospect of Sophie Handley in it.

As the carriage continued its interminable journey east, Charlie prayed. He prayed as he never had a chance to during the battle. For wisdom, for courage and, most of all, for love. There was nothing he could do without love. He realized that now—his entire work and life's purpose was built around giving back love.

The carriage entered the Park gates and continued meandering up the long gravel driveway that banked to a tight C-shape in front of the massive stone facade of the house. He had not been here in many months, and yet nothing had changed so far as he could tell. This house was as dignified as his mother's home was smug. Despite his uncertainty, Brookes Park welcomed him.

He quit the carriage as soon as it halted. "I'll send someone down to attend the horses," he called over his shoulder to the coachman.

A pair of boots crunched on the gravel. "I'll see to them," a familiar, rough voice called.

Charlie turned, a grin breaking across his face. How good to see Stoames. "Ho there, my good man," he called.

"Good morning, Lieutenant. How are you doing? The captain wasn't expecting you, was he? He didn't mention your visit to me this morning." Stoames held out his weather-beaten hand.

Charlie grasped his had warmly. "My visit is a surprise, I must confess. Is the captain at home?"

Stoames nodded. "He's in the study, working on his morning ledgers." He coughed and then lowered his voice. "Mrs. Brookes and Miss Sophie have walked into the village." He cocked a knowing glance at Charlie, a half smile tugging at his lips.

A rush of heat swept over Charlie, and he was powerless to fight it. He was blushing like a schoolboy, but there was nothing he could do about it now. "Oh, yes. I'll go see the captain right away, then."

"Need me to do a bit of announcing?" Stoames eyed him warily. "From what I gathered, the captain is not exactly pleased with your family right now."

Ah, just as he had suspected. And Brookes had a formidable temper when provoked. He would have to proceed with caution. "No, thank you, Stoames. Brookes is right to be upset. But I have come to make amends."

"Very good, Lieutenant." Stoames bowed respectfully and indicated the house with a wave of his hand. "In that case, you know the way to the study."

"I do." As Charlie mounted the steps, he racked his brains for a way to talk to Brookes without infuriating him further. He was right to be upset.

Charlie's boots rang hollowly on the parquet as he strode down the hallway to the study. Were the tables turned, Charlie would have been absolutely livid. It would take all his soldierly instinct and diplomacy to find a way to broach the matter delicately.

He pushed open the study door, and paused on the threshold. "What ho, Brookes?"

Brookes glanced up, his expression turning from mild surprise to frank distaste upon seeing his old friend. "You—you blackguard," he thundered, coming around the desk with his unusual loping gait, the result of his war injury. "How dare you show your face here, after breaking my sister-in-law's heart?"

Charlie held his hands up to signal a truce. "You are perfectly right to plant me a facer, Brookes. But first, you should hear why I have come."

"The only way I could be angrier is if you brought that scoundrel Bradbury with you," Brookes roared, his face turning a darker shade of red. "How dare you treat Sophie in that way?"

"Brookes, hark what I am saying." Charlie took a step backward. "I have come to make amends. After you hear me out, you can throw me out on my ear, I promise."

Brookes paused, clenching his teeth. A muscle in his jaw-line twitched. "Very well. I will listen to you for five minutes. Not a second more."

"I'll only need three." With that, Charlie stepped into the study and closed the door behind him.

"Aren't you glad you posted the letter?" Harriet said in her best elder-sister tone, as they neared the outskirts of the village, walking arm in arm.

"Yes." Sophie sighed. "But there is something so unseemly in writing to Charlie. As though I am begging for his attention."

"Don't be so prideful," Harriet admonished. "Pride has been the downfall of many a person in our family. And besides, you said nothing you did not mean. All you told him was how very grateful you are to have met him, and how profoundly he changed your life. Would you be upset or mortified to receive such a letter?" Harriet steered Sophie from the well-worn village path to the sweet meadow grasses that led toward Brookes Park.

"No, I would not be angry to get a letter like that. Especially not from Charlie." But her inner coquette would not be shushed. It was the man's job to chase, and the woman's job to dangle herself alluringly, just out of reach enough to tantalize. She had been taught so from infancy, and it felt wrong to go against that ingrained practice.

The sun was hidden behind some gathering clouds—another storm was surely on the way. The two sisters trudged down the meadow, which smelled sweetly damp as the long grasses were ruffled by the eastern wind. They walked on in companionable silence, as Sophie grew absorbed in her thoughts.

Soon Brookes Park—familiar, safe, comfortable—loomed into view. Sophie smiled as she gazed at it.

"I love it here." She blurted the words out before she even knew what she was saying.

"Hmm. I agree. As I once told John, I feel closer to God out here, as though I can touch the sky. But I thought the splendors of Bath were more in keeping with your style." Harriet stumbled slightly as her skirts caught in the moor grass. Sophie steadied her with a gentle hand and held her arm more tightly.

"I once thought so. But no more. I love this gentle peace, the sight of the clouds clustered on the horizon, the tiny waves that lap the mill pond. Thank you for allowing me to stay at the Park. I cannot express my gratitude enough."

"Oh, Sophie. You know that the Park will always be your home, no matter what the future holds." Harriet squeezed her arm more tightly about Sophie's waist. "I would reserve your planning, though, until you have heard back from the lieutenant."

They entered the Park gates and crossed the driveway toward the large fountain. "Girls!" a familiar voice cried. Sophie looked up as Rose scurried toward them, her half boots sending the gravel flying. "Such a to-do! Upon my word!" Her bonnet strings streamed out behind her.

"Rose? Whatever is the matter?" Harriet broke into a run, tugging Sophie along with her. "Is the captain all right?"

"Slow down, Harriet. You'll harm yourself or the baby," Sophie warned. She pulled at Harriet's arm until she was obliged to slow her steps to a trot. "Rose," she called. "Is everything all right?"

Rose ran up to the sisters and clutched their shoulders, her breath coming in short pants. "Mr. Stoames told me about it first," she gasped. "Lieutenant Cantrill has returned. The pair of them are locked up in the captain's study, and what a rumpus has ensued. They have been shouting at each other for well nigh on a quarter of an hour at least."

"Dear me," Harriet gasped. She sat on the side of the fountain, her eyes darkened so blue they were almost black.

Sophie stood, shaking, staring up at the window of Brookes's study. The man she adored was there, arguing with her brother-in-law. Yelling at him, in point of fact. What did it signify? Why was he here? The blood pounded in her ears, and she had trouble focusing her vision. It was blurred with unshed tears.

"Harriet, Rose," she murmured, her voice trembling. "I think I must go to see the lieutenant now."

Every footstep was like moving through molasses. Every sound was muted to a strange hush, a buzz sounding in her ears. She was going to see her beloved. For, no matter what he had to say or why he had come, Lieutenant Charles Cantrill would always be the only man she had ever loved, and he must know that. She must tell him that.

Chapter Twenty-Five

"Name one good reason why I shouldn't drive you out of this house right now," Brookes thundered, pounding his fist on his desk. "Your family has behaved in an infamous manner toward my sister-in-law. She fled Bath in tears after your rejection and Bradbury's untoward offer. How dare you even show your face at Brookes Park?"

"You have a right to be angry, Brookes. But please, hear what I have to say." Charlie was poised for a fight, his defenses rising. Brookes would likely throw a punch in a matter of moments unless he spoke quickly and cleverly to quash his anger.

"Your brother sent some hired minion to check up on the Handley family," Brookes countered, his eyes blazing the same steely gray as the sword he carried into battle. "How dare you, sir? What makes the Cantrill clan—a passel of shopkeepers, no less—think themselves so far above the Handleys, who are nobility? How dare you question the lineage of my wife and her sister?"

"I don't." That cut about the Cantrills being shopkeepers aroused his ire, and he struggled to keep his own temper in check. "Robert was checking up on the Handleys and their refusal to support Miss Sophie and Miss Harriet after their father passed. He was looking after my best interests, but he did so without my knowledge or consent."

"Are you under your brother's thumb? Or are you a man?" Brookes challenged, poking his forefinger at Charlie's face. "From what I understand, my sister-in-law offered to help you, so that you could cut yourself free of your mama's apron strings." His face contorted in a mocking grin. "And after she did all of that for you, you have the gall to allow your family to run roughshod over her—"

"Enough," Charlie barked. He took a deep breath. Matters were getting well out of hand. Brookes was well on his way to inciting fisticuffs unless they both calmed down. "Sophie offered to help me, and I deeply appreciated her offer. She is the dearest, sweetest girl I know, and it was a dream come true for a wretch like me to even pretend to court her."

Brookes said nothing, his jaw clenched and his hands doubled up into fists at his side. The situation was still precarious. He must proceed with caution.

"I am not proud of what my family has done, and I told them so in no uncertain terms. They know now that what they did was wrong—unforgiveable, even."

The door to the study opened, and Sophie stood on the threshold. Her skin was so pale it shone with translucence, her eyes like wide reflecting pools of uncertainty and astonishment. He took two steps forward, ready to crush her in an embrace.

"Stand right where you are," Brookes admonished him. Then he turned to Sophie. "Sister, I must ask you to leave. We are having a discussion—"

"It sounds rather like a fight," Sophie replied calmly. "And I have no intention of leaving. Brookes, I appreciate all you are doing. You are a dear for defending me so. But you must know that I sent Charlie away. I behaved awfully to him. I broke our engagement."

"Is that true?" Brookes asked, staring daggers at Charlie.

"It is. But I knew she never meant it." He crossed over to Sophie and caught her around the waist. "Sweetest Sophie, I knew what you did—you drove me away because you thought it was the right thing to do. But it wasn't. It was cruel and foolish. We are meant to be together, you and I. And I will never leave your side again." He pressed her close, relishing the sight of her golden curls and dimpled cheeks. He kissed the top of her head reverently, drinking in the scent of her—a scent of violets and fresh moor air.

"I ask your forgiveness, Sophie," he murmured. "I fought my love for you for too long. I was so hurt by being jilted, and so determined to be right, that I pushed you away at every turn. And you, my darling, returned each time, so full of forgiveness and love that it shamed me. When I found what my family had done and what Bradbury asked you to do—" Sophie squirmed in his embrace, hiding her face on his shoulder "—no need to be embarrassed, Sophie. You chose the right path. And I was determined to also do the right thing, and I have taken a journey of forgiveness. Forgiving others and asking them to do the same."

He bent down, peering into her face. "Can you forgive me, Sophie?"

Unshed tears sparkled in her eyes. "Of course," she whispered. "Do you forgive me for the awful things I said?"

"I never believed them for a moment." He nuzzled her forehead with his lips. "I've already forgotten them."

"Harrumph," Brookes coughed. Charlie glanced up, still holding Sophie tightly. He had forgotten that Brookes was even in the room.

"So if I understand matters, it would be most unsporting of me to throw Charlie out on his ear?" Brookes queried Sophie, his eyebrows quirked in a rueful manner.

"Quite," she chuckled.

"I suppose, then, that I should leave you two in peace for a few moments." As he passed by them, he gave Charlie's shoulder a brotherly slug. "Too bad. I was enjoying the thought of knocking you on your bum."

Charlie threw back his head, laughing. "Brookes, I must ask your forgiveness, too, and Harriet's. I must tender my apologies on behalf of my family. I know that both Robert and Mother are truly sorry for criticizing the Handley clan."

"All is well," Brookes replied evenly. "And now, I must go find my wife. I am sure she is beside herself with wonderment, and will want to know exactly what has transpired." He left, closing the door to the study behind him.

Charlie led Sophie over to the settee, settling her on his lap as he wrapped his injured arm around her waist. "Sophie, before I can ask you what I have come to ask, I must tell you one thing. I fought my love for you for so long because I could not reconcile my desire for austerity with the need to provide for a wife. I was afraid I couldn't give you the life you deserved while still following my life calling."

"That doesn't matter, Charlie," she whispered, stroking his chin with the tip of her forefinger. "I don't care for fine clothes or a large home. All the things that my mother taught me to value I realized long ago don't matter a bit. What matters is that you opened my eyes to an entirely new world. I am a better person because of you."

He struggled against the rising tide of emotion in his chest—gratitude, humble awe and an overwhelming sense of finally being at peace with the world. He closed his eyes and said a silent prayer—beseeching God that he would be worthy of this woman now and forever.

"I can finally ask you this question because the way has been cleared for me to have the best of both possible worlds—my work with the soldiers and my love for you. I am now an independent man, Sophie. My uncle Arthur has given me a living so that I might continue working with the soldiers. I can hold out no longer—Sophie, will you please do me the honor of becoming my wife?"

He said the words. The words she longed to hear ever since she first bumped into him on the rainy streets of Bath, and he had saved her from being lost and unprotected. And he wasn't saying them out of a sense of obligation. He wasn't saying them because they were pretending to be courting and matters went too far. He had come all this way and faced Brookes's anger to say them to her, and her alone.

She trembled a little in his embrace. Love swept over her like a wave. How marvelous to be by his side for the rest of their lives, working together, hoping and planning together. Except—

"Your family must still object to me. Robert said—"

"Never mind what Robert said," Charlie interrupted, squeezing her tight. "I had a long talk with my mother and my brother. I explained what you meant to me, how profoundly you changed my life. How working with you to benefit the soldiers was the purpose of my life—indeed, my calling. And how you had sacrificed everything—including that bracelet—to help make my dreams a reality." He chuckled softly, leaning his forehead against hers. "Naturally, that overcame every objection they had."

She leaned against his warmth, savoring the feeling of his strong embrace. They sat so in silence, broken only by the ticking of the clock on the mantelpiece and the beating of his heart against her ear. At length, Charlie murmured, "Sophie?"

"Yes?"

"Are…are you going to marry me?" His voice betrayed a hint of uncertainty. Oh, dear. She had been so wrapped up in the security of his arms that she forgot to say the words.

"Charlie," she replied, gazing deeply into his dark brown eyes. "I can think of nothing I want more in this life than to become your wife."

"Thank you. I am so blessed to have you, my darling." With that, he lowered his head to hers and captured her lips sweetly. She returned the kiss with all the pent-up longing and warmth she had held for him in her heart all these long months. When they broke apart, he clasped her closer, and she laid her head back against his chest, relishing the closeness of her beloved.

"Charlie, where will we live?" His work took him to Bath, and yet she wasn't sure she wanted to live there. Too many memories. Most of them bad, and most of them fairly recent.

"I don't know. I was going to let you decide. My flat in Bath is, I fear, not comfortable enough for a wife and—" his face reddened adorably "—children. We can live anywhere you wish. Now that I am independent, we can settle where we choose."

"I know your work is in Bath, but I feel I must stay close to Harriet," she responded. "Now that she is increasing—"

"Harriet is increasing? That is wonderful news." He grinned at her, a sweet, boyish grin that caused her heart to leap in her chest. "Of course you want to stay close to her during this time."

"But how can we reconcile my need to stay in Tansley with your work in Bath?" Sophie wondered aloud, plucking at his shirtsleeve. "I don't want to halt your progress with the fund, and I do want to work with the widows to start a sewing bee of sorts. What say you, Charlie? How shall we do everything we want?"

He sat for a moment, running his fingers over the top of her hand. She shivered a little at his touch.

"We could settle in Tansley for part of the year, and then go to Bath during the other portion to work on the fund," he replied. "I could ask the reverend to help with managing things whilst I am gone, and perhaps you could have someone help with running your sewing bee. We could even give the reverend and your helper a stipend so they are able to help us while still earning a bit of an income."

"That's a wonderful idea, Charlie. I could appoint Lucy." Lucy would be attending all the veterans' meetings, anyway, if for no other reason than to pay a call on the ensign. "I was thinking today about how wonderful Tansley is, and how much it has become my home. Now I shall have the best of everything—my beloved husband, my family and our work that brings us such peace and joy."

She reached up and kissed the rough stubble of his chin, and he responded by gathering her close and kissing her dimples. A discreet knock at the door, and they sprang apart.

"Sophie? May I come in?" Harriet called.

"Of course," Sophie responded, tumbling off Charlie's lap. They both stood and faced the door expectantly, Charlie standing protectively by her side.

Harriet pushed open the door, Brookes hovering in the background. "Charlie," she said with a hesitant smile. "How lovely to see you again."

He bowed. "Mrs. Brookes. You look radiant."

"Such formality!" Sophie chuckled. "After all, he will be your brother soon."

Harriet's grin widened, her dark blue eyes sparkling. "Lieutenant, is this true?"

"Quite," he responded. "Your sister has turned me into a changed man. Thanks to her, I released all the rankling bitterness in my heart, and opened myself to love. And all I can do to thank her is offer her myself—a very poor consolation prize, indeed."

"I couldn't agree more," Brookes grumbled from behind Harriet. She turned and smacked his shoulder playfully.

"What? Why strike me?" Brookes responded. "As far as I can tell, he has not even given your sister a ring."

"That's quite enough," Harriet admonished, and enveloped both Charlie and Sophie in a warm embrace despite her round belly. She turned to Sophie, placing both hands on her shoulders.

"Are you still glad you posted your letter today?"

Her letter! Likely it would reach Charlie's flat in just a matter of days. What an astonishing day it had been. She had woken this morning full of heartache and longing, and now—now she had everything she wanted. "Yes. It will be my wedding gift to my husband."

Charlie was looking at them both, his brow furrowed, a smile tugging at the corners of his mouth. "What letter? Did you decide to jilt me once and for all?"

"On the contrary. I threw myself at your head. Fortunately, I have a famous novelist for a sister, one who can help me craft the most romantic letters of our age." Sophie winked at Harriet. "I am sure my missive will soothe your masculine pride to no end once you read it."

"Then I cannot wait to receive it." Charlie fumbled in his jacket pocket and produced a small box. "As my astute brother in arms just reminded me, I have a gift for you, as well." He opened the box, extracting his grandmother's ring—the ring she had worn so proudly for those few glorious days in Brightgate.

Sophie extended her left hand, and he slipped the

ring on her finger. Unlike the glittering fetter the diamond bracelet from Lord Bradbury had become, this ring was a glowing promise of a bright future. She clasped her hands together, staring at the prisms of light reflected in the jewels.

"That's better, Cantrill. Now, we should all sit down over luncheon and discuss what the wedding plans will be," Brookes reminded them in his gruff voice. "After all, it's quite likely that Aunt Katherine is already on her way to take over all the plans. If she finds that Harriet and Sophie haven't even considered her dress, or that you and I haven't seen to reading the banns, then she will be all a-swither."

"Very true, John." Harriet took his hand. "I believe Rose has already set out our repast in the dining room and even included an extra place for Charlie. Shall we go?"

"Indeed." Sophie took Charlie's hand, and smiled up at him. "'Whither thou goest, I will go,'" she whispered.

"'Thy people shall be my people,'" Charlie murmured, turning that same crooked grin on her that always reduced her knees to jelly. She was the luckiest woman in the world. She had her beloved, her family and a purpose beyond her own whims and desires.

Life was complete. She could ask for nothing more.

Chapter Twenty-Six

November, 1818
St. Mary's church, Crich, Derbyshire

"Nervous?" Brookes joked, coming to stand by Charlie at the altar.

"A bit, yes." There was no use hiding his feelings from anyone. Surely every person crowding the tiny country chapel this morning could see his shaking hand, his profusely sweating forehead. He patted it once more with his handkerchief and tucked the scrap of linen back into his pocket.

"Don't worry." Brookes slapped him heartily on the shoulder. "Just say 'I will' to everything the reverend asks you, and you will make out just fine."

Charlie nodded. He cast a glance around the pews. Aunt Katherine sat in the front row, decked out in violet, plying herself with a silk fan even though it threatened to snow outside. Lord Bradbury and his two daughters sat behind them, the girls flaunting two gowns that Sophie had made for them during her last few weeks in Bath. Veterans and widows alike filled two rows within the chapel, their transportation from Bath to Derbyshire arranged by his lordship, who, it must be admitted, had become quite a patron of their organization.

Brookes grinned. "Try not to look so much like a green lad gawking about," he admonished. "In no time at all, you'll be wed and wondering how on earth you deserve such a glorious creature. I know. I felt the same way when I married her sister. Speaking of whom, I must check on my wife. I don't want her on her feet all day when she's in such a state."

Brookes disappeared up the aisle just as Mother and Robert entered the chapel. Mother bustled up to him, the feathers on her cap fluttering as she scurried. "Darling, I have just seen Sophie," she breathed, catching his arm. "She looks beautiful. Simply radiant."

"Where is she?" Charlie's heart beat a nervous tattoo against his rib cage. Surely the ceremony would be starting soon. He didn't exactly relish being on display like this, even if it was his own friends and family eyeing him expectantly.

"She's putting the finishing touches on her appearance over at Reverend Kirk's house. I must say, it's very odd for you to have two men of the cloth performing your ceremony. Wouldn't one be ample?" Mother quirked her eyebrow and looked at Robert. "Don't you agree, my boy?"

"I think it's a grand gesture. Reverend Kirk has meant a lot to Sophie's family, and Reverend Stephens brought the two of them together," Robert replied with a shrug.

"Precisely." Charlie smiled at his brother.

The two reverends entered the chapel at that moment, talking together cordially as they walked up the aisle. Mother gave his cheek a quick peck, then she and Robert both took their seats in the pews.

The ceremony must be about to start. For there was Brookes, escorting a considerably rounder Harriet to their pew, and an expectant hush fell over the assembled crowd. Lucy Williams, clad in a dark rose gown that Sophie had stitched, paused at the top of the aisle, smiling broadly. Yes, it was beginning.

His every nerve was trained on the lovely creature in white who walked slowly up the aisle. Her very presence drew all the air out of the chapel. He fought to catch his breath as she turned toward him and smiled. How unreal, how very unbelievable, that she was coming to stand by him, to pledge her troth, her undying love, for the rest of their days.

He was the luckiest man alive.

Reverend Kirk spoke first, asking Sophie in his kind but gruff old voice if she would honor and love Charlie for the rest of his days. Her voice, clear as a bell, rang out every response. "I will."

Then Reverend Stephens took over, asking Charlie the same questions. His mind echoed Brookes's advice, and he merely parroted "I will," whenever the reverend paused. He could barely understand anything that was being said, as he contemplated his lovely bride with growing wonderment.

And then the ceremony ended and the entire company spilled across the frozen church lawn, streaming into Reverend Kirk's manse, which had been prepared especially for the assembled company to partake in a hearty, old-fashioned wedding breakfast. Charlie caught his bride's hand and led her into the vicarage, still in awe that he was married. To Sophie Handley. No, not Sophie Handley any longer. She was Sophie Cantrill.

"Are you all right?" she whispered, clutching his hand more tightly. "You look rather pale."

"I'm fine." He could not even begin to articulate how he was feeling, especially not with so many people about. He would tell her everything tonight, when they would be finally and blessedly alone.

She smiled, but her eyes held a worried and puzzled glint. He patted her back in what he hoped was a reassuring manner, and led her toward the breakfast room.

Harriet rounded the corner, nearly colliding with them both. "Sophie! Charlie, may I borrow my sister for a moment?"

"Of course." He bowed and released his hold on her back.

"Harriet, whatever is the matter? We are supposed to start the wedding breakfast."

"I know, but I have a surprise for you." Harriet grabbed Sophie's hand and tugged her down the hallway. "We will return shortly, Charlie."

Whatever was Harriet about? The crowd was milling around, waiting patiently for breakfast. The enticing scents of bacon and fried potatoes wafted through the little house. His stomach gurgled. He had been too nervous to even eat the roll Stoames had brought him while he was dressing that morning. Now that the ceremony was over and his nervousness ebbed, hunger gnawed at his insides like a hungry wolf. If only they would hurry up.

"Scone, Lieutenant?" Reverend Stephens passed him

a packet wrapped in a handkerchief, which gave forth the mouthwatering scents of vanilla and lemon peel.

"Dare I eat while the assembled company waits?" he asked with a laugh.

The reverend smiled. "In my experience, the bride and groom have precious little time to partake of wedding breakfasts, so occupied are they with good wishes and congratulations," he replied. He beckoned Charlie to an abandoned corner of the room. "Eat quickly. It will help you make it through the morning."

Charlie unwrapped the scone with a grateful sigh. "This must be Rose's cooking. Heavenly."

The reverend nodded. "I poached one from the breakfast table this morning, after I conferred with Reverend Kirk." He gave a conspiratorial wink. "Now that you are receiving a little sustenance to make it through the day, how do you feel?"

"Better. Awestruck. Unworthy. But better." Charlie polished off the last of the scone, and brushed the crumbs off his fingertips.

Reverend Stephens gave him a crooked grin. "Always with the eternal tally, eh, Lieutenant? Isn't that what got you in trouble the first time around? Always checking in to see who was right, who was wrong and who was deserving of what they received? Surely you learned something from the task I gave you. You forgave everyone else. Now you must forgive yourself."

"Forgive myself for what?" The reverend's words made no sense.

"For being human." The reverend turned and left, leaving Charlie alone in the corner.

The wedding guests milled around, talking, laughing and embracing one another. Aunt Katherine chatted with Stoames and Rose, who stood side by side. Ensign Rowland listened, his eyes wide with fascination, as Lucy talked to him, her lips moving a mile a minute. Lord Bradbury held the hands of his two daughters and twirled them around, smiling at Mother and Robert. They were all here to celebrate his union with Sophie. His heart surged with gratitude, and he said a silent prayer of thanks for them—flawed, exasperating and wonderful as they were—who all occupied a space in his life and a place in his heart.

Sophie sat in the same spare bedroom she had dressed in earlier that morning, and reread the letter Harriet handed to her. "I don't understand this at all. None of it makes sense."

"I don't understand it, either," Harriet replied, her eyebrows drawn together. "I knew nothing of it until Reverend Kirk gave me the letter this morning."

"Why did he send the letter to Reverend Kirk? Why not send it directly to you?"

"I don't know. Maybe he was unsure of where to send it. Or perhaps he wanted the reverend to act on his behalf, in case we were unhappy with the contents of the letter for any reason." Harriet shrugged.

Sophie reread the letter aloud.

"'Dear Misses Harriet and Sophie,

"A misunderstanding has long existed between our families, and I have decided that it is time to heal the breach. My family wishes to extend our deepest sympathy to you for your mother's recent passing, and to congratulate Miss Harriet on her marriage to Captain

John Brookes. We also understand that Miss Sophie will also soon be wed to Lieutenant Charles Cantrill, and we wish to tender our congratulations for that blessed event, as well…'"

"How did they know I was going to be married?" Sophie asked, glancing up at Harriet from the sheet of foolscap.

"Gossip, perhaps? I really have no idea. Keep reading. I still cannot fathom it myself." Harriet plucked at the fringe of the coverlet.

"Put your feet up on the bed, or they'll start to swell," Sophie admonished. Then she turned her attention back to the letter.

"'As the head of the Handley clan, I wish to state emphatically that we do not have any objection to your family connections, and would welcome you to our home at any time, should you choose to return to Liverpool. As a sign of our good faith, I am reinstating the living your father would have left to you, had his fortunes not collapsed. The sum of three thousand pounds per annum shall be settled on you each.

"I am, most affectionately, your uncle

"David Handley."'

"So Papa's brother magically decides to gift us with a living after years of penury and neglect? Why so?" Harriet nibbled her thumbnail. "I am not sure we should accept."

"Stop biting your nails," Sophie admonished. "Of course we will accept. And we will forgive them, too. Charlie has taught me the value of forgiveness. I shall never harbor bitterness in my heart again." She folded up the foolscap and tossed it aside. "I have no need of his money, so I shall gift it all to the Veterans' Fund."

"I shall, too." Harriet struggled to get off the bed. Sophie laughed and walked around to her sister's side, giving her hands a mighty pull.

"I suppose we should return to the breakfast. Your guests will be getting hungry, and poor Charlie probably thinks I have kidnapped you forevermore," Harriet puffed, tugging her dress down over her broad middle.

Sophie nodded, and followed her sister out the bedroom door. She paused in her descent down the staircase, staring at Charlie, who was talking earnestly with Brookes and Stoames.

Charlie had done it. She was sure he had done it. She knew not how, but he was the reason that her uncle was suddenly so willing to let bygones be bygones.

Her beloved must have felt her eyes on him, for he turned, a grin lighting his thin face. She rushed down the staircase and flung herself into his embrace. "Thank you." She sighed, closing her ears to the laughter of the assembled company.

"For what?" He held her tightly—so tightly she could scarcely draw breath.

"For being wonderful." She would spend the rest of her life trying to keep that same crooked, boyish grin on her beloved's face.

Smoke curled lazily from the chimney of Tansley Cottage as Charlie and Sophie's carriage wound its way down the rocky path. "Look, Rose kept the fire going all day, even when we were at Crich. How marvelous she is." Sophie brushed a minuscule speck of dust from her white woolen frock. It was one of her finest creations, and she had no wish for it to be marred by dirt before the day was even over.

"What a pretty little cottage," Charlie observed. "Just the right size for us two."

"Until our family grows," Sophie added, her face heating to her hairline.

Charlie reddened, too, and his eyes flashed with a dangerous light. "Of course. But it will do quite nicely until we find our permanent home. Isn't this a lovely place to live, all tucked up against the moor like this? It quite puts my flat in Bath to shame."

"Yes, in some ways. But you must understand, back then we had so very little. And Mama was quite ill. I didn't realize it at the time, but Hattie was protecting me from a great deal of bald truths about our poverty." She looked over at him, batting her eyelashes like a practiced coquette. "I know you won't believe this, but I was quite ignorant of anything beyond my own small world back then."

"Perish the thought," he replied gallantly, kissing her hand.

"No, it's true." She sidled closer to him. "And because I am now realizing all she has done for me, I am making sure that I cultivate gratitude for every kindness that has been shown to me. I know, for example, that you are likely the reason the Handley clan has suddenly changed their long-held opinion of my family. Why, Hattie showed me a letter this morning from Papa's brother David, who insists that the family harbors no ill will toward us."

"Ah, what good news," her husband replied. "I am glad to hear it."

She touched his cheek, her glove catching slightly on his beard stubble. "He has even settled an allowance on us both, which we are giving to the Veterans' Fund."

"That is too good of the Handley gels," he rejoined, turning the palm of her hand toward his lips.

"The Handley gels have you to thank for it, Lieutenant Cantrill."

He smiled briefly as the carriage rolled to a halt. "I must disagree, Mrs. Cantrill. It seems to me that the head of your family merely did the right thing. At long last." He opened the carriage door and boosted her to the ground, swinging her in a slow circle until her toes touched the frozen earth.

"Come, sweetheart. Let's go home." He swept her up, holding her in the crook of his injured arm, and opened the door latch.

Unlike her undignified mistake in Bath, she was going in the front door. In point of fact, her darling husband was carrying her over the threshold.

Sophie laughed, smiling up into her beloved's handsome face, and kicked the door shut with her slippered foot.

* * * * *

If you enjoyed Lily George's book,
be sure to check out the other books this month
from Love Inspired Historical!

Dear Reader,

When I started to write book two of the Brides of Waterloo series (known to you now as *The Temporary Betrothal*), my wonderful editor, Melissa Endlich, had one clear directive: "Bring back Aunt Katherine."

I must say it was a delight to immerse myself back in the world of Tansley Village and the Handley girls, and yes, to listen and report everything Aunt Katherine had to say. Even though Sophie leads a much more cosmopolitan life in Bath than her sister, Harriet, leads in Tansley Village, she finds the simple life infinitely more attractive than a life of abundance and elegance. And helping Sophie learn that important lesson has been so much fun. I hope you enjoy her story as much as I enjoyed writing it.

While it's true that Charlie helps bring Sophie closer to God, it's also true that Sophie rekindles Charlie's belief in himself. He becomes, through her example, as generous with himself as he is toward others in need. Together they embark on a life filled with a sense of mission and purpose. If only Sophie's dear friend Lucy could find such fulfillment in her life....

I enjoy hearing from all my readers, so please feel free to send me an email at Lily@lilygeorge.com. Thank you for allowing me to share the Handley girls, and their trials and triumphs, with you.

Blessings,
Lily George

Questions for Discussion

1. Sophie Handley feels that the only way to find independence is to become a seamstress for Lord Bradbury and his daughters. Why does she consider this her only option? Is independence important to you? Do you agree with her choice?

2. Lieutenant Charles Cantrill is immediately attracted to Sophie, but distrusts her beauty and her reputation for being flighty. Why does he feel wary of beautiful women? Have you distrusted someone based solely on the way they looked, even though you knew nothing about them? What did you do?

3. Charlie never lost his faith during the horrible Battle of Waterloo. Yet he tries to overcome feelings of inadequacy and embarrassment after he fainted during the battle. Does he try to overcompensate by helping others? Do you often find yourself overcompensating to make up for a perceived mistake or flaw?

4. Sophie has never really thought deeply about God. Her heart and mind are opened to God during a sermon on the Beatitudes. Is there a point at which you felt your life open to God?

5. Sophie accepts the gift of a bracelet from Lord Bradbury. Was that a wise decision? What would you have done?

6. Sophie later sells the bracelet to finance a sewing circle with the widows of Waterloo soldiers. Was that a good way to use the money from Lord Bradbury's gift?

7. Charlie's brother, Robert, distrusts Sophie immediately, even though their mother is in awe of Sophie's family background and beauty. What is your feeling about first impressions? Has there ever been a time when you were mistaken about your first impression of someone?

8. Sophie breaks off her engagement to Charlie because Robert orders her to do so. Was this the right thing to do? What would you have done?

9. Sophie declines Lord Bradbury's offer to become his mistress, and flees back to Tansley Village to be with her sister. Was this the right choice? How would you have handled Lord Bradbury's offer?

10. Reverend Stephens teaches Charlie a powerful lesson in forgiveness. Have you ever had to forgive someone for a transgression? How did you feel after doing so?

11. Charlie goes on a journey to forgive several people and to ask their forgiveness in turn. Why does he feel this is a crucial step before seeking Sophie's hand in marriage?

12. Charlie is determined to live a life of simplicity, even though his family is against his choice of life-

style. Have you ever gone against someone's expectations of you, even though you knew it would be difficult to do so?

13. The Handley family finally acknowledges the Handley girls, and promises to reinstate their inheritance. Both girls decide to give the money to charity. Is this a wise choice?

14. Have you ever met anyone like Moriah Cantrill, Charlie's mother, who is so devoted to appearances? How do you feel about appearances and wealth?

15. Lucy Williams, Sophie's friend, feels that Sophie has been impractical for turning down two marriage proposals *and* a proposal to be Lord Bradbury's mistress. How do you feel about Sophie's choices? Was she right to wait, and marry for love?

REQUEST YOUR FREE BOOKS!

2 FREE INSPIRATIONAL NOVELS
PLUS 2
FREE
MYSTERY GIFTS

Love Inspired.
HISTORICAL
INSPIRATIONAL HISTORICAL ROMANCE

YES! Please send me 2 FREE Love Inspired® Historical novels and my 2 FREE mystery gifts (gifts are worth about \$10). After receiving them, if I don't wish to receive any more books, I can return the shipping statement marked "cancel". If I don't cancel, I will receive 4 brand-new novels every month and be billed just \$4.49 per book in the U.S. or \$4.99 per book in Canada. That's a saving of at least 22% off the cover price. It's quite a bargain! Shipping and handling is just 50¢ per book in the U.S. and 75¢ per book in Canada.* I understand that accepting the 2 free books and gifts places me under no obligation to buy anything. I can always return a shipment and cancel at any time. Even if I never buy another book, the two free books and gifts are mine to keep forever.

102/302 IDN FEHF

Name	(PLEASE PRINT)
Address	Apt. #
City	State/Prov.	Zip/Postal Code

Signature (if under 18, a parent or guardian must sign)

Mail to the **Reader Service:**
IN U.S.A.: P.O. Box 1867, Buffalo, NY 14240-1867
IN CANADA: P.O. Box 609, Fort Erie, Ontario L2A 5X3

Not valid for current subscribers to Love Inspired Historical books.

Want to try two free books from another series?
Call 1-800-873-8635 or visit www.ReaderService.com.

* Terms and prices subject to change without notice. Prices do not include applicable taxes. Sales tax applicable in N.Y. Canadian residents will be charged applicable taxes. Offer not valid in Quebec. This offer is limited to one order per household. All orders subject to credit approval. Credit or debit balances in a customer's account(s) may be offset by any other outstanding balance owed by or to the customer. Please allow 4 to 6 weeks for delivery. Offer available while quantities last.

Your Privacy—The Reader Service is committed to protecting your privacy. Our Privacy Policy is available online at www.ReaderService.com or upon request from the Reader Service.

We make a portion of our mailing list available to reputable third parties that offer products we believe may interest you. If you prefer that we not exchange your name with third parties, or if you wish to clarify or modify your communication preferences, please visit us at www.ReaderService.com/consumerchoice or write to us at Reader Service Preference Service, P.O. Box 9062, Buffalo, NY 14269. Include your complete name and address.

LIH11B

When Greta Goodloe is jilted by her longtime sweetheart, she takes comfort in matchmaking between newcomer Luke Starns and her schoolmarm sister. Yet the more Greta tries to throw them together, the more Luke fascinates her.

Read on for a sneak peek of A GROOM FOR GRETA by Anna Schmidt, available October 2012 from Love Inspired® Historical.

***

"So what do you intend to do about this turn of events, Luke?"

"Do? Your sister made her feelings plain last evening. She does not wish to spend her time with me."

Greta sighed heavily. "She does not know what she wants. The question is, are you serious about finding a wife for yourself or not?"

"I am quite serious."

"Then—"

"What I will not do," Luke interrupted, "is go after a woman who has declared openly that she has no interest in making a home with me."

"And what of her idea that you and I should…" She let the sentence trail off.

"That depends," he said slowly.

"On what?"

"On whether or not you are able to put aside your feelings for Josef Bontrager. Your sister believes that your feelings for him were not as strong as they should be for two people planning a life together. Do you agree?"

"Lydia is…I mean…oh, I don't know," Greta replied.

"How can either of you expect me to know what it is that I'm feeling these days? It's too soon."

"If Josef came to you and asked for your forgiveness and pleaded with you to reconsider, would you?"

"No," she finally whispered. "I would not."

Luke felt his heart pounding, and he realized that over the months he had been in Celery Fields, he had taken more notice of the beautiful Greta Goodloe than he had allowed himself to admit. He had learned a hard lesson back in Ontario and he had been determined not to make the same mistake twice.

But if Greta had come to realize that Josef was not for her...

On the other hand, surely the idea that she might be firm in her decision to be rid of Josef did not mean that she was ready for someone new.

***

Don't miss A GROOM FOR GRETA by Anna Schmidt, the next heartwarming book in the AMISH BRIDES OF CELERY FIELDS *series, on sale October 2012 wherever Love Inspired® Historical books are sold!*